A
Werewolf
Problem
IN
Central Russia

AND

OTHER STORIES

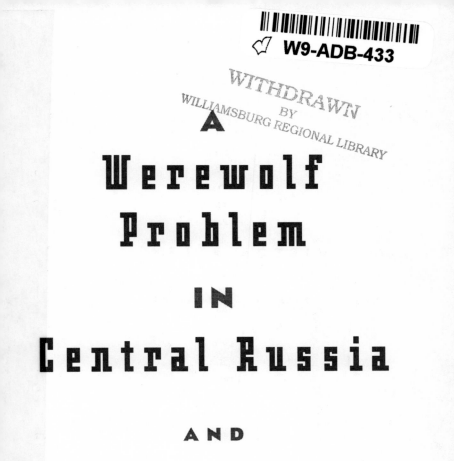

VICTOR PELEVIN

a Werewolf Problem in Central Russia

and Other Stories

Translated by **Andrew Bromfield**

New Directions

Published by arrangement with Harbord Publishing Limited, 58 Harbord Street, London SW6 6PJ, and the Watkins/Loomis Agency

Manufactured in the United States of America
New Directions Books are printed on acid-free paper.
First published as New Directions Paperbook 959 in 2003
Published simultaneously in Canada by Penguin Books Canada Limited

Library of Congress Cataloging-in-Publication Data

Pelevin, Viktor.
    [Short stories. English. Selections]
    A werewolf problem in Central Russia and other stories / Victor
Pelevin : translated by Andrew Bromfield.
        p. cm.
    Contents: Vera Pavlovna's ninth dream—the ontology of childhood
—Sleep—Tai Shou Chuan USSR (A Chinese folk tale)—The Tarzan
swing—A werewolf problem in Central Russia—Bulldozer driver's
day—Prince of Gosplan.
        ISBN 0-8112-1394-3 (alk. paper)
        ISBN 0-8112-1543-1 (pbk.)
        1. Pelevin, Viktor—Translations into English. I. Bromfield,
    Andrew. II. Title.
    PG3485.E38A23   1998
    981.73'44—dc21   98-17488
                                                CIP

New Directions Books are published for James Laughlin
by New Directions Publishing Corporation
80 Eighth Avenue, New York 10011

Table of Contents

A Werewolf Problem in Central Russia

AND

OTHER STORIES

A Werewolf Problem in Central Russia

JUST FOR A MOMENT SASHA thought that the battered Zil would stop for him: it was so old and rattled so loudly, and was so obviously ready for the scrap heap, that it should have stopped—if only the law by which old people who have been rude and inconsiderate all their lives suddenly become helpful and obliging shortly before they die had applied to the world of automobiles—but it didn't. With a bucket clanking beside its gas tank with a drunken, senile insolence, the Zil rattled past him, struggled up a small hill, giving vent to a whoop of indecent triumph and a jet of gray smoke at the summit, and disappeared silently behind the asphalt rise. Sasha stepped off the road, dropped his small backpack on to the grass and sat down on it. Something in it bent and cracked and Sasha felt the spiteful satisfaction of a person in trouble who learns that someone or something else is also having a hard time. He was just beginning to realize how serious his own situation was.

There were only two courses of action open to him: either he could go on waiting for a lift or head back to the village—a three mile walk. As far as the lift was concerned, the question seemed as good as settled already. There were obviously certain regions in the country, or a least certain roads, where all the drivers belonged to some secret brotherhood of black-hearted villains. Hitchhiking became impossible, and you had to take great care the passing cars didn't splash you with mud from the puddles as you walked along the side of the road. The road from Konkovo to the nearest oasis on the railway line—a straight stretch of 15 miles—was one such enchanted highway. Not one of the five cars that had passed him had stopped, and if not for one aging lady wearing purple lipstick and an "I still love you" hairstyle who stuck her long arm out of the window of a red Niva to give him the finger, Sasha could have believed he'd become invisible. He'd still been hoping for that mythical driver, the kind you encounter in newspaper stories and films, who would stare silently through the dusty windscreen of his truck at the road ahead for the entire journey and then refuse any payment with a curt shake of his head (at this point you suddenly notice the photograph hanging above the steering wheel, showing a group of young men in paratrooper uniforms against a backdrop of distant mountains)—but when the Zil rattled past, even this hope had died.

Sasha glanced at his watch—it was twenty minutes past nine. It would get dark soon. He looked around. Beyond a hundred yards or so of broken ground (tiny hillocks, scattered bushes, and grass that was too high and luscious for his liking, because it suggested it was growing on a bog) there was the edge of a forest, thin and unhealthy looking, like the sickly offspring of an alcoholic. All the vegetation in the neighborhood looked strange, as though anything bigger than flowers and grass had to strain and struggle to grow, and even when it eventually reached normal size, it still gave the impression of only having grown under the threat of violence—otherwise it would have flattened itself against the ground like lichen. It was an unpleasant sort of place, oppressive and deserted, as though it was ready for removal from the face of the earth—but then, Sasha thought, if the earth does have a face, it must be somewhere else, not here.

Of the three villages he had seen that day only one had appeared more or less convincing—the last one, Konkovo; the others had been deserted, with just a few little houses inhabited by people waiting to die. The abandoned huts had reminded him more of an ethnographic exhibition than human dwellings. Even Konkovo, distinguished by a plaster sentry standing beside the road and a sign which read "Michurin Collective Farm," only seemed like a human settlement in comparison with the desolation of the other nameless villages nearby. Konkovo had a shop, and there was a poster for the village club, with the title of an avant-garde French film traced in green watercolor, flapping in the wind, while a tractor whined somewhere behind the houses— but even there he hadn't felt comfortable. There was no one on the streets—only one woman dressed in black had passed him, crossing herself hurriedly at the sight of Sasha's Hawaiian shirt with its design of multicolored magical symbols, and a man in spectacles had ridden by on a bicycle with a string shopping bag dangling from the handlebars. The bicycle was too big for him, so he couldn't sit in the saddle and stood instead on the pedals, looking as though he was running in the air above the heavy rusty frame. All the other villagers, if there were any, must have been staying indoors.

He had imagined his trip would be quite different. He would get off the small flat-bottomed riverboat, walk to the village, and there on the *zavalinkas*—Sasha had no idea what a *zavalinka* was, but he imagined it as a comfortable wooden bench set along the log wall of a peasant hut—there would be half-crazy old women sitting peacefully among the sunflowers, and clean-shaven old men playing chess quietly beneath the broad yellow discs of the blossoms. In other words, Sasha had imagined Tverskoi Boulevard in Moscow overgrown with sunflowers—with a cow occasionally lowing in the distance. After that he would make his way to the edge of the village to find a forest basking in the sun, a river with a boat drifting by on it or some country road cutting through an open field, and whichever way he walked, everything would be simply wonderful: he could light a fire, he could remember his childhood and climb trees—if, that is, his memories told him that was what he used to do. In the evening he would hitch a lift to the train.

What had actually happened was very different. It had been a colored photograph in a thick, tattered book that was to blame for everything, an illustration with the title "The ancient Russian village of Konkovo, now the main center of a millionaire collective farm." Sasha had found the spot from which the photograph that caught his eye had been taken, roundly cursed the American word "millionaire" and marveled at how different the same view can appear in a photograph and in real life.

Having promised himself never again to set out on a senseless journey purely on impulse, Sasha decided that at least he would watch the film in the village club. After buying a ticket from an invisible woman—he had to conduct his conversation with the plump freckled hand in the window, which tore off the blue scrap of paper and counted out his change—he made his way into the half-empty hall, spent one and a half bored hours there, occasionally turning to look at an old man who sat in his chair straight as a ramrod and whistled at certain points in the action—his criteria for whistling were quite incomprehensible, but his whistle had a wild bandit ring to it, a lingering note from Russia's receding past.

Afterwards, when the film was over, he looked at the whistler's straight back as it retreated from the club, at the street lamp under its conical tin cap, at the identical fences surrounding the little houses, and he shook the dust of Konkovo from his feet, with a sideways glance at the eroded hand and raised foot of the plaster Lenin in the plaster hat, doomed to stride for all eternity towards his brother in oblivion who stood, as if waiting for him, by the highway. Sasha had waited so long for the truck which finally dispelled his illusions that he had almost forgotten what he was waiting for. Standing up, he slung the backpack over his shoulder and set off back the way he had come, wondering where and how he would spend the night. He didn't want to try knock-

ing on some woman's door—most of the women who let people
in to spend the night live in the same mythical places as nightin-
gale-whistling bandits and walking skeletons, and this was the
"Michurin Collective Farm" (which was actually no less magical
an idea, if you thought about it, but one with a different kind of
magic, not one that offered any hope of a night's lodging in a
stranger's house). The only reasonable way out Sasha was able to
think of was to buy a ticket for the last showing at the club and
hide behind the heavy green curtain after the film and spend the
night there. If it was to work, he would have to leave his seat before they switched on the lights, so that he wouldn't be noticed by
the woman in the homemade black uniform who escorted the
customers to the exit. He'd have to watch the same dark, depressing film again, but he'd just have to put up with that.

As he was thinking all this through, Sasha came to a fork in
the road. Passing this way twenty minutes before, he had thought
that the road he was walking along was joined by a smaller side
road, but now as he stood at the junction he couldn't decide
which was the road he had come along—they both looked exactly
the same. Probably it was the one on the right—there was that
big tree by the road. Yes, that must be it—he had to go right. And
surely there was a gray telephone pole in front of the tree. Where
was it now? There it was—but it was on the left, and there was a
small tree beside it. It didn't make sense. Sasha looked at the telephone pole, which had once supported wires, but now looked like
a huge rake threatening the sky. He went left.

After he'd walked twenty steps, he stopped and looked back.
Clearly visible against the dark stripes of the sunset, a bird which
he had previously taken for an insulator caked with the dirt of
many years launched itself into the air. He walked on—he had to
hurry to get to Konkovo in time, and his road lay through the
forest.

It occurred to him how incredibly unobservant he was. On
the way from Konkovo he hadn't noticed this wide cut opening
on to a clearing. When you're absorbed in your own thoughts, the

world around you disappears. He probably wouldn't have noticed it this time either, if someone hadn't called out to him.

"Hey," the drunken voice shouted, "who are you?"

Several other voices broke into coarse laughter. In among the trees on the edge of the forest, right beside the cut, Sasha caught a quick glimpse of people and bottles—he refused to turn his head and only saw the young locals out of the corner of his eye. He started walking more quickly, believing that they wouldn't pursue him, but still he was unpleasantly alarmed.

"Whoa, what a wolf!" someone shouted after him.

"Maybe I'm going the wrong way?" Sasha thought when the road took a zig-zag that he didn't remember. But no, it seemed right—there was a long crack in the road surface that looked like the letter "W"; he'd seen something like that the last time. It was gradually getting dark and he still had a long way to go. To occupy his mind, he began thinking of ways of getting into the club once the film had started—from explaining that he'd come back for a cap he'd left behind to climbing down the chimney (if there was one, that is).

Half an hour later it became clear that he had taken the wrong road—the air was already blue and the first stars had broken through the sky. What made it obvious was the appearance of a tall metal pylon supporting three thick cables at the side of the road and a quiet crackling of electricity: there definitely hadn't been any pylons like that on the road from Konkovo. Everything was quite clear now, but still Sasha went on walking automatically until he reached the pylon. He stared with fixed concentration at the metal plaque with the lovingly executed drawing of a skull and the threatening inscription, then looked around and was astonished to think that he had just walked through that dark, terrifying forest. Walking back to the fork would mean another encounter with the young guys sitting beside the road, and discovering what state they had got into under the influence of fortified wine and evening twilight. Going forward meant walking into the unknown—but then, a road has to lead somewhere, surely?

The humming of the power cables served as a reminder that there were normal people living somewhere in the world, producing electricity by day and watching television with its help by night. If it came to spending the night in the forest, Sasha thought, the best thing would be to sleep under the pylon—it would be something like sleeping in a front hallway, and that was a well-tried move, absolutely safe. In the distance he heard a roaring which seemed to be filled with some ancient anguish—he could hardly make it out at first, and not until it became incredibly loud did Sasha realize that it was an airplane. He lifted his gaze to the sky in relief, and soon he could see above his head the triangle defined by its three different colored lights: as long as he could see the airplane, Sasha actually felt comfortable standing there on the dark forest road. When it moved out of sight, he walked on, looking straight ahead down the road that was gradually becoming the brightest thing in his surroundings.

The road was illuminated by a weak light, and he could walk along without any fear of stumbling. For some reason, probably simply the habit of a city dweller, Sasha felt sure that the light came from widely spaced street lamps, but when he tried to spot one, the truth struck him—of course there were no street lamps, it was the moon shining, and when Sasha looked upwards he could see its crisp white crescent in the sky. After gazing upwards for a while, he noticed that the stars were different colors—he'd never noticed that before, or if he had, he'd forgotten it ages ago.

Eventually the darkness became complete—that is, it became clear that it wasn't going to get any darker. Sasha took his jacket out of the backpack, put it on and closed all the zips—that made him feel more prepared for any further surprises the night might have in store. He ate two crumpled wedge-shaped pieces of "Friendship" processed cheese—the foil wrapping with the word "Friendship" printed on it gleamed dully in the moonlight, vaguely reminding him of the pennants that the human race is constantly launching into space.

Several times he heard the roar of engines as cars or trucks passed by in the distance. At one point the road emerged from the forest and ran through an open field for about five hundred yards, then plunged into another forest where the trees were older and taller. At the same time it narrowed, as did the strip of sky above his head. He had the feeling that he was plunging deeper and deeper into some abyss which the road would never lead him out of—it would take him into some dark thicket and end there in a kingdom of evil, among huge oak trees waving their branches like arms—just like in those children's horror films, where the victory of the hero in the red shirt makes you feel sorry for the wicked witch and the walking skeleton who fall victim to his triumph.

He heard the sound of an engine up ahead once again, but this time it was closer, and Sasha thought that he might actually get a lift somewhere where he would be enclosed by walls, with an electric lightbulb above his head, where he could fall asleep without feeling afraid. The sound of the engine grew closer and closer, then suddenly died away—the car had stopped. He started walking more quickly, and soon he heard the engine again—but this time it was far away, as though the car had taken a silent leap a mile back and was heading back over the journey it had already made. He realized he was hearing another car that was also traveling in his direction. In the forest it's hard to tell just how far away a sound is, but when the second car stopped, Sasha thought that it must be about a hundred yards away: he couldn't see any headlights, but there was a bend ahead.

This was very strange indeed—two cars one after the other suddenly stopping in the forest in the middle of the night. Just to be on the safe side Sasha went over to the edge of the road, ready to dive into the forest if circumstances required it, and then walked on stealthily, staring hard into the darkness. His fear gradually evaporated and he felt sure that he would either soon be getting into a car or he would just keep on walking the way he was. Just before the bend in the road he saw faint gleams of red on the leaves and heard voices talking and laughing. Another car drove up and stopped somewhere close by, slamming its doors. Since whoever it was ahead was laughing, there was probably nothing very frightening going on. Or perhaps just the opposite, he thought suddenly. He turned into the forest and moved on, feeling his way through the darkness with his hands, until he reached a spot from which he could see what was going on around the bend. He hid behind a tree and waited for his eyes to adjust to the new level of darkness, then he took a cautious peep.

Ahead of him there was a large clearing: about six cars were parked haphazardly on one edge, and the whole area was illuminated by a small campfire, around which people of different ages were standing, dressed in various ways, some of them holding sandwiches and clutching bottles. They were talking to each other and generally conversing like any group gathered around a fire at night—the only thing lacking was the music of a tapedeck straining against the silence. As though he had heard what Sasha was thinking, a thickset man walked over to a car and stuck his hand in through its window, and suddenly loud music began playing—only it wasn't the right kind of music for a picnic: it was the howling of hoarse, dark-toned horns. The group made no gesture of complaint—in fact, when the man who had switched on the music came back to the others, he received several slaps of congratulation on the shoulders. Looking closer, Sasha began to notice other things that were strange.

Standing alone by the fire was a military figure—he looked like a colonel. Everybody kept their distance from him, and sometimes he raised his hand in the direction of the moon. Several other men were dressed in suits and ties, as though they had come to the office, not the forest. A man in a loose black jacket wearing a leather hairband around his forehead came over to the near edge of the clearing and Sasha pressed himself tightly against his tree. Someone else turned a face distorted by the dancing firelight in Sasha's direction. But no, no one had seen him. He thought how easily it could all be explained: they'd probably been at some formal reception and had headed off into the forest out of boredom. The Colonel was there to protect them, or maybe he was selling tanks. But then why that music?

"Hey!" said a quiet voice behind him. Sasha turned cold. Slowly turning around he saw a girl in a tracksuit with an Adidas lily on her breast. "What are you doing here?" she asked in the same low voice. He forced his mouth open to answer:

"I . . . just happened along."

"How did you happen along?"

"I was just walking along the road and I ended up here."

"Just ended up here?" said the girl in astonishment. "You mean you didn't come with us?"

"No."

She made a movement as though she was about to spring away from him, but stayed where she was.

"You mean you came on your own? You just walked here?"

"What's so strange about that?" Sasha asked.

He thought for a moment that she was teasing him, but the girl shook her head in such sincere astonishment that he abandoned the idea and began to feel that he really must have made an outlandish gaffe. She thought for a minute without saying anything, then asked:

"So now what are you going to do?"

Sasha decided she must be talking about his status as a solitary pedestrian stranded in the night, and he said:

"What am I going to do? Ask someone to drive me to some station or other. When are you going back?"

She didn't answer. He repeated his question and she twirled her hand in an indefinite gesture.

"Or I'll keep on walking," Sasha blurted out.

The girl looked at him pityingly.

"Listen to me: don't even try to run. I mean it. You'd better wait about five minutes and then walk over to the fire as if you belong here. And make wild eyes. They'll ask you who you are and what you're doing here. You tell them that you heard the call. And sound as though you mean it. All right?"

"What call?"

"Just the call. I'm the one giving the advice here."

The girl looked Sasha up and down one more time, walked around him and went towards the clearing. When she got close to the fire a man wearing running shoes patted her on the head and gave her a sandwich.

"She's making fun of me," Sasha thought. But then he looked closely at the man with the leather band on his forehead who was still standing at the edge of the clearing, and decided that the girl must be serious: there was something very strange in the way the man was peering into the night. And in the center of the clearing he suddenly noticed a skull on a wooden stake thrust into the earth—the skull was long and narrow, with powerful jaws. A dog maybe? No, more like a wolf.

He gathered himself together, stepped out from behind the tree, and walked towards the orange-red blur of the campfire. He swayed as he walked, without understanding why, and his eyes were glued to the flames. The voices in the clearing instantly fell silent.

"Stop," said a hoarse voice by the stake with the skull.

He didn't stop—they came running over to him and he was seized by large male hands.

"What are you doing here?" asked the voice that had ordered him to stop.

"I heard the call," Sasha replied in a dull, expressionless voice, staring down at the ground.

"Aha, the call . . ." several voices repeated. They released him, the others suddenly laughed and someone said. "A new boy."

They gave Sasha a sandwich and a glass of water, and he was immediately forgotten. He remembered the backpack he had left behind the tree. "Just too bad," he thought, and started eating the sandwich. The girl in the tracksuit walked past him.

"Hey!" he said, "what's going on here? A picnic?"

"Wait a while and you'll find out."

She crooked her little finger at him in a gesture that looked cryptically Chinese, and went back to the group standing by the stake. Someone tugged at Sasha's sleeve. He turned around and shuddered: it was the army officer.

"There you go, new boy," he said, "fill that in."

A sheet of paper with lines of print and a pen appeared in Sasha's hands. The fire lit up the officer's high cheekbones and the writing on the sheet of paper: it was a standard form. Sasha squatted down on his haunches and writing awkwardly on his knee, began filling in the answers—where he was born, when, why, and so on. It certainly felt strange to be filling in a form in the forest in the middle of the night, but the presence of a man in uniform towering over him somehow balanced things out. The officer waited, occasionally sniffing at the air and glancing over Sasha's shoulder. When the last line had been filled in, he grabbed the pen and the form, bared his teeth in a smile and set off towards the car with a strange springy run.

While Sasha was filling in the form there had been obvious changes over by the fire. The people were still talking, but now their voices seemed to bark, and their movements and gestures had become smooth and dexterous. A man in an evening suit was squirming agilely in the grass, moving his head in an attempt to free it from his dangling tie. Another had frozen motionless on one leg like a stork and was gazing prayerfully at the moon, and through the tongues of flame Sasha could see someone else standing on all fours. Sasha himself could hear a ringing in his ears and his throat was dry. It was all definitely caused in some strange way by the music: it was faster now, and the hoarse notes of the horns were more and more strident, increasingly resembling a car alarm. The horns suddenly broke off on a sharp note that was followed by the howling of a gong.

"The elixir!" the Colonel ordered.

Sasha saw a skinny old woman wearing a long jacket and red beads. She was carrying a jar covered with paper—the kind they sell mayonnaise in. Suddenly there was a slight commotion by the stake with the skull.

"Well, look at that!" someone said in admiration, "without any elixir . . ."

Sasha glanced in that direction and saw the girl in the track-suit kneeling on the ground. She looked very odd—her legs seemed to have grown shorter, while her face had stretched out into an incredible, fearsome muzzle almost like a wolf's.

"Magnificent," said the Colonel, looking around and inviting everyone to admire the event. "No other word for it! Quite magnificent! And they say young people today are good for nothing!"

A tremor ran through the body of the terrifying creature, followed by another and another, until it was shuddering violently. After a minute a young female wolf was standing among the people in the clearing.

"That's Lena from Tambov," someone said in Sasha's ear, "she's really talented."

The conversation died away, and everyone lined up in a rough row. The woman and the Colonel walked along it, giving everyone in turn a sip from the jar. Sasha, totally stupefied by what he'd just seen, found himself in the middle of the line. For a few minutes he couldn't take anything in, and then he saw the woman with the beads standing in front of him and holding out the jar. Sasha smelled something familiar—like the way leaves smell if you rub them against your palm. He started back, but the woman's hand reached further and thrust the rim of the jar up to his lips. Sasha took a little sip, at the same moment feeling that he was being held from behind. The woman walked on. He opened his eyes. As long as he held the liquid in his mouth, the taste actually seemed quite pleasant, but when he swallowed it, it almost made him sick.

A pungent smell of vegetation welled up and filled Sasha's empty head as though someone had suddenly pumped a jet of gas into a balloon. The balloon grew and stretched, straining upwards with ever greater force until suddenly it broke the slim thread binding it to the earth and soared upwards—leaving the forest and the clearing with the fire and the people far below, and the scattered clouds came rushing towards him, followed by the stars. Soon he couldn't see anything below him. He began looking upwards and saw he was getting close to the sky, which turned out to be a sphere of stone with shiny metal spikes protruding from its inner surface. From down below the spikes looked like stars, and one of the gleaming points was hurtling directly towards Sasha, and there was nothing he could do to prevent the collision—he was soaring up faster and faster. Finally he hit the spike and burst with a loud bang. All that was left of him was the stretched skin, swaying in the air, which began slowly sinking back down to earth. He fell for a long, long time, for a thousand years, until he finally felt solid ground under his feet. It felt so good that Sasha wagged his tail vigorously in pleasure and gratitude, got up from his belly on to his four paws and howled gently.

There were several wolves standing beside him. He immediately recognized Lena among them, although he couldn't understand exactly how. The human features which had struck him earlier had disappeared, of course, and now she had those of a wolf. He would never have imagined that the expression of a wolf's muzzle could be simultaneously so mocking and dreamy if he hadn't seen it with his own eyes. Lena noticed his gaze.

"Like what you see?" she asked.

She didn't speak in words. She whined gently, whimpering—it was nothing like human speech, but Sasha not only understood her question, he even caught the familiar tone she imparted to her howling. He wanted to answer "Great!" What came out was a brief barking sound, but it expressed exactly what he wanted to say. Lena lay down in the grass and lowered her muzzle between her paws.

"Rest," she whined, "we'll be running for a long time."

Sasha looked around. By the stake the Colonel was rolling

about on the ground, with fur growing right over his greatcoat: a thick bushy tail was appearing out of his trousers as fast as a blade of grass in a school biology film.

The clearing was now full with the wolf pack, and only the woman with the beads who had handed out the elixir was still in human form. She walked rather apprehensively around two large male wolves and climbed into a car. Sasha turned to Lena and whined:

"Isn't she one of us?"

"She just helps us. She turns into a cobra."

"Is she going to do that now?"

"It's too cold for her now. She goes to Central Asia."

The wolves were prowling around the clearing, going up to each other and barking quietly. Sasha sat on his haunches and tried to appreciate every aspect of his new condition.

He could sense numerous smells impregnating the air, in a way which felt like a second gift of sight—for instance, he could immediately smell his own backpack behind a tree that was quite a long way off, as well as the woman sitting in the car, the scent of a ground squirrel that had recently run along the edge of the clearing, the reliable, brave smell of the older wolves and the gentle aura of Lena's smell—perhaps the freshest and purest note in the entire unimaginably wide gamut of scents.

He felt a similar change in his perception of sounds: they had become far more meaningful, and their variety had increased significantly. He could distinguish the creaking of a branch in the wind a hundred yards from the clearing and the chirping of a cricket coming from precisely the opposite direction. He could follow the fluctuations in both sounds simultaneously, without dividing his attention.

But the greatest transformation that Sasha sensed was in his own awareness of himself. This was something very difficult to express in human language, and he began barking, whining and howling to himself in the same way that he used to think in words. The change in his self-awareness had affected the meaning of life, and he realized that people could talk about it, but they couldn't feel the meaning of life in the same way as they felt the wind or the cold. But now Sasha was able to feel it, he felt the meaning of life continuously and clearly as an eternal quality of the world itself, and that was the greatest charm of his present condition. No sooner did he realize this than he also realized that he was not likely ever to return to his former existence of his own free will—life without this feeling seemed like a long, tormenting dream, dim and incomprehensible.

"Ready?" the Colonel barked from the direction of the stake.

"Ready!" a dozen throats howled in response.

"Hang on . . ." someone wheezed behind him. "I can't finish changing . . ."

Sasha tried to look around, but he couldn't manage it. It turned out that his neck didn't bend very well, and he had to turn his entire body. Lena came over, stuck her cold nose in his side and whined softly:

"Stop trying to turn around, just move your eyes. Like this." When she swiveled her eye it flashed red. Sasha tried doing the same, and he found that by turning his eyes he could see his back, his tail and the dying camp fire.

"Where are we going to run to?" he asked.

"To Konkovo," Lena replied, "there are two cows in a field there."

"But aren't they locked away now?"

"It's all been arranged. Ivan Sergeievich arranged a call from the top"—Lena jerked her muzzle upwards—"to say they were studying the effect of night grazing on milk yields, or something like that."

"You mean we have people up there"—Sasha repeated her gesture—"as well?"

"What do you think?"

Ivan Sergeievich, who before had been the man in the black jacket with the leather band on his forehead—it had turned into a strip of dark fur—nodded his muzzle significantly. Sasha squinted around at Lena. Suddenly she seemed incredibly beautiful—her smooth, shiny fur, the delicate curve of her spine, her slim, powerful hind legs, fluffy young tail and shoulder blades moving so touchingly beneath her skin—in her he sensed at one and the same time strength, a slightly reticent thirst for blood, and that special charm peculiar to young she-wolves that is quite impossible to express in wolf howls.

Noticing his glance, Lena felt embarrassed and moved off to the side, lowering her tail so that it lay on the grass. Sasha also felt embarrassed and he pretended to be biting burrs out of the fur on his paw.

"One more time, is everybody ready?" barked the leader in a low voice that filled the entire clearing.

"Ready!" they all howled together.

"Then, forward!"

The leader trotted to the edge of the forest—he seemed deliberately to be moving slowly and loosely, like a sprinter warming up before settling on the starting blocks in order to emphasize even more the speed and concentration he would demonstrate after the starting shot. At the edge of the clearing the leader bent his muzzle down to the ground, sniffed, howled, and suddenly leapt forward into the darkness. The others hurtled after him, barking and whining. For the first few seconds of this wild pursuit through a night studded with sharp branches and thorns, Sasha felt as if he'd dived into water without knowing how deep it was—he was afraid of splitting his head open. But it turned out that he could sense approaching obstacles and avoid them quite easily. Having realized that, he relaxed, and running became easy and enjoyable—his body seemed to be hurtling along by itself, simply releasing the power concealed within it.

The pack stretched out and formed itself into a diamond shape. The powerful, full-grown wolves raced along at its edges, while the she-wolves and cubs stayed in the center. The cubs somehow managed to play as they ran along, grabbing each other by the tail and making all sorts of unimaginable leaps and bounds. Sasha's place was at the leading corner of the diamond, just behind the leader, somehow he knew this was a place of honor which he had been granted today as a newcomer. The forest came to an end and they moved on through a large deserted field and on to a road—the pack raced along the asphalt, picking up speed and stretching out into a ribbon of gray along the edge of the highway. Sasha recognized the road. On his way to the clearing it had seemed dark and empty, but now he could see life everywhere: field mice darted across the road and disappeared down their burrows as soon as the wolves appeared; on the shoulder a hedgehog curled up into a ball of prickles and bounced off into the grass when it was struck lightly by a wolf's paw, two hares swept by like a jet plane, leaving a thick trail of scent which made it clear that they were frightened to death and that one of them was also a total idiot. Lena was running alongside Sasha.

"Be careful," she howled, pointing upwards with her muzzle.

He looked up, allowing his body to find its own way along. There were several owls flying along above the road at exactly the same speed as the wolves. The owls hooted threateningly, and the wolves growled in reply. Sasha felt a strange connection between the owls and the pack. They were hostile to each other, but somehow alike.

"Who are they?" he asked Lena.

"Were-owls. They're tough customers—if they catch you alone."

Lena growled something else and looked up with hate in her eyes. The owls began moving away from the road and climbing higher—they flew without flapping their wings, simply stretching them out in the air. Circling once, they turned towards the rising moon.

"They're heading for the poultry farm," Lena growled, "during the day they're the sponsors there."

They had reached the fork in the road. There ahead was the familiar telephone pole and the tall tree. Sasha sensed the scent trail he had left when he was still human, and even an echo of the thoughts that had come into his head on the road several hours ago—the echo lingered in the smell. The pack flowed smoothly around the bend and raced on towards Konkovo. Lena had fallen back a little, and now the Colonel was running along beside Sasha—he was a large reddish wolf with a muzzle that looked as though it had been singed. There was something strange about the way he moved—when Sasha looked more closely he noticed that the Colonel sometimes fell into a canter.

"Comrade Colonel!" he howled. The actual sound was something like "Rrrr-uuu-vviii," but the Colonel understood perfectly and looked around in a friendly fashion.

"Are there many werewolves in the army?" Sasha asked, without really knowing why.

"Yes," answered the Colonel.

"Have they been there for long?"

They leapt high, flew over a long puddle and went racing on.

"From the very beginning," barked the Colonel, "how d'you think we drove the Whites all the way across Siberia?"

He gave a series of short growls rather like chuckles and moved ahead, his tail raised high like a flag on the stern of a ship. The plaster watchman hurtled past them, followed by the sign for the "Michurin Collective Farm," and there in the distance were the sparsely scattered lights of Konkovo. The village had prepared itself well for the encounter. It was like a ship consisting of several watertight compartments. When night came to the streets, of which there were only three, an impenetrable darkness descended, the houses' hatches were firmly battened down, each maintaining the yellow electric gleam of rational life in isolation from the others. Konkovo met the werewolves with a yellow glow behind curtained windows, silence, empty streets, and a series of entirely autonomous human dwellings: there was no village any longer—only a few spots of light in the midst of the darkness covering the world. The long gray shadows rushed along the main street and circled in front of the club as they abandoned the momentum of their run. Two wolves separated from the pack and disappeared among the houses, while the rest remained sitting in the square. Sasha stayed in their circle and stared at the club building where only recently he had intended to spend the night. He turned to Lena:

"Lena, where have they . . ."

"They'll be back in a minute," she interrupted. "Shut up."

The moon had gone behind a long tattered cloud, and now the square was only lit by a single lamp under a tin cone that swayed in the wind. Looking around, Sasha found the scene sinister and beautiful: the steel-gray bodies sat motionless around an empty space like an arena, the dust raised by the wolves was settling, their eyes and fangs were gleaming. The humans' little painted houses with the TV aerials and chicken houses stuck to them and the crooked parthenon of the club building seemed less like a stage set for the reality which had focused itself in the center of the square than a parody of a stage.

Several minutes passed in motionless silence, then something moved out of a side alley on to the main street and Sasha saw the silhouettes of three wolves trotting towards the square. He knew two of them—Ivan Sergeievich and the Colonel—but the third was unknown to him. Sasha sniffed his scent, full of putrid self-satisfaction and at the same time fear, and he wondered who it could be.

As the wolves approached, the Colonel dropped back a little, before running up and knocking the third wolf into the ring with his chest. Then he and Ivan Sergeievich took the places that had been left for them. The circle was completed and the stranger was left in the center. Sasha took a good sniff at him. The impression he received was like that of a man of about fifty with a body shaped like a broad-based cone and a fat, insolent face—but somehow at the same time very lightweight, as though filled with air. The newcomer peered at the wolf who had shoved him from behind and said with uncertain humor:

"So Colonel Lebedenko's pack is all present and accounted for. But what's all the drama about? Why this circle in the night?"

"We want to have a word with you, Nikolai," their Colonel answered.

"Glad to oblige," howled Nikolai. "Any time—for instance, we could talk about my latest invention. I call it the soap bubble game. You know I've always been fond of games, and just recently . . ."

Sasha suddenly realized that he was not following what Nikolai said, but the way he said it—he spoke rapidly, so that his words tumbled over each other, and he seemed to be using the words to defend himself from something which he found extremely unpleasant—as if the thing was scrambling up the stairs and Nikolai (for some reason Sasha imagined him in his human form), standing on the landing, was throwing everything that came to hand at it.

". . . to create a smooth and shiny model of what is happening."

"What's the point of the game?" asked the leader of the pack. "Tell us. We like games too."

"It's very simple. You take a thought and you blow it up into a soap bubble. Shall I show you?"

"Yes, show us."

"For instance . . ." Nikolai thought for a moment. "For instance, let's take something close at hand: you and I."

"Us and you," echoed the leader.

"Right. You're sitting around me and I'm standing in the center. That's what I'm going to blow into a bubble. And so . . ."

Nikolai lay down on his belly and assumed a relaxed pose.

"And so, now you're standing and I'm lying in the center. What does that mean? It means that certain aspects of the reality drifting past me can be interpreted in such a fashion that I, having been dragged from my home in a somewhat crude fashion, appear to have been brought here and set in the center of a circle of what are apparently wolves. Perhaps I'm dreaming it, or perhaps you're dreaming it, but one thing is certain: something is going on. Now, we've skimmed the surface and the bubble has begun to inflate. Let us turn to the more subtle fractions of the current event and you will see what delightful colors start playing on its thinning walls. I can see from your muzzles that you've come with the usual collection of stinging reproaches. I don't have to listen to you, I know what you're going to say. That I'm not a wolf but a pig—I eat off the garbage dump, live with a mongrel bitch, and so on. You think that's debased. And you think your crazy obsessive activity is exalted. But now the walls of my bubble reflect gray bodies that are absolutely identical—any of yours and mine—and they reflect the sky—and honestly, looking down from there a wolf and a mongrel and everything they do look very much the same. You run in order to get somewhere and I lie among a pile of old newspapers on my dump—how trifling the difference is in essence! What's more, if we take your state of motion as the starting point—note this, now!—it turns out that in fact I am running and you are simply jumping up and down on the spot." He licked his lips and continued:

"Now the bubble is half-ready. Next we come to your major complaint against me: I break your laws. Note that: your laws, not mine. But if I am bound by laws, they are of my own making, and I believe that is my right—to choose which authority to submit to and in what way. You are not strong enough to allow yourselves that, but in order not to seem like idiots in your own eyes, you convince yourselves that the existence of individuals like me can harm you."

"You've hit the nail on the head there," the leader observed.

"Well now, I don't deny that, hypothetically speaking, I could cause you a certain degree of inconvenience. But if that does happen, why should you not regard it as a kind of natural calamity? If a hailstorm starts, surely instead of remonstrating with it, you try to take shelter. And am not I—from the abstract point of view—a natural phenomenon? In fact, it turns out that in my piggishness, as you call it, I am stronger than you are, because I don't come to you, but you come to me. That's another given. See how the bubble is growing. We just have to give it a final puff of air. I'm fed up with these nocturnal visits. It wasn't so bad when you came one at a time, but this time the whole pack has turned up. But now that it's happened, let's get things clear between us once and for all. What can you actually do to stop me? Nothing. You can't kill me—you know why yourselves. As for changing my mind—you simply haven't got the brains to do it. So what's left is just your word and mine, and on the walls of the bubble they are equal. Only mine is more elegant—though, in the final analysis that's a matter of taste. In my view, my life is a magical dance and yours is a senseless dash through the darkness. So wouldn't it be best for us to go our separate ways as quickly as possible? There, the bubble has separated now, it's flying. How do you like it?"

While Nikolai was howling, gesticulating with his tail and his left forepaw, the leader listened to him without speaking, looking down into the dust and occasionally nodding. Having heard Nikolai out, he slowly raised his muzzle and at that very moment the moon came out from behind a cloud, and Sasha saw its light gleam on the leader's fangs.

"Nikolai, you obviously think you're performing for stray dogs at the dump. I personally have no intention of arguing about life with you. I don't know who has been to visit you,"—the leader glanced around at the other wolves—"that's news to me. We're here on business."

"On what business?"

The leader addressed the circle.

"Who has the letter?"

A young she-wolf came out of the circle and dropped a rolled piece of paper from her jaws. The leader straightened it out with a paw that just for a moment became a human hand and read:

"'Dear Editor . . .'"

Nikolai, who had been wagging his tail, now dropped it into the dust.

"'This letter comes to you from one of the women of

Konkovo. Our village is not far from Moscow, and the full address is shown on this envelope. I don't mention my name for reasons which will be clear from what follows. Recently there has been a series of articles in the press about phenomena which science previously dismissed out of hand. I wish to inform you of a remarkable phenomenon which from the scientific point of view is much more interesting than the phenomena which have been attracting so much attention, such as x-ray vision or Assyrian massage. You might take what I have to tell you as a joke, so let me tell you straight off that it is not. You have probably come across the word "werewolf" more than once, in the sense of a human being who can turn into a wolf. The point is that there is a real natural phenomenon behind the word. You could call it one of the most ancient traditions of our homeland, one which has miraculously survived all of the trials of the years of oppression. Our village is the home of Nikolai Petrovich Vakhromeiev, a man of great modesty and kindheartedness, who possesses this ancient knowledge. Probably only he can tell you what the essential nature of the phenomenon is. I myself would never have believed such things were possible if I had not accidentally witnessed how Nikolai Petrovich turned into a wolf and saved a little girl from a pack of wild dogs. . . .'"

"Is this all lies, or have you been conspiring with your old buddies?" the leader asked, interrupting himself.

Nikolai said nothing, and the leader carried on reading:

"'I gave Nikolai Petrovich my word that I wouldn't tell anyone about what I had seen, but I am breaking my promise because I believe that this remarkable natural phenomenon should be studied. Because of the promise I cannot give you my name, and I ask you please not to tell anyone about my letter. Nikolai Petrovich himself has never told a lie in his life and I do not know how I shall ever look him in the face if he finds out. I confess that apart from a desire to assist the development of our science I do have another motive. Nikolai Petrovich lives in very poor circumstances, with no income but a meager pension, which he generously shares with all comers. Although Nikolai Petrovich himself regards this side of life as entirely unimportant, I make bold to assert that the value of his knowledge for all of humanity is so great that he should be provided with quite different conditions. Nikolai Petrovich is such a kind and considerate man that I am sure he would not refuse to cooperate with scientists and journalists. I can tell you the small amount of information that Nikolai Petrovich has given me in our conversations—in particular several historical facts. . . .'"

The leader turned the letter over.

"Now . . . nothing interesting here . . . rubbish . . . what's Stenka Razin got to do with it? . . . where is it now . . . ah, here it is: 'Incidently, it is an insult that a foreign word is still used for a fundamentally Russian concept. I would prefer the word *werevolk*—the Russian root indicates the origin of the phenomenon and the romance prefix sets it in the general European cultural context.'

"That final phrase," said the leader, "makes it perfectly clear that the kind and considerate Nikolai Petrovich and the anonymous inhabitant of Konkovo are one and the same."

For several seconds there was silence. The leader tossed the piece of paper aside and looked at Nikolai.

"They'll come here," he said sadly. "They're quite stupid enough to do that. They might have been here already if Ivan hadn't seen the letter. But you sent it to other journals as well, didn't you?"

Nikolai slammed his paw down into the dust.

"Listen, what's the point of all this hot air? I do what I think is right, there's no point in trying to change my mind, and I must confess that I don't much care for your company. So let's leave it at that." He raised his belly from the earth, as if to stand.

"Wait! Don't be in such a hurry. It's sad, but it looks as though your magical dance on the dump is about to come to an end."

"What does that mean?" asked Nikolai, pricking up his ears.

"Just that soap bubbles have a habit of bursting. We can't kill you, it's true. But take a look at him."

"I don't know him," yelped Nikolai. He looked down at Sasha's shadow. Sasha also looked down and his head spun with the shock: all the others had the shadows of humans, but he had the shadow of a wolf.

"He's new. He can take your nominal place in the pack if he defeats you. What do you think off that?" The leader's final question was phrased in obvious mimicry of Nikolai's typical bark.

"It seems you're quite a specialist on the ancient laws," Nikolai replied, attempting an ironical growl.

"Like yourself. Aren't they the commodity you intend to trade in? But you're not so clever. Who's going to pay you? Most of what we know is of no use to anyone."

"That still leaves something," Nikolai muttered, probing the circle with his gaze. There was no way out—the circle was closed. Sasha finally understood the meaning of what was happening: he would have to fight with this fat old wolf.

"But I only ended up here by accident," he thought. "I didn't hear any call—I don't even know what it is!"

He looked around—all eyes were fixed on him. "Maybe I should tell them everything? They might let me go . . ."

He remembered his transformation, and then the way they had raced through the dark forest and along the road: it was the most beautiful thing he had ever experienced. "You're nothing but an impostor. You haven't got a chance," said a familiar voice inside his head. But at the same moment a different voice—the leader's—said:

"Sasha, this is your chance."

He was about to confess everything, but his paws stepped forward of their own accord and he heard a voice hoarse with excitement bark:

"I'm ready."

He realized that he had said it and immediately felt calm.

The wolf in him had taken control of his actions—he no longer had any doubts. The pack growled in approval. Nikolai slowly raised his dull yellow eyes to look at Sasha.

"Remember, my young friend, that it's only a very small chance," he said. "Very small indeed. It looks as though this is going to be your last night."

Sasha didn't reply. The old wolf lay on the ground in the same position.

"We're waiting for you, Nikolai," the leader said quietly.

Nikolai yawned lazily—and suddenly leapt into the air. His legs, rapidly straightening, threw him upwards like a spring, and when he struck the ground again there was nothing left in him of the old tired dog—this was a real wolf, filled with calm ferocity: his neck was tensed and his eyes stared right through Sasha. Once again a growl of approval ran through the pack. The wolves discussed something rapidly: one of them ran over to the leader and put his muzzle close to his ear.

"Yes," said the leader, "definitely." He turned to Sasha. "Before the fight there should be an exchange of insults. The pack desires it."

Sasha yawned nervously and glanced at Nikolai, who set off around the circle without taking his eyes off some object located just beyond Sasha—then Sasha also set off along the living wall, following his foe. They walked around the circle several times and then stopped.

"Nikolai Petrovich, I find you repulsive," Sasha managed to squeeze out.

"You can tell that to your daddy," Nikolai replied readily. Sasha felt the tension slip away.

"Why not," he said, "at least I know who he is."

He thought that was a phrase from an old French novel—it would have been more appropriate if the moonlit bulk of Notre Dame had been towering up behind him, but he couldn't think of anything better.

"I must keep it more simple," he thought, and asked:

"What's that wet spot under your tail?"

"That's where I smashed out the brains of a kid called Sasha," Nikolai growled. They started off again, along a slowly narrowing spiral, facing each other all the while.

"I suppose all sorts of things probably happen at the dump," said Sasha. "Don't you find the smells there irritating?"

"I find your smell irritating."

"Be patient. It'll pass—soon you'll be dead."

Nikolai stopped. Sasha stopped too and screwed up his eyes against the painful glare of the street lamp.

"Your stuffed body," Nikolai said softly, "will stand in the local secondary school next to the globe and they'll use it for the ceremony when children join the Pioneers."

"Enough," said Sasha, "let's finish on a more intimate note. Do you like Yesenin, Nick?" Nikolai replied with an obscene variation of the deceased poet's name.

"That's wrong of you. I can remember a quite remarkable line: *You whine like a bitch in the moonlight.* Good isn't it, terse yet expressive . . ."

Nikolai Petrovich pounced.

Sasha had not the slightest idea of what a werewolf fight was like, but everything became clear in the course of events. While he and his opponent were walking around the circle and insulting each other, he had realized that the idea was not just to amuse the pack, but to allow the opponents to take a good look at each other and choose the moment to attack. He had made a mistake in getting carried away by the exchange of insults and his opponent had jumped at him while he was blinded by the light of the street lamp.

As soon as Nikolai's front paws and gaping jaws rose into the air, Sasha instantly thought through several possible courses of action, and his racing thoughts were entirely calm. He jumped to one side, first giving his body the command, then flying up from the earth into the dense gray air, making way for the heavy gray carcass as it fell. Sasha realized he had the advantage of being lighter and more agile. But his opponent was more experienced and stronger and was sure to know some special tricks—that was what Sasha had to watch out for.

When he landed he saw that Nikolai was standing sideways next to him, half-squatting and turning his muzzle in Sasha's direction. Nikolai's flank seemed to be exposed, and Sasha leapt, reaching with his open jaws for the patch of light fur which he somehow knew was the most vulnerable spot. Nikolai leapt as well, but in a strange way, twisting in the air. Sasha couldn't understand what was happening—Nikolai's entire hindquarters were exposed, he seemed to be laying himself open to Sasha's fangs. When he realized, it was too late—a tail like a whip of iron lashed across his eyes and nose, blinding him and depriving him of his sense of smell. The pain was unbearable, but Sasha knew that nothing serious had happened to him. The danger was that the second's blindness might be enough for his enemy to make another, decisive leap.

As he fell onto his outstretched paws, feeling that he was already defeated, Sasha suddenly realized that his enemy must once again be standing side on to him, and instead of jumping aside as instinct and pain prompted, he darted forwards, still unable to see, with the same feeling of fear he'd had during his first leap as a wolf—that leap from the clearing into the darkness among the trees. For a moment he hung in the air, and then his numbed nose rammed into something warm and yielding, and he closed his jaws as hard as he could.

The next second they were standing facing each other as they had at the beginning of the fight. Time had accelerated once again to its normal speed. Sasha shook his head as he recovered from the terrible blow of Nikolai's tail. He was waiting for his enemy to make another leap, but suddenly he noticed that Nikolai's front paws were trembling and his tongue was hanging out. A few more seconds passed, then Nikolai slumped over on to his side and a dark stain began to spread over the ground beside his throat. Sasha took a quick step forward, but he caught the leader's eye and stopped.

He looked at the dying werewolf. Nikolai shuddered a few times, then lay still. His eyes closed. Then his body began to tremble, but in a different way this time—Sasha could sense very clearly that the body was already dead, and the sight was terrifying. The outline of the recumbent figure began to blur, the stain beside the throat disappeared, and a fat man in his underpants and vest appeared on the trampled surface of the earth. He was snoring loudly, lying on his belly. His snores suddenly broke off, he turned on his side and made a movement with his hand as though he was straightening his pillow. The hand closed on emptiness, and the surprise was enough to wake him. He opened his eyes, looked around, and closed them again. A second later he opened them again and instantly burst into a wail so piercing that Sasha thought you could tune the most ear-rending police siren to it. He leapt to his feet, jumped clumsily over the nearest wolf and ran off into the distance along the dark street, all the while howling on the same note. When he eventually disappeared around the bend his wailing finally ceased.

The pack laughed wildly. Sasha glanced at his shadow and instead of the long silhouette of a muzzle he saw the outline of a rounded head and two protruding ears—his own, human ears. When he looked up he saw the leader staring directly at him.

"Do you understand?" the leader asked.

"I think so," said Sasha. "Will he remember anything?"

"No. For the rest of his life—if, of course, you can call it a life—he will think that he had a terrible nightmare," the leader replied and turned to the others: "Let's go."

Sasha retained no memory of their journey back. They went a different way, straight through the forest—it was shorter, but it took just as long because they had to run more slowly than on the highway. In the clearing the final embers of the fire were fading. The woman with the beads was dozing behind the windshield of a car: when the wolves appeared she opened her eyes, waved, and smiled. But she didn't get out of the car.

Sasha was sad. He felt rather sorry for the old wolf whom his bite had turned back into a human being. When he remembered the exchange of insults, and especially the change that had come over Nikolai a minute before the fight began, he almost felt a liking for him. He tried not to think about what had happened, and after a while he managed to forget it. His nose was still stinging from the blow. He lay down on the grass to think.

For a while he lay there with his eyes closed. Then he sensed how heavy the silence was and raised his muzzle—on every side the wolves were staring at him without speaking. They seemed to be waiting for something. "Shall I tell them?" Sasha thought.

He decided he would. Rising on to his paws, he set off around the circle as he had in Konkovo, but this time there was no opponent walking ahead of him. The only thing moving with him was his shadow—a human shadow like that of every member of the pack.

"I want to confess everything," he howled softly. "I have deceived you." The pack said nothing.

"I didn't hear any call. I don't even know what it is. I ended up here entirely by accident."

He closed his eyes and waited for a response. There was a moment's silence, followed by an explosion of barking, howling laughter. He opened his eyes.

"What are you laughing at?"

The reply was another eruption of laughter. Eventually the wolves calmed down and the leader asked him:

"How did you get here?"

"I lost my way in the forest."

"That's not what I mean. Try to remember why you came to Konkovo."

"No special reason. I like trips to the country."

"But why here?"

"Why? Let me think—That's it.—I saw a photograph that I

liked; it was a very beautiful view. And the caption said it was the village of Konkovo near Moscow. Only everything here turned out quite different . . ."

"And where did you see the photograph?"

"In a children's encyclopedia."

This time they all laughed even longer.

"All right," said the leader, "and what were you looking for in there?"

"I . . ." Sasha suddenly remembered, and it was like a blinding flash of light inside his skull. "I was looking for a photograph of a wolf! Yes, I'd just woken up and I wanted to see a photograph of a wolf! I searched through all my books. I wanted to check something—and then I forgot—so that was the call?"

"Precisely," replied the leader.

Sasha looked at Lena, who had hidden her muzzle in her paws and was shaking with laughter.

"Then why didn't you tell me right away?"

"What for?" asked the old wolf, maintaining a calm expression among the general merriment. "Hearing the call's not the most important thing. That doesn't make you a werewolf. Do you know when you really became one?"

"When?"

"When you agreed to fight with Nikolai, believing that you had no chance of winning. That was when your shadow changed."

"Yes. Yes. That's right," several voices barked in unison.

Sasha said nothing for a while. His thoughts were a confused turmoil. Then he raised his muzzle and asked:

"But what was that elixir we drank?"

The wolves laughed so loudly that the woman in the car wound down the window and stuck her head out. The leader could hardly control himself—his muzzle twisted into a crooked smile.

"He liked it," he said, "give him some more elixir!"

Then he began to laugh as well. A small bottle fell on the

ground by Sasha's paws. Straining his eyes, he read: Forest Joy. Elixir for the Teeth. Price: 92 kopecks.

"That was just a joke," said the leader. "But if you could have seen the way you looked when you were drinking it— Remember, a werewolf changes into a human being and back again as he wishes, at any time and in any place."

"But what about the cows?" Sasha asked, this time ignoring the howls of laughter. "You said we were running over to Konkovo to . . ."

He didn't finish the sentence and simply waved his paw in the air. Laughing, the wolves scattered over the clearing and lay down in the tall grass. The old wolf stayed sitting opposite Sasha.

"There's another thing I have to tell you," he said. "You must always remember that only werewolves are real people. If you look at your shadow you'll see that it's human. But if you look at people's shadows with your wolf's eyes, you'll see the shadows of pigs, cocks, toads . . ."

"And spiders, flies, and bats, too," said Ivan Sergeievich, who had stopped beside them.

"That's right. And then there are the monkeys, the rabbits, and the goats. Not to mention . . ."

"Don't frighten the boy," growled Ivan Sergeievich. "You're just making it all up as you go along. Don't you listen to him, Sasha." The two old wolves looked at each other and laughed.

"I might be making it up as I go along," said the leader, "but it's still true."

He turned to go, but stopped when he saw Sasha's inquiring gaze.

"Did you want to ask something?"

"What are werewolves, really?"

The leader looked him in the eye and bared his teeth slightly.

"What are people, really?"

Left on his own, Sasha lay down in the grass to think again. Lena came across and settled down beside him.

"The moon's about to reach its zenith," she said.

Sasha looked up.

"Surely that's not the zenith?"

"This is a special zenith, you have to listen to the moon, not watch it. Try it."

He pricked up his ears. At first all he could hear was the wind stirring the leaves on the trees and the buzzing of nighttime insects, and then another sound appeared, something like the sound of singing or music in the distance, when you can't tell whether it's an instrument or a voice. Once he'd picked up the sound, Sasha separated it out from all the others and it began growing stronger, until after a while he could listen to it without any strain. The melody seemed to be coming straight from the moon and it sounded like the music that had been played in the clearing before their transformation. It had sounded dark and menacing then, but now it was soothing. It was beautiful, but there were annoying gaps in it, empty patches. Suddenly he realized that he could fill them in with his own voice, and he began howling, quietly at first, then louder, raising his muzzle to the sky and forgetting everything else—and just then the melody blended with his howling and became perfect. Other voices sprang up beside his. All of them were quite different, but they didn't clash at all.

Soon the entire pack was howling. Sasha could understand the feelings expressed in every voice and the meaning of the whole business. Every voice howled its own theme: Lena was howling about something light and gentle like a drop of rain falling on a ringing tin roof; the leader's deep bass was howling about the immeasurably deep abysses he had crossed in great soaring leaps; the descant howling of the cubs was about their joy at being alive, the fact that morning came in the morning and evening came in the evening, and about a strange sadness that is like a joy. And all together they were howling about the incomprehensible beauty of the world, the center of which lay in the grass of the clearing. The music became louder and louder, the moon swam towards Sasha's eyes, covering the entire sky, and then came tumbling down on him—or perhaps he floated up from the earth and fell on to its advancing surface.

When he came around, he could feel a gentle jolting and hear the sound of an engine. He opened his eyes and discovered that he was half-slumped on the back seat of a car. His backpack lay at his feet, Lena was sleeping beside him with her head on his shoulder, and the leader of the pack, Colonel Lebedenko, was sitting in the driver's seat.

Sasha was about to say something, but he saw the Colonel press his finger to his lips in the rearview mirror. Sasha turned toward the window. A long line of cars was racing along the highway. It was early in the morning, the sun had only just appeared, and the surface of the road ahead looked like an endless pink ribbon. On the horizon he could see the tiny doll's houses of the approaching city.

Vera Pavlovna's Ninth Dream

Here we see that solipsism, strictly thought through,
coincides with pure realism.
                                        —Ludwig Wittgenstein

PERESTROIKA ERUPTED INTO
the public lavatory on Tverskoy Boulevard from several directions at once. The clients began squatting in their cubicles
longer, reluctant to part with the new sense of boldness they discovered in their scraps of newspaper. The spring light illuminating the stony faces of the gays jostling in the small tiled entranceway brought the intimation of long-awaited freedom, distant, as
yet, but already certain: those sections of obscene monologues in
which the leaders of the Party and the government were coupled
with the Lord God grew louder; the water and the electricity
were cut off more often.

Nobody caught up in all of this could make any real sense of
his involvement—nobody, that is, except Vera, the cleaning lady
in the men's toilet, a being of indeterminate age, and entirely sex-
less like all the rest of her colleagues. The changes that had set in
came as something of a surprise to Vera as well, but only to the
extent of the precise date at which they began and the precise

form in which they manifested themselves, because she herself was their source and origin.

It all began on that afternoon when Vera thought for the first time, not of the meaning of existence, as she usually did, but of its mystery. This resulted in her dropping her rag into the bucket of murky, sudsy water and emitting a sound something like a rather quiet "ah." The thought was quite unexpected and unbearable, and most remarkable of all, quite unconnected with anything in her surroundings. It simply manifested itself in a head into which nobody had invited it, leading to the conclusion that the long years of spiritual endeavor spent in the search for meaning had been wasted—because meaning was itself concealed within mystery. Vera nonetheless somehow managed to calm herself down and go on washing the floor.

When ten minutes had passed and she had already worked her way across a substantial portion of the tiles, a new consideration suddenly occurred to her, which was that this same idea could well occur to other people engaged in intellectual activity, and must, in fact have occurred to them, especially the older and more experienced ones. Vera began figuring out which members of her circle that might be, and quickly reached the certain conclusion that she did not have to look very far and could talk about it with Manyasha, the cleaner from the toilet next door, which was just like this one, only for women.

Manyasha was a little older, a skinny woman also of indeterminate but decidedly advanced age. For some reason, perhaps beause Manyasha always wove her hair into a gray plait at the back of her head, the sight of her always reminded Vera of the phrase "Dostoyevsky's Petersburg." Manyasha was Vera's oldest friend: they often exchanged photocopies of Blavatskaya and Ramacharaka, whose real name, according to Manyasha, was Silberstein. They went to the *Illusion* cinema to see Fassbinder and Bergman, but they hardly ever spoke about serious matters. Manyasha's mentorship of Vera's intellectual life was exercised in a quite unobtrusive and tangential fashion, and Vera never really felt aware of it.

No sooner had Vera recalled Manyasha, than the small employees' door between the two toilets opened (they had separate entrances from the street) and Manyasha herself appeared. Vera immediately launched into a confused explanation of her problem, and Manyasha listened without interrupting.

"So it turns out," Vera was saying, "that the search for the meaning of life is itself the only meaning of life. No, that's not it, it turns out that knowledge of the mystery of life, as distinct from an understanding of its meaning, makes it possible to control existence, that is, actually to put an end to an old life and begin a new one. Once the mystery has been mastered, no problem remains with the meaning."

"That's not exactly right," Manyasha interrupted, after listening attentively for a long time. "Or more precisely, it is absolutely right in every respect except that you fail to take into account the nature of the human spirit. Do you seriously believe that if you discovered this mystery you could solve every problem that arises?"

"Of course. I'm sure of it. But how can I discover it?"

Manyasha thought for a second, then she seemed to come to some decision and said:

"There's a rule involved here. If someone knows this mystery and you ask them about it, then they have to reveal it to you."

"Then why doesn't anyone know it?"

"Why do you think that? Some people do know it, and the others, obviously, never think to ask. Have you, for instance, ever asked anybody?"

"Well, let's say that I'm asking you now," Vera replied quickly.

"Then put your hand on the floor," Manyasha said, "so that you will bear the full responsibility for what is about to happen."

"Couldn't we do it without any of this playacting?" Vera grumbled, leaning down to the floor and placing her palm on a cold, square tile.

"Well, then?"

Manyasha beckoned Vera to come closer, then she took her head in her hands, tilted it so that Vera's ear was directly opposite her mouth, and whispered briefly into it. At that very moment there was a loud booming sound outside the walls of the lavatory.

"What, is that all?" Vera asked, straightening up. Manyasha nodded. Vera laughed doubtfully. Manyasha shrugged, as if to say she wasn't the one that thought it up, so she wasn't to blame. Vera stopped laughing.

"You know," she said, "I always suspected something of the sort."

Manyasha laughed.

"They all say that."

"Well then," said Vera, "for a start I'll try something simple. For instance, make pictures appear on the walls here and have some music playing."

"I think you'll be able to manage that," Manyasha said, "but don't forget that your efforts might produce unexpected results, something that seems to be entirely unrelated to what you're try-ing to do. The connection will only become clear later."

"But what could happen?"

"You'll see that for yourself."

It was some time before she did see, several months in fact, dur-ing those repulsive November days when it might be snow your feet are plowing through or it might be water, and it might be mist hanging in the air or it might be steam obscuring the sight of blue militia caps and the crimson bruises of banners held aloft.

What happened was that several proletarians in a festive mood descended into the toilet bearing a large quantity of ideo-logical equipment: immense paper carnations on long green poles and incantations on special plywood sheets. Having relieved themselves, they set their bicolored lances against the walls, fenced off the urinals with their sodden plywood placards (the upper one bore the incomprehensible inscription: "Ninth Pipe-Drawing Brigade") and settled down for a small picnic in the narrow space in front of the mirror and the washbasin. The smell of fortified wine rapidly overpowered the smell of urine and chlorine. At first there was laughter and conversation, then a sudden silence fell, broken by a coarse male voice:

"You pouring that on the floor deliberately, you fucker?"

"No, 'course not," an unconvincing tenor replied hastily, "it's not the usual kind of bottle, the neck's shorter. I was listening to what you were saying. Try it yourself, Grigory, my hand just automatically . . ."

There was the sound of a blow striking against something soft and voices raised in approving obscenity, and after that the picnic somehow came to a rapid conclusion and the voices withdrew, echoing hollowly on the staircase up to the boulevard before they finally disappeared. Vera plucked up the courage to glance out of her corner.

A young man with his face beaten to pulp was sitting in the middle of the floor, spitting out blood at regular intervals onto the tiles that were awash with fortified port wine. At the sight of Vera he took fright, leapt to his feet and ran out on to the street, leaving behind in the entranceway a damp, broken carnation and a small board bearing the inscription: "There is no alternative to the paradigm of Perestroika!" Vera had not the slightest idea of the meaning contained in these words, but from her long experience of life she was quite certain that something new had begun, though she could not really believe that she had started it. Just to be on the safe side she picked up the gigantic flower and the placard and carried them into her own small room, which was made out of the two end cubicles. The partition between them had been removed and there was just enough space for a bucket, a mop, and a chair, in which she was able to take an occasional nap.

After this incident everything went on in the same old way for a long time. After all, what can happen in a toilet? Life proceeded smoothly and predictably, only the number of empty bottles that arrived each day began to fall, and people became less friendly.

One day a group of people appeared in the toilet who were clearly not there to relieve themselves. They were dressed in identical denim suits and dark glasses and they brought a folding ruler and one of those special things on a tripod stand (Vera didn't know what it was called) that people on the street sometimes look through at a stick with special markings held by someone else. The visitors measured the doorway, carefully surveyed the entire premises, and left without making any use of their optical device. A few days later they appeared again, accompanied by a man in a brown rain coat, carrying a brown briefcase (Vera knew him, he was the head of all the toilets in the city). This time the group behaved in a very strange manner: they didn't discuss anything or measure anything, they just walked backwards and forwards, with their shoulders bumping against the backs of the workers relieving themselves into the urinals (what an uncertain place this world is!) occasionally halting to peer meditatively at something invisible to Vera and the other visitors. Whatever it was, it must have been quite beautiful—she could tell from the smiles on their faces and the remarkably romantic poses they assumed.

Vera could never have expressed her feelings in words, but she understood everything perfectly, and for a few moments there arose before her inner eye a vision of the picture that used to hang in her nursery school: "Comrades Kirov, Voroshilov, and Stalin at the Building of the White Sea Baltic Canal." Two days later Vera learned that she was now working in a cooperative.

Her duties, by and large, remained the same as before, but everything in her surroundings changed. Gradually, and yet rapidly, with no delays or stoppages, the place was repaired. First the pale Soviet tiles on the wall were replaced with large tiles bearing images of green flowers. Then the cubicles were remodeled, their walls were paneled with imitation walnut formica, the severe white porcelain bowls of triumphant socialism were replaced by festive pinkish-purple chalices, and a turnstile was installed at the entrance, just like in the subway, except that entrance cost ten kopecks, not five.

When these transformations were completed Vera was given a raise of an entire 100 rubles a month and issued with new work clothes: a red peaked cap and a black garment halfway between overalls and an overcoat. Everything, in fact, was just like in the subway, except that the buttonholes and cockade were not adorned with the letter "S," but with two crossed streams of gold forged in thin copper. The double cubicle, where previously she could at least take a nap, was now transformed into a closet for toilet paper, and there was no way she could even squeeze inside.

Vera now sat beside the turnstiles, in a special booth like the throne of the Martian Communists in the film *Aelita*, smiling and changing money. Her movements acquired a smooth joyful rhythm, just like a sales assistant in the Eliseev shop she saw once in her childhood and remembered for the rest of her life. Bright blonde, with a generous, womanly figure, the sales assistant was slicing salmon against the background of a fresco depicting a sun-drenched valley where a cool bunch of grapes hung just half a meter outside reality, and it was morning, and the radio was playing softly, and Vera was a little girl in a red cotton dress.

The money jingled merrily in the turnstiles—every day they took in one and a half or two sacks full of it. "I seem to remember," Vera thought vaguely, "that somewhere Freud compares excrement to gold. He was certainly no fool, that's for sure—Why do people hate him so much? And then, that Nabokov . . ." She became absorbed in her usual unhurried stream of thought, but most of the thoughts consisted of no more than beginnings which had not yet crept as far as their own ends before they were overtaken by others. Life was gradually getting better and better. Green velvet curtains had appeared at the doorway, so that anyone entering had to separate them with his shoulder, and on the wall by the door hung a picture that was bought from a bankrupt diner: in rather strange perspective it depicted a troika of white horses harnessed to a hay-filled sleigh in which three passengers were paying not the slightest attention to the pack of wolves galloping after them in earnest pursuit. There were two men dressed in unbuttoned fur jackets playing accordions, and a woman without an accordion (which made the accordion a sexual characteristic).

The only thing that bothered Vera was the distant rumbling or roaring that she sometimes heard beyond the walls of the toilet—she had no idea what could possibly make such a strange sound under ground, but then she decided it must be the subway and stopped worrying. The cabins were filled with the rustling of genuine toilet paper—a far cry indeed from the old days. Pieces of soap appeared on the sinks, and beside them hung the boxes of electrical hand dryers. In short, when one regular client told Vera that he visited the toilet as he would a theater, she was not surprised at the comparison, and not even particularly flattered.

The new boss was a young, ruddy-faced guy dressed in a denim jacket and dark glasses, but he only showed up very occasionally, and Vera gathered he had another two or three toilets to keep an eye on. In Vera's eyes he seemed a mysterious and extremely powerful individual, but one day something happened which made it clear he was by no means in control of everything. When he came in from the street the ruddy-faced young guy usually thrust aside the green velvet curtain with a short, powerful movement of his open hand, then his face appeared, with two black glass ellipses in place of eyes, followed by the sound of his high-pitched voice. This time everything came in reverse order—first Vera heard his high, challenging tenor ringing out on the staircase, answered condescendingly by a gruff bass, and then the curtains parted. But instead of the hand and the dark glasses, what appeared was a denim-clad back that wasn't so much hunched over as folded. Vera's boss came backing in, trying to explain something as he went, and striding in after him came a fat elderly gnome with a big red beard, wearing a red cap and a red foreign T-shirt, on which Vera read the words: WHAT I REALLY NEED IS LESS SHIT FROM YOU PEOPLE.

The gnome was tiny, but the way he carried himself made him look taller than everyone else in the place. Glancing quickly around the premises, he opened his briefcase, took out a bundle of seals and applied one of them to a sheet of paper hastily proffered by Vera's boss. Then he uttered some brief instruction, prodded the young guy with the dark glasses in the belly with his finger, chuckled, and left. Vera didn't even notice him go. He was standing opposite the mirror, and then he was gone, as though he'd just plunged into the open mouth of some special gnome subway. Following the disincarnation of the midget with the seals Vera's boss calmed down, grew a lot taller and spoke a few phrases to no one in particular, from which Vera gathered that the gnome really was a very big man; he ruled over all the toilets in Moscow.

"What strange bosses we have nowadays," Vera muttered to herself, jangling the money in the bowl in front of her and handing out disposable paper towels. "It's really awful." She liked to pretend she took everything that happened in just the same way as some abstract Vera working as a cleaner in a toilet ought to take it, and she tried to forget that she herself had stirred up these forces of the underworld, stirred them up for no more than a joke, just so that she could have a picture hanging on the wall (as far as the music was concerned, she felt that wish had already been granted in the two accordions it included). Where Vera's life had previously been boring and monotonous, it was now eventful and full of meaning. Quite often now Vera saw various remarkable people, such as scientists, cosmonauts, and performers, and once the toilet was even visited by the father of a fraternal nation, General Pot Mir Soup, who was caught short on his way to the Kremlin. He had masses of people with him, and while he was sitting in the stall, three touchingly made-up Young Pioneers played a mournful, drawn-out melody on long flutes right beside Vera's booth. It was so moving that Vera shed a furtive tear.

One day soon after this incident Vera's boss arrived with a cassette deck and speakers, and the following day the toilet had music. Vera now had the additional responsibility of turning the cassettes over and changing them. The morning usually began with Giuseppe Verdi's "Requiem," and the first excited visitors usually appeared when the passionate soprano in the second movement was imploring the Lord to save her from eternal death.

"*Libera me domini de morte aeterna*," Vera sang along quietly, jangling the copper in her bowl in time with the powerful blows of the invisible orchestra. After that they usually put on Bach's "Christmas Oratorio" or something of the kind, something spiritual in German, and Vera, who could only follow that language with a certain effort, listened as the thin-voiced children merrily gave the Lord who had dispatched them to the world below an assurance of something or other.

"Then for what has the Lord created us?" inquired the doubting soprano, forcefully escorted by two violins.

"In order," the choir replied confidently, "that we might glorify him."

"Can this be so?" the soprano queried with renewed doubt.

"Beyond all doubting!" the children's voices sang in confirmation.

Then, as the time approached two or three o'clock, Vera would put on Mozart, and her troubled soul would slowly settle into calmness as it glided over the cold marble floor of an immense hall, in which two grand pianos jangled against each other in a minor key. When the evening was really close, Vera put on Wagner, and for a few seconds the Valkyries were confused in their flight into battle by the sight of tiled walls and sinks flickering past beneath their wildly careering steeds.

Everything would have been just wonderful, if not for one strange thing, which at first was hardly noticeable, in fact it almost seemed like a hallucination. Vera began to notice a strange smell, or to put it more bluntly, a stink, to which she had not paid any attention before. For some inexplicable reason the stink appeared when the music began to play, or rather, that was when it manifested itself. It was there all the rest of the time as well, in fact it was a fundamental element of the place, but it went pretty well unnoticed as long as it remained in harmony with everything else. When the pictures appeared on the walls, though, and then on top of that they started playing music, she began to smell that genuine, inexpressible toilet stench that no words can possibly describe, and which is merely hinted at even by the phrase "Mayakovsky's Paris."

One evening Manyasha dropped in to see Vera and while they listened to the overture to *The Corsair*, she suddenly noticed the stink as well.

"Vera," she asked, "have you never thought about how our will and imagination form these lavatories around us?"

"I have thought about it," Vera answered. "I've been thinking about it for ages and I can't understand it. I know what you're going to say. You're going to say that we ourselves create the world around us and the reason we're sitting in a public lavatory lies in our own souls. Then you'll say there really isn't any public lavatory, there isn't anything but a projection of inner content on to external object, and what seems like a stink is simply an exteriorized component of the soul. Then you'll quote something from Sologub . . ."

"And heaven's lamps to me proclaimed," Manyasha interrupted her in a sing-song voice, "that I created nature . . ."

"That's it, or something like it. Am I right?"

"Not entirely. You're making your usual mistake. The fact is that the only interesting thing about solipsism is its practical side. You've already managed to do something in this line—this picture with the troika, for example, or these dulcimers—zing, zing! But that stink, why, at what precise moment, do we create that?"

"From the practical point of view I can tell you for certain that it's no problem for me to clean up the stink, and the toilet as well."

"Me too," Manyasha answered, "I clean up the toilet every

evening. But what would come after that? Do you really think it's possible?"

Vera was about to open her mouth to reply, but she suddenly began coughing into her palm, and then carried on coughing for a long time. Manyasha stuck her tongue out at her.

Two or three days went by, and then the green curtains at the entrance were thrust aside by a group of visitors who immediately reminded Vera of that first group, in denim jackets, that had started everything happening. These people were dressed in leather and were even more ruddy-faced, but apart from that they behaved exactly the same as the first group. Soon Vera learned that they were closing down the toilet and turning the place into a shop selling goods on commission.

They kept her on as cleaner this time too, and even gave her paid leave while the repairs were going on, so that Vera got a good rest and reread several books on solipsism that she hadn't been able to get around to for ages. When she went back to work the first day, there was nothing left to remind her that the place had once been a toilet. Now just to the right of the entrance there was a long row of shelves where they sold all sorts of knick-knacks. Further in, where the urinals used to be, was a long counter, with a display stand and electronics counter opposite it. Hanging at the far end of the hall were winter clothes—leather raincoats and jackets, sheepskin coats and ladies' coats, and behind each counter stood a salesgirl. There was a lot less work for her to do now, and just loads of money. Vera now walked around the premises in a new blue overall coat, politely pushing her way through the crowd of customers and wiping the glass surfaces of the counters with a dry flannel rag. Glimmering and glittering behind the glass, like bright, multicolored Christmas-tree tinsel ("All the thoughts of the centuries! All the dreams! All the worlds!" Vera whispered to herself) lay various brands of chewing gum and condoms, plastic clip-on earrings and brooches, spectacles, hand mirrors, jewelry chains and elegant little pencils. After that, during the lunch break, she had to sweep up the dirt that the customers brought in, and then she could take it easy until evening.

Now the music played the whole day long—sometimes even several different types of music—and the stink had disappeared, as Vera proudly informed Manyasha one day when she appeared through the door in the wall. Manyasha frowned.

"I'm afraid it's not quite that simple. Of course, from one point of view, we really do create our own surroundings, but from another, we ourselves are merely the reflection of all that surrounds us. And therefore the fate of any individual in any country repeats in metaphorical terms what happens to that country— while what happens to the country is made up of thousands of separate lives."

"So what?" Vera asked, puzzled. "What's that got to do with what we're talking about?"

"Well, this," said Manyasha. "You tell me that the stink has disappeared. But it hasn't really disappeared at all. You're going to come up against it again."

Since they had transferred the men's toilet to Manyasha's side and combined it with the women's, Manyasha had changed a great deal—she spoke less and she came visiting less often too. She herself explained this by the fact that she had achieved equilibrium between Yin and Yang, but in her heart of hearts Vera believed her heavy work load and her envy of Vera's new lifestyle were really to blame—an envy that was merely masked by her philosophical attitude.

Through all of this, Vera gave not a single thought to the person who had taught her everything required to achieve this metamorphosis. Manyasha sensed Vera's changed attitude toward her, but she took it calmly, as though that was the way things ought to be—and she simply came to visit less often. Vera soon came to realize that Manyasha was right, and it happened like this: one day as she was straightening up after wiping down the glass counter, she noticed something strange out of the corner of her eye—a man smeared all over with shit. He was carrying himself

with great dignity as the crowd parted before him on his way to
the electronics counter. Vera shuddered and even dropped her
feather duster, but when she turned her head for a better look at
the man, it turned out to be nothing but a trick of the light—he
was actually wearing a russet-brown leather jacket.

After that first instance, however, tricks of the light began to
happen more and more often. Vera would see crumpled pieces of
paper on the glass surface of the counter, and she would have to
stare hard for a few seconds before she could see them as anything else. She began to feel it was no accident that the expensive
decorative bottles with the fairy tale names—each of them cost-
ing three or four Soviet monthly salaries—stood on the long shelf
behind the salesgirl in exactly the same spot where the urinals
used to gurgle so boisterously. Even the very name "toiletries"
scrawled on cardboard with a red felt tip pen suddenly became a
mere euphemism. Behind the walls now there was something
rumbling quietly but menacingly almost all the time, like a whispering giant; although the sound was not loud, it conveyed a
sense of incredible power.

Vera began looking carefully at customers as they came in.
The first thing she noticed were certain oddities in their dress:
certain things they wore simply insisted on resembling shit, or
just the opposite, the shit daubed on them simply insisted on resembling certain things. Many of their faces were smeared with
shit in the form of dark glasses; it covered their shoulders in the
form of leather jackets and encased their legs in the form of
jeans. They were all smeared with it to a greater or lesser degree:
three or four of them were completely covered from head to toe,
and one had several layers; the crowd showed him very particular
respect.

There were lots of children running around. One boy reminded Vera very much of her brother, who drowned at a Young
Pioneer Camp, and she watched very carefully to see what would
happen to him. At first he simply used to tell the customers what
they could buy from each of the shit-smeared individuals,

and he would even run up to customers as they came in and ask them:

"What do you want?"

Soon he was selling trinkets himself, and then one day, as Vera was shifting her bucket across the floor toward the counter with the huge black lumps of shit with serious-sounding Japanese names, she looked up and saw his face beaming with happiness. Looking down, she saw that his feet, which had been wearing shoes, were now thickly plastered with the same substance that covered most of the people standing around him. In a purely instinctive response she ran her duster over the boy, and the next moment he shoved her away rudely.

"Watch where you're going, you old fool," he said, brandishing the finger he had taken out of his pocket, and then, after a second's thought, transforming the gesture into a fist. Vera suddenly realized that while she was ruling the universe, old age had overtaken her, and now all that lay ahead was death.

Vera had not seen Manyasha for a long time. Recently their relationship had become a lot cooler, and the door in the wall that led to Manyasha's half of the premises remained locked for long periods. Vera began trying to recall the circumstances under which Manyasha usually appeared, and discovered that she could say nothing on that score except that sometimes she simply did.

Vera began recounting the history of their acquaintance to herself, and the longer she spent remembering, the more convinced she became that Manyasha was to blame for everything. Just exactly what this "everything" was she would hardly have been able to say, but she decided to take her revenge anyway, and began preparing a treat for the next meeting with Manyasha—that was how she thought of this thing she was preparing, a "treat," not even calling things by their real names to herself, as though behind the wall Manyasha might be frightened by reading her thoughts and decide not to come.

Manyasha evidently didn't read anything from behind the wall, because one evening she turned up. She seemed tired and unsociable, which Vera automatically explained by the fact that she had so much work to do. Forgetting about her plans for the moment, Vera told Manyasha about her hallucinations, and Manyasha livened up a bit.

"That's natural enough," she said. "After all, you understand the mystery of life, which means you can perceive the metaphysical function of objects. But since you don't know the meaning of life, you can't distinguish their metaphysical essence. And so you think that what you see is a hallucination. Have you tried explaining it for yourself?"

"No," said Vera, after a moment's thought. "It's very difficult to understand. Probably there's something that turns things into shit. It affects some things and it doesn't affect others—no—A-ha—I think I've got it now. The things themselves are not actually shit. It's when they find their way in here that they—or not even that—the shit that we live in becomes visible when it gets onto them. . . ."

"That's a bit nearer the mark," said Manyasha.

"Oh, my God—There was I thinking about pictures and music, and all the time this place was just a toilet; what music could there possibly be in here. But whose fault is it? As far as the shit's concerned, it's clear enough, it was the Communists who opened the valve."

"In what sense?" Manyasha asked.

"In both senses. No, if there's anyone to blame, Manyasha, then it's you," Vera concluded unexpectedly, and gave her former friend an unfriendly look, such a very unfriendly look that Manyasha took a small step backwards.

"Why me? On the contrary, how many times have I told you that all these mysteries would do you no good unless you came to grips with their meaning? Vera, what are you doing?"

Looking down and off to the side somewhere, Vera advanced on Manyasha, and Manyasha backed away, until they came to the narrow, awkward door leading to Manyasha's half of the premises. Manyasha stopped and lifted her eyes to Vera's face.

"Vera, what have you decided to do?"

"I want to smash your head in with an ax," Vera replied in a crazed voice, and from under her overall coat she pulled out her terrible treat, with a projection for extracting nails sprouting from its heel.

"Right across the braid, just like in Dostoyevsky."

"Well, of course, you can do that," Manyasha said nervously, "but I warn you, if you do, you'll never see me again."

"That much I can work out for myself, I'm not a total idiot," Vera whispered exaltedly as she swung her arm and brought down the ax with all her strength on Manyasha's gray head. There was a ringing and a rumbling, and Vera fainted.

When she came to she found herself lying in the changing room clutching the ax in her hands, with a tall mirror almost the height of a man, towering over her, and in it a gaping hole with the contours of an immense snowflake.

"Yesenin," thought Vera.

What frightened her most of all was that there was no door in the wall, and now she had no idea what to do with all those memories which involved the door. But even this ceased to be important when Vera suddenly realized that she herself had changed. It was as though part of her soul had disappeared, a part that she had only just become aware of, in the same way that some people are tormented by pain in amputated limbs. Everything still seemed to be in the right place, but the most important thing, which lent meaning to all the rest, had disappeared. Vera felt as though it had been replaced by a two-dimensional drawing on paper, and her two-dimensional soul generated a two-dimensional hatred for the two-dimensional world around her.

"Just you wait," she whispered to no one in particular, "I'll show you."

Her hatred was reflected in her surroundings: there was something shuddering behind the wall, and the customers in the shop, or the toilet, or the subterranean niche where she had spent her entire life—Vera was no longer sure of anything—would sometimes break off their inspection of the shit plastered along the shelves and look around in startled anxiety.

Some tremendous force was pressing against the walls from the outside; there was something trembling and quivering behind the thin surface as it flexed inwards—as though some immense fist was squeezing a paper cup on the bottom of which Vera's tiny figure was sitting, surrounded by counters and changing rooms, squeezing it only gently as yet, but capable at any moment of totally crushing Vera's entire reality. One day, at precisely 19:40 (the exact moment when Vera thought the green figures on the three identical lumps of shit on the shelf were showing the year of her birth), this moment came.

Vera was standing holding her bucket, facing the long counter with the clothes—where the sheepskin coats, leather rain slickers, and obscene pink blouses hung jumbled together—looking absentmindedly at the customers as they fingered the sleeves and collars that were so close and yet so far beyond their reach, when she felt a sudden jab of piercing pain in her heart. Instantly, the rumbling outside became unbearably loud. The walls began to tremble; they bulged inwards, then cracked open. And flowing out of the crack, overturning the counter with the clothes as it advanced on the terrified shrieking people, came a repulsive black-brown flood tide.

"Aagh!" Vera just had time to sigh before she was lifted from the floor, whirled around, and flung hard against the wall. The last memory retained by her consciousness was the word "Karma" written in large black letters on a white background in the same typeface as the title of the newspaper *Pravda*. She was brought back to her senses by another blow, this time a weak one, as she came into contact with some twigs. The twigs proved to be on the branches of a tall old oak tree, and for a moment Vera was at a loss to understand how, from her position on a tiled floor she knew every inch of, she could have been thrown up against any branches. It turned out that she was floating along Tverskoy Boulevard on a foul-smelling, black-brown flood which was already lapping at the windows on the second and third stories of the buildings. Glancing around, she caught sight of something that looked like a hill rising up above the surface of the slurry, formed by a fountain that sprang from the very spot where her underground passage had been.

The current carried Vera on in the direction of Tverskaya Street. The surface of the slurry was rising at a fantastic speed, the two- and three-story houses at the side of the road were no longer visible, and the huge ugly theater next to them resembled an island of gray granite. Standing on the brink of its towering shoreline were three women in white muslin dresses and an officer of the White Guards who was shading his eyes as he gazed into the distance. Vera realized they must have been performing *The Three Sisters*.

She was borne on further and further. A stroller drifted past her, carrying a baby dressed in a blue cap with a big red star, who stared around in wide-eyed astonishment. Then she found herself at the corner of a house crowned by a round columned turret, on which two fat soldiers in peaked caps with blue bands were hastily readying a machine gun for firing. Finally the current carried her out onto Tverskaya Street, which was almost totally submerged, and off in the direction of the somber distant peaks with their summits crowned by barely visible ruby-red pentagrams.

The flood tide was flowing faster now. Behind her to the right, above the roofs protruding from the brownish black lava, she could see an immense rumbling geyser that obscured half the sky; its rumbling mingled with the barely distinguishable chatter of a machine gun.

"Blessed is he who has visited this world," Vera whispered, "in its fateful moments. . . ."

She saw a globe of the earth floating alongside her, and realized that it must have come from the wall of the Central Telegraph Building. She rowed it over to her and grabbed hold of Scandinavia. The electric motor that turned the globe had obviously also been ripped from the wall of the Central Telegraph, and it lent the entire structure stability—on her second attempt Vera managed to scramble up onto its blue dome, seat herself on the red highlighted surface of the workers' state, and look around her.

Away in the distance she could see the television tower at Ostankino, some roofs still visible as islands, and ahead a red star seemed to be drifting toward her over the surface of the water; when Vera drew level with it, its lower points were already below the surface. She grabbed hold of one of its cold glass ribs and brought her globe to a standstill. Alongside her on the surface of the slurry there were two soldier's caps and a soaked tie, blue with small white polka dots—they weren't moving, which suggested that the current here was weak.

Vera took another look around and was amazed for a moment at the ease with which a centuries-old city had disappeared, until the thought came to her that all changes in history, when they happen, take place exactly like that: as though they are entirely natural. She didn't want to think at all; she wanted to sleep, and stretched out on the convex surface of the USSR, resting her head on her mop-callused hand.

When she woke, the world consisted of two parts—the early evening sky and an infinite smooth surface, which had turned quite black in the dim light. There was nothing else to be seen, the ruby-red stars had long ago sunk out of sight and God only knew what depth they were at now. Vera thought of Atlantis, then about the Moon and its ninety-six laws, but all of these comfortable, familiar old thoughts, inside which only yesterday her soul could nestle and curl up into a tight ball, were out of place now, and Vera dozed off again. Through her drowsiness she suddenly noticed how quiet it was—she noticed because she heard a gentle splashing coming from the direction where the magnificent red hill of the sunset rose up above the horizon.

An inflatable dinghy was moving towards her, with a tall, broad-shouldered figure in a peaked cap standing in it, holding a long oar. Vera pushed herself up with her hands, thinking as she looked at the approaching figure that on her globe she must look like an allegorical figure; she even realized what the allegory was—it was an allegory of herself, drifting on a globe with a dubious history across the boundless ocean of existence. Or of nonexistence—but that made no difference at all. The boat drew close, and Vera recognized the man standing in it. It was Marshal Pot Mir Soup.

"Vera," he said, with a strong Eastern accent, "do you know who I am?"

There was something unnatural about his voice.

"I know," answered Vera, "I've read a bit. I realized everything a long time ago, only there was a tunnel through what I read. There has to be to be some kind of tunnel."

"That can be arranged."

Vera felt the surface of the globe she was riding open inward, and she tumbled into the gap. It happened very quickly. She managed to get a grip on the edge of the breach, and began flailing her feet to find some support, but there was nothing beneath her but black emptiness into which the wind blew. Above her head there remained a patch of the mournful evening sky, shaped exactly like the outline of the USSR (her fingers were straining with all their might against the southern border). The familiar silhouette—which all her life had reminded her of a beef carcass hanging on the wall of the meat department in her local food store—suddenly seemed the most beautiful thing it was possible to imagine. And apart from it there was nothing else left at all.

From out of the fleeting world, Vera heard a splash, and a heavy oar struck her right, and then her left hand. The bright silhouette of the motherland swirled away and disappeared into the distance far below. Vera felt herself floating in a strange space—it couldn't really be called falling because there was no air, and even more importantly, because she herself was not actually there. She tried to catch a glimpse of at least some part of her body and failed, although she was staring at her arms and legs.

There was nothing left but this looking, and it didn't see anything even though the looking, as Vera realized with a fright, was in all directions at once, and there was no need at all to try and look in any particular direction. Then Vera noticed that she could hear voices—but not with her ears, she was simply aware of someone else's distant conversation. It concerned herself.

"There's one here with third degree solipsism," said what seemed to be a low and rumbling voice. "What do we recommend for that?"

"Solipsism?" broke in what might have been another voice, thin and high pitched. "That's not very pleasant at all. Eternal confinement in the prose of socialist realism. As a character."

"There's no vacancies left," said the low voice.

"What about Sholokhov's Cossacks?" the high voice asked hopefully.

"Full up."

"Then what about that, what do they call it . . ." the high voice began enthusiastically, "war prose? Maybe some two-paragraph Lieutenant in the NKVD? Does nothing but appear around the corner, wiping the sweat from her brow, and gazing piercingly at the bystanders? Nothing there at all except a cap, sweat, and a piercing gaze? For the rest of eternity, eh?"

"I told you, there's no room left."

"Then what is to be done?"

"Let her tell us," the low voice rumbled in the very center of Vera's being. "Hey, Vera! What is to be done?"

"What is to be done?" Vera repeated. "What do you mean what is to be done?"

Suddenly it felt as though a wind had risen—it wasn't real wind, but it reminded Vera of it, because she felt herself being carried off somewhere like a floating leaf.

"What is to be done?" Vera repeated out of sheer inertia, and then suddenly understood what was happening.

"Mmm!" the low voice growled tenderly.

"What is to be done?" Vera screamed in horror. "What is to be done?"

Every scream lent strength to this likeness of the wind; she hurtled through emptiness with ever-increasing speed, and after the third scream she sensed that she had entered the gravitational field of some immense object which had not existed before the scream, but which became so real after it that she found herself hurtling toward it as if falling out a window.

"What is to be done?" she screamed for the last time, before crashing into something with terrifying force.

She fell asleep at the moment of impact—and through her sleep she could hear a monotonous, mechanical-sounding voice:

". . . the position of assistant manager, I set the following condition: that I can start the job when I want, in a month or two, say. I want to make good use of the time off. I haven't seen the old folks in Ryazan for five years—I'll go visit them. Goodbye, Verochka. Don't get up. There'll be time tomorrow. Sleep."

Chernyshevsky, *What Is To be Done?*, Chapter XXVII:

When Vera Pavlovna emerged from her room the following day, her husband and Masha were already packing two suitcases.

Sleep

AT THE VERY START OF THE third semester, in one of the lectures on Marxism-Leninism, Nikita Dozakin made a remarkable discovery. Something strange had been happening to him for quite some time now: as soon as the small senior lecturer with the big ears—the one who looked like a priest assailed by blasphemous thoughts—entered the lecture hall, Nikita was overcome by the urge to sleep, as though he was exhausted. And when the lecturer began speaking and pointing up at the light fixture, Nikita just couldn't resist anymore, and fell asleep.

At first it seemed as though the lecturer was not talking about philosophy, but about something from Nikita's childhood—about attics, sand pits, and burning garbage dumps. Then the pen in Nikita's hand would mount diagonally to the very top of his sheet of paper, trailing some illegible phrase in its wake, and finally his head would droop and he would plummet down into darkness— only to emerge from it a second or two later, when the same sequence of events would be repeated.

His notes looked very odd and were totally useless for study: short paragraphs of text were cut through by long diagonal sentences about cosmonauts lost in space or a visit to Moscow by the Mongol Khan, all in small, jerky handwriting. At first Nikita was very upset by his inability to sit through a lecture in the proper fashion, but then he began wondering whether the same thing happened to the other students—and that was when he made his discovery. It turned out that almost everyone else in the hall was sleeping, but they did it a lot more cleverly than he did—with their foreheads leaning against the open palm of one hand, so that their faces were hidden. At the same time they hid their right hands behind their left elbows, so that it was quite impossible to tell whether or not they were writing as they sat there.

Nikita tried sitting in this position and he found that the quality of his sleep changed immediately. Before he used to switch suddenly back and forth between total oblivion and star-tled wakefulness, but now the two states were combined—he fell asleep, but not completely, not so deeply that he was totally oblivious. His state of consciousness was like that morning drowsiness, when any thought is easily transformed into a moving colored picture that you can watch while you wait for the ring of the alarm clock you've set back an hour. He discovered that this new state was actually more convenient for making notes on the lectures—all he had to do was to let his hand move on its own, allowing the lecturer's mumbling to skip straight from his ears to his fingers, but on no account allowing it to enter his brain—then Nikolai would have woken up, or fallen into a deeper sleep, losing all contact with what was happening.

Gradually, balancing between these two states, he grew so adept at sleeping that he learned how to pay attention to several subjects simultaneously with that tiny part of his consciousness that was responsible for contact with the external world. He might, for instance, have a dream in which the action unfolded in a women's bath house (a frequent and rather strange vision, in-cluding a number of quite astonishing absurdities: on the log walls there were handwritten posters with versified appeals to people to save bread; and thickset red-haired women hold-ing rusty washbasins, dressed in short ballet dresses made of feathers)—at the same time he was able to follow the streak of egg yolk on the lecturer's tie, while listening to the joke about three Georgians in space that the student next to him recited constantly.

For several days, waking up after Philosophy, Nikita was filled with joy at his new abilities, but the self-satisfaction evaporated when he realized that as yet all he could do in his sleep was listen and write, but the other student could tell a joke while he was asleep! It was obvious from that special oily gleam in his eyes, his general pose, and a number of other small but telling details. So one day, when he fell asleep at a lecture, Nikita tried telling a joke of his own in reply. He deliberately chose the shortest and most simple one, about an international violinists' competition in Paris. He almost got through it, but stumbled right at the very end and started talking about Dnepropetrovsk geysers instead of Dzerzhinsky's mauser. His neighbor didn't notice anything, though, and chortled in a deep bass when three seconds had gone by without Nikita saying anything, and it was clear the joke was over. What astonished Nikita most of all was the deep, viscous quality his voice acquired when he was talking in his sleep. But it was dangerous to pay too much attention to this, or he would begin to wake up.

Speaking while he was asleep was hard, but possible, and the lecturer served as an example of the extent to which human mastery of this skill could be taken. Nikita would never have guessed that the lecturer was asleep too, if he hadn't noticed that when the lecturer leaned against the tall lectern in his usual fashion, from time to time he would turn over to his left side and end up with his back to the auditorium and his face to the board (in order to justify his impolite pose he would gesture feebly in the direction of his numbered list of premises). Sometimes when the lecturer turned his back, his speech would slow down and his utterances would become so liberal, they incited a fearful joy—but he gave most of the course propped up on his right side.

Nikita soon realized that sleeping was convenient not only in lectures, but at seminars too, and gradually he was able to manage a few simple movements—he could get to his feet without waking up and greet the lecturer, he could go up to the board and wipe it clean, and even look for chalk in the nearby lecture halls. When he was called on, at first he used to wake up, become alarmed, and start confusing words and concepts, at the same time feeling a profound admiration for the sleeping lecturer's ability to frown, clear his throat and bang his hand on the table, all while keeping his eyes open and actually maintaining some semblance of expression. The first time Nikita managed to answer a question in his sleep it was unexpected and completely without any preparation—he simply became aware at the boundary of his consciousness that he was reciting some "fundamental premises." At the same time he was on the upper landing of a tall bell tower, where a small wind ensemble was playing, conducted by Love, who proved to be a short, yellow-haired old woman who moved with monkey-like agility.

Nikita was given straight A's, and from then on he even took notes from primary sources while he was still asleep, and only reverted to full wakefulness in order to leave the reading hall. Little by little his mastery increased, and by the end of second year he was already falling asleep as he entered the subway in the morning, and waking up when he left the same station at night.

But something began to frighten him. He noticed that he had begun to fall asleep unexpectedly, without being aware that he was doing so. It was only when he woke up that he realized, for instance, that Comrade Lunacharksy's visit to their institute on a carriage with three black horses wearing bells was not part of the program of ideological studies devoted to the 300th anniversary of the first Russian balalaika (the entire country was preparing for the big date at the time), but just an ordinary dream.

It was all very confusing, and in order to be able to tell whether he was asleep or not at any particular moment, Nikita began carrying a small pin with a big, round, green head in his pocket, and whenever he was in any doubt, he pricked his thigh, and everything became clear. Then, of course, there was the new fear that he might simply dream that he was pricking himself with the pin, but Nikita drove that thought out of his mind as quite unbearable. His relations with fellow students at the institute improved noticeably—the Communist Youth League organizer Seryozha Firsov, who could drink eleven glasses of beer in his sleep without stopping, confessed that he always used to think that Nikita was crazy, or at least that there was something strange about him, but now it was clear he was a good guy. Seryozha was about to add something else, but his tongue ran away with him, and he suddenly started talking about Spartak and Salavat Yulaev's chances in soccer this year, from which Nikita, who was dreaming at that moment about the Battle of Kursk, concluded that his friend was having a highly confused Romano-Pugachevian dream of some sort. Nikita gradually stopped being surprised that the sleeping passengers in the subway were able to swear and argue, stand on each other's feet and hold up those heavy bags filled with toilet paper and pickled seaweed—he had learned to do all of that himself. But he was astounded by something else. As soon as they reached an empty seat, many of the passengers in the subway would immediately drop their heads on to their chests and fall asleep—not the way they had been sleeping a minute earlier, but much deeper, completely cutting themselves off from everything around them. And yet when they heard the name of their station announced through their dreams, they never woke up completely, they slid straight back with astounding precision into the state from which they had previously taken their dive into temporary oblivion.

Nikita noticed this for the first time when a man sitting in front of him wearing a blue overall coat, who was snoring so loudly the sound filled the entire car, suddenly jerked up his head, marked his place in the book lying open on his knees with his travel-pass, closed his eyes, and fell into a state of motionless, inorganic torpor; after a while the carriage was shaken violently and the man jerked his head and began snoring again. Nikita guessed the same thing must be happening to the others, even if they weren't snoring.

At home he began observing his parents closely and soon noticed that he could never catch them awake, no matter how hard he tried—they were asleep all of the time. Just once his father, sitting in the armchair, let his head droop and dozed off into a nightmare: he shrieked, waved his arms about, leapt to his feet, and woke up—Nikita could tell that from the expression on his face—but then he swore, fell back asleep, and sat down closer to the television, where the blue flickering screen was purveying some historical epic of communal dozing.

On another occasion his mother dropped the iron onto her foot, giving herself a nasty bruise and a burn. Until the paramedics arrived, she sobbed so pitifully in her sleep that Nikita couldn't bear it any longer and fell asleep himself until the evening, when his mother was already dozing peacefully over *One Day in the Life of Ivan Denisovich*. The book had been brought over by a neighbor attracted by the smell of bandages and blood, an old anthroposophist by the name of Maximka, who had reminded Nikita, ever since his childhood, of a decayed biblical patriarch. Maximka was only visited very rarely by any of his numerous criminal grandchildren, and he was quietly sleeping out his life in the company of several intelligent cats and a dark-colored icon with which he argued every morning.

After the incident with the iron Nikita's relations with his parents moved into a new phase. It turned out to be quite easy to avoid all the scandals and misunderstandings if you simply went to sleep at the beginning of the conversation. One time he and his father discussed the state of the country, and during the discussion Nikita squirmed and shuddered on his seat because Senkievich, the smirking host of "Traveler's Club," had tied him to the mast of his papyrus boat and was whispering something into Thor Heyerdahl's ear. The boat was lost somewhere in the Atlantic, and Heyerdahl and Senkievich were walking around openly in their black Masonic caps.

"You're showing a bit more intelligence," said his father, gazing up with one eye at the ceiling, "only I don't know who can have been feeding you all that rubbish about caps. They have aprons, long ones down to here," his father demonstrated with his hands.

And so it turned out that no matter what form of human activity Nikita tried to adjust to, difficulties only existed until the moment he fell asleep, and after that, without the slightest real involvement on his part, he did everything that was required, and so well that when he woke up he was amazed. This applied both to the institute and to his free time, which used to be something of a torment to him because it just dragged on for so long. In his sleep Nikita devoured many of the books which had previously resisted his attempts to decipher them, and even learned to read newspapers, which finally reassured his parents, who had frequently whispered their bitter disappointment about him to each other.

"It's just like you've been reborn!" said his mother, who loved a pompous turn of phrase. This phrase was usually pronounced in the kitchen, while the borscht was being prepared. As the beets fell into the water, Nikita would begin dreaming of something out of Herman Melville. The smell of fried seaweed would fly out through the window, and mingle with the bovine lowing of a French horn. Then the music would fade away and the radio voice would begin speaking: "Today at seven o'clock we present for your attention a concert by master artists which sounds, so to speak, the final chord of the symphony of festivities devoted to the 300th anniversary of the Russian balalaika!"

In the evening the family gathered round the blue window into the universe. Nikita's parents had a family favorite: "The World in the Eye of the Camera." His father came out to see it dressed in his gray striped pajamas and curled up in the armchair. His mother came in from the kitchen with a plate in her hand, and for hours at a time they would sit there enchanted, following the landscapes drifting across the screen through half-closed eyes.

"If you long to try the taste of fresh bananas and wash them down with coconut milk," said the television, "if you long to delight in the roaring of the surf, the golden warmth of the sands and the gentle sunshine, then . . ."

At this point the television paused intriguingly. ". . . then that means you long to be among the bananas and lemons of Singapore."

Nikita snored along with his parents. Sometimes the name of the program would reach him, refracted through the prism of his dreams, and the content of his dreams would assume the form of a screen. Several times during the program "Our Garden," Nikita dreamed about the inventor of a popular sexual perversity; the French marquis was dressed in a cranberry-red robe with gold lace trimming, and he was inviting Nikita to go with him to some women's hostel.

Sometimes everything deteriorated into total confusion and the archimandrite Julian, an essential participant for any self-respecting "round table," would peer out of his long Zil with the flashing light on the top and say: "Till we meet again on the airwaves."

As he spoke he would jerk his finger upwards in a frightened manner toward the empty heavens. One of his parents would change the channel, and when Nikita half-opened his eyes he would see on the screen a major wearing a light-blue beret, standing in a hot mountain ravine.

"Death?" the Major would say with a smile. "You're only afraid of that at the beginning, just for the first few days. Serving here has really been an education for us—we've taught the spirits, and the spirits have taught us. . . ."

The off-switch would click, and Nikita would go to his own room to sleep under a blanket on the bed. In the morning, when he heard footsteps in the corridor or the alarm clock ring, he would open his eyes carefully, taking his time to adjust to the daylight, then get up and go to the bathroom, where various thoughts usually came into his head and his nightdreams gave way to the first of his daydreams.

"How very lonely a human being really is," he would think, twisting the toothbrush in his mouth. "I don't even know what my parents are dreaming about, or what the passersby on the street or old grandpa Maximka are dreaming about. I wish I could at least ask someone why we're all asleep."

Then he would panic at the thought of how impossible it was to discuss the question. Not even the most brazen of the books that Nikita had read had so much as mentioned it, and he had never heard anyone speak about it aloud. Nikita could guess what the problem was. This was not one of the ordinary things that simply go unspoken, it was a kind of universal joint on which people's entire lives turned. Even if someone shouted out that they should tell the whole truth, it wasn't because he really hated things being left unspoken, but because he was forced to by this most important thing in existence being left unspoken.

Once, when he was standing in a slow-moving line for seaweed that filled half the supermarket, Nikita even had a special dream on this subject. He was in a vaulted corridor, where the ceiling was decorated with moldings of vine leaves and snub-nosed female profiles, and the floor was covered with a red runner of carpet. Nikita set off along the corridor, turned several corners, and found himself in a dead end that ended with a painted-over window. One of the doors in the short cul-de-sac opened and a plump man in a dark suit peeped out. His eyes gleamed happily and he waved Nikita in.

Sitting at a round table in the center of the room were a group of about fifteen men, all in suits and ties and all rather similar to each other—balding, aging, with the shadow of the same inexpressible thought on their faces. They paid no attention to Nikita.

"Beyond a shadow of doubt!" said the one who was addressing the others. "We have to tell the whole truth. People are fed up."

"Why not? Of course!" responded several cheerful voices, and everyone began speaking at once; there was nothing but confused hubbub until the one who happened to be speaking smacked the table really hard with a file bearing the inscription "Far East Fish"—Nikita realized that the words were not on the file at all, but on the tin of seaweed from his other dream. The full surface of the file hit the table, and though the sound was not loud, it was very solid and prolonged, like the sound of a church bell with a muffler. Silence fell.

"Clearly," said the one who had struck the table, "we first have to find out what will come of all this. Let's try setting up a commission, say with three members."

"What for?" asked a girl in a white gown.

Nikita realized she was there because of him, and he held out the money for his five cans of seaweed. The girl's mouth gave out a sound like the rattling and buzzing of a cash register, but she didn't even glance at Nikita.

"In order," the man answered her—even though Nikita had moved on past the cash register and was already on his way towards the supermarket doors, "in order that the members of the commission can first try telling each other the whole truth."

Agreement was quickly reached on the membership of the committee—it was made up of the speaker himself and two men in light blue three-piece suits and horn-rimmed glasses, who looked like brothers: both of them even had dandruff on their left shoulder. (Nikita was perfectly well aware, of course, that neither the dandruff on the shoulders nor their simple way of speaking was genuine, but were simply elements of the accepted aesthetics in dreams of this kind.) The others went out into the corridor, where the sun was shining, the wind was blowing, and car motors were roaring, and while Nikita was walking down the steps into the pedestrian passageway, they locked the door of the room, and to make sure nobody could peep in, they filled the key-hole with caviar from a sandwich.

They waited. Nikita walked past the monument to the antitank gun and the tobacco shop, and had reached the huge obscene inscription on the wall of the concrete slab Palace of Weddings— which meant that he had only five more minutes to walk before he was home—when suddenly from inside the room, where so far he had heard only a hubbub of indistinguishable voices, there came a gurgling and crackling, which was followed by total silence. The whole truth had apparently been told. Someone knocked at the door.

"Comrades! How are things going?"

There was no reply. The people in the small crowd at the door began exchanging glances, and a suntanned European-looking man exchanged glances with Nikita by mistake, but immediately averted his eyes and muttered something in irritation.

"We'll break in!" they finally agreed in the corridor.

The door gave way at the fifth or sixth blow, just at the moment when Nikita was entering the hallway of his house, and he and the door-breakers found themselves in a completely empty room with a large puddle covering most of the floor. At first Nikita thought that it was the puddle he'd seen in the elevator, but when he compared their outlines, he decided it wasn't. Although the long tongues of urine were still creeping toward the walls, there was nobody there, not under the table or behind the curtains, and three empty suits that were left dangling on the chairs were all hunched over and scorched on the inside. A pair of cracked horn-rimmed glasses gleamed beside the leg of an over-turned chair.

"That's the truth for you," someone whispered behind his back. Nikita was already thoroughly fed up with this dream, which showed no sign of coming to an end, and he reached into his pocket for his pin. Trust his bad luck, it wasn't there. He went into the apartment, threw the bag with the cans onto the floor, opened his wardrobe, and began going through the pockets of all the trousers hanging there. In the meantime all the others went out into the corridor and started whispering in alarm; the sun-tanned guy almost whispered something to Nikita again, but

stopped himself in time. They decided they had to phone somewhere urgently, and the suntanned guy, who was given the responsibility of phoning, was already on his way to the telephone,
when suddenly all of them began howling triumphantly—the
vanished trio had appeared right there in the corridor in front of
them. They were wearing light blue shorts and runners and
looked ruddy and cheerful, as though they'd just come from the
bath house.

"There!" shouted the one who had been speaking at the very
beginning of the dream, gesturing with his arm. "It's a joke, of
course, but we wanted to show certain impatient comrades . . ."

In his fury Nikita jabbed himself several times with the pin,
harder than necessary, and he never knew what happened after
that. He picked up the bag and carried it into the kitchen, and
then went over to the window. Outside there was a summer wind,
people were walking along talking happily, and it was just as
though each of the passersby really was walking under Nikita's
windows, and not actually in some dimension known only to him.

As he gazed at the tiny human figures, Nikita thought
gloomily that he still didn't know the content of their dreams, or
the relationship between sleeping and waking in their lives. He
had nobody to complain to about his recurrent nightmares or to
tell about the dreams that pleased him. He suddenly wanted very
badly to go out into the street and start talking to someone—it
didn't matter in the slightest who it was—about everything that
he had come to understand. And no matter how crazy the idea
might be, today he was going to do it.

About forty minutes later he was already striding away from
one of the outlying subway stations up an empty street that rose
towards the horizon. It was like an avenue of lime trees that had
been sawed in half—where the second row of trees should have
been there was a broad paved road. He had come out this way because there were quiet places here, places the militia patrols
hardly ever visited. That was important—Nikita knew that you
can only run away from a sleeping militiaman in a dream, and

adrenaline in the blood is a very poor soporific. Nikita walked up the slope, pricking his leg with the pin and admiring the immense lime trees, like frozen fountains of green ink: he was so absorbed in them that he almost missed his first client.

He was an old man with several different colored badges hanging on a decrepit brown jacket, probably out for his usual evening stroll. He darted out of the bushes, squinted at Nikita, and set off up the hill. Nikita caught up with him and started walking beside him. From time to time the old man would raise his hand and move his thumb through the air with a forceful gesture.

"What's that you're doing?" Nikita asked after a while.

"Bedbugs," replied the old man.

"What bedbugs?" Nikita was puzzled.

"Ordinary ones," the old man said, and sighed. "From the apartment above. All the walls here are full of holes."

"You need Desinsectal," said Nikita.

"No need. In one night I'll squash more with my thumb than all your chemicals. You know the way Utyosov sings it: 'Our enemies . . .'"

Then he fell silent, and Nikita never did find out about the bedbugs and Utyosov. They walked on for several yards without speaking.

"Splat," the old man suddenly said, "splat."

"Is that the bedbugs cracking?" Nikita asked, hazarding a guess.

"No," said the old man with a smile, "bedbugs die quiet. That's the caviar."

"What caviar?"

"Well, just think about it," said the old man, livening up, his eyes beginning to gleam with the crazed cunning of a Suvorov, "d'you see that kiosk?"

Standing on the corner there was a newspaper and magazine kiosk.

"Yes," said Nikita.

"Good. Well now, imagine there's a crooked little hut standing right there, and they sell caviar there. You've never seen caviar like it and you never will—every grain the size of a grape, unnerstand? And then the woman serving, that great lazy creature, when she's weighing you out half a kilo she just grabs it out of the barrel with her scoop and slaps it onto the scales. By the time she's ladled out half a kilo for you she's dropped as much on the ground—splat! Unnerstand?"

The old man's eyes stopped gleaming. He looked around, spat, and went across the road, sometimes stepping around something invisible—perhaps the heaps of caviar lying on the asphalt in his dream.

"All right," Nikita decided, "I have to ask directly. Otherwise you can't tell what anybody's talking about. If they call the militia, I'll run for it."

It was already quite dark on the street. The street lamps were on, but only half of them were working, and most of those gave off a weak purple glow which colored the pavement and the trees rather than illuminating them, making the street look like some harsh scene from the afterlife. Nikita sat on a bench under the lime trees and froze into immobility. A few minutes later something that squeaked and squealed and consisted of a dark spot and a light spot appeared on the edge of the hemisphere of visibility that was bounded by twilight. It came closer, its movement interrupted by brief pauses during which it rocked to and fro, giving out an insincerely reassuring whisper.

When he looked more closely, Nikita could make out a woman of about thirty in a dark jacket, pushing a light-colored perambulator in front of her. It was quite obvious that the woman was asleep: every now and then she adjusted an invisible pillow under her head, pretending through the force of habitual female hypocrisy that she was tidying her piebald hair. Nikita got up off his bench. The woman trembled but didn't wake up.

"Excuse me," Nikita began, angry at his own embarrassment, "may I ask you a personal question?"

The woman drew her plucked eyebrows up onto her fore-head and stretched her thick lips from ear to ear, which Nikita took to indicate polite incomprehension.

"A question?" she asked in a low voice. "All right."

"What is it you're dreaming about at the moment?"

Nikita made an idiotic gesture, gesturing at everything around them with his hand, and lapsed into final and utter confusion when he realized that his words had had an entirely inappropriate suggestive note to them. The woman laughed like a pigeon cooing.

"You silly thing," she said tenderly, "I don't like that type."

"What type then?"

"With Alsatians, you silly. With big Alsatians."

"She's making fun of me," thought Nikita.

"Please don't misunderstand me," he said. "I realize that I'm stepping out of bounds, so to speak."

The woman shrieked quietly, turned her eyes away from him, and began walking quickly.

"You see," Nikita continued, becoming excited. "I know that normal people don't talk about it. Perhaps I'm not normal. But surely you must have wanted to talk about it with someone sometime?"

"Talk about what?" the woman asked, as though she was playing for time in a conversation with a lunatic. She was almost running now, peering intensely ahead into the gloom: the stroller was bouncing over the surface of the asphalt, and something in it was beating against its oilcloth sides.

"I'll tell you what about," Nikita answered, breaking into a trot, "take today for instance. I switch on the television, and there it is—I don't know which is more frightening, the audience or the presidium. I watched for a whole hour and I didn't see anything new, except perhaps for a couple of unfamiliar poses. One person sleeping in a tractor, another sleeping in an orbital space station, one talking about sports in his sleep, and even the ones jumping from the springboard—they were all asleep. And it turns out I have nobody to talk to."

The woman frantically adjusted her pillow and began running quite openly. Nikita ran alongside, trying to get his breath back after the effort of speaking, and the green star of a traffic light loomed rapidly towards them.

"For instance, take you and me. I'll tell you what, let me stick a pin in you! Why didn't I think of that before? Shall I?"

The woman flew out into the intersection and then stopped so sharply that something in the stroller shifted bodily and almost broke through the front of it, and before he could stop himself he had flown on several yards beyond her.

"Help!" shouted the woman.

As luck would have it, standing about twenty feet away in an alley there were two men with armbands on their sleeves, both wearing identical white jackets which made them look like angels. Their first response was to back away, but when they saw Nikita standing under the traffic light and not displaying any signs of hostility, they grew bolder and slowly came closer. One of them started talking to the woman, who was wailing and moaning and waving her arms about and kept repeating the words 'pester' and 'maniac,' and the second man came over to Nikita.

"Out for a walk?" he asked in a friendly voice.

"Something like that," answered Nikita.

The volunteer militiaman was a head shorter than Nikita and was wearing dark glasses—Nikita had noticed a long time ago that some people found it hard to sleep in the light with their eyes open. The patrolman turned to his partner, who was nodding sympathetically to the woman and writing something down on a sheet of paper. At last the woman finished what she was saying, glanced triumphantly at Nikita, adjusted her pillow, turned her stroller around, and pushed it off up the street. The other volunteer came over. He was a man of about forty with a thick mustache and a cap pulled right down over his ears to prevent his hair from being ruffled during the night, and a bag slung over his shoulder.

"On the money," he said to his partner. "It was her."

"I realized it right away," said the one in glasses, and turning to Nikita, he said, "and what's your name?"

Nikita introduced himself.

"I'm Gavrila," said the one in glasses, "and this is Mikhail. Don't you be alarmed, she's the local idiot. They mention her at all our briefings. When she was little two border guards raped her in the middle of a cinema, during the film *Here, Mukhtar!* and she's been touched ever since. She's got a bust of Dzerzhinsky wrapped in diapers in the stroller. Every evening she phones the station and complains they're trying to screw her, and she pesters the dog catchers, trying to get them to let an Alsatian loose on her. . . ."

"I did notice," Nikita said, "that she was a bit strange."

"Never mind her. You drinking?"

Nikita thought for a moment.

"Yes," he said.

They sat down on the very same bench where Nikita had been sitting only a few minutes earlier. Mikhail took a bottle of Moscow Special export vodka out of his bag, separated the bronzed cap from its fixing ring with a key ring charm shaped like a small sword, and twisted it off with a single complicated movement of his wrist. He was obviously one of those natural talents you can still meet in Russia who open bottles of beer on their eye socket and with a single firm slap of the hand can knock the cork half-way out of a bottle of dry Bulgarian wine, so that it can easily be grasped in their firm white teeth.

"Perhaps I should ask them?" Nikita thought, as he took the heavy paper cup and the seaweed sandwich. "But I'm afraid to. There are two of them, after all, and that Mikhail's a big guy."

Nikita breathed out heavily and fixed his gaze on the complex interwoven pattern of shadows on the asphalt under his feet. The pattern changed with every gust of the warm evening wind: at first there were clear images of horns and banners, then suddenly there was the outline of South America, or three Adidas stripes from the wires hanging under the tree, or else it all looked like nothing more than the shadows cast by light shining through leaves. Nikita raised his cup to his lips. The liquid that was intended to represent his country in foreign parts slipped down with remarkable gentleness and tact, no doubt in the belief that the action was taking place somewhere in the Western Hemisphere.

"By the way, where are we right now?" Nikita asked.

"Route number three," replied Gavrila in the glasses, downing a cupful.

"You blockhead," laughed Mikhail. "Just because some pig writes something down on the map does that mean it really is 'route number three'? It's Stenka Razin Boulevard."

Gavrila toyed with the empty cup, then for some reason he prodded Nikita with his finger and asked:

"Shall we finish it?"

"What do you think?" Mikhail asked Nikita seriously, tossing the cap up and down on his palm.

"All the same to me," said Nikita.

"Well, in that case . . ."

The cup made its second round in silence.

"That's it," Mikhail said thoughtfully. "Nothing else for the workers to look forward to for the time being."

He swung back his arm and was about to toss the bottle into the bushes, but Nikita managed to grab his sleeve.

"Let me have a look," he said.

As Mikhail handed him the bottle Nikita noticed a tattoo on his wrist—it looked like a man on horseback thrusting his lance into something under the hooves of his horse—but Mikhail immediately hid his hand away in his pocket, and it would have been awkward to ask specially to look at the tattoo. Nikita looked closely at the bottle. The label was exactly the same as on Moscow Special for the domestic market, except that the writing was in Latin characters and the Special Limited Extra Export Product emblem—a stylized globe with "SLEEP" inscribed on it in big letters—gazed out from the white background like an eye.

"Time to go," Mikhail said suddenly, glancing at his watch.

"Time to go," Gavrila repeated like an echo.

"Time to go," Nikita repeated for some reason.

"Put on your armband," said Mikhail, "or else the captain'll raise hell."

Nikita reached down into his pocket, pulled out a crumpled armband and slipped it over his arm; the tapes were already tied. The word 'patrolman' was back to front, but Nikita made no effort to fix it. "It won't be for long anyway," he thought to himself.

When he got up off the bench, he felt really unsteady and he was even afraid for a second that he'd be spotted at the base, but then he remembered what state the captain himself was in at the end of the last shift, and felt calmer.

The three of them walked in silence as far as the traffic light and turned on to a side street, in the direction of the base, which was ten minutes' walk away. Perhaps it was the vodka, perhaps something else, but it was a long time since Nikita had felt such a lightness in every part of his body—he felt as though he wasn't walking but soaring straight up into the sky, borne aloft on currents of air. Mikhail and Gavrila walked on each side of him, surveying the street with drunken severity. Every now and then they encountered groups of people. First there were some emptyheaded girls, one of whom winked at Nikita, then a pair of obvious criminals, then some people eating a cake right there on the street, and various other rather dubious individuals.

"It's a good thing," Nikita thought, "there's three of us. Or else they'd tear us to pieces—just look at their ugly mugs."

Thinking was hard. Inside his head the words of a children's song kept flaring up like bright neon lights—with words about how the best thing on earth was to step out side by side across the open country and sing together. Nikita didn't understand the meaning of the words, but that didn't worry him.

Back at the station they found that everyone had already gone home. The duty officer said they could have come in an hour earlier. While Nikita looked for his bag in the dark room where they usually held the briefings and assigned people their routes, Mikhail and Gavrila left—otherwise they would have missed their train. Once he'd handed in his armband, Nikita pretended that he was in a hurry too. The last thing he felt like doing was walking to the subway with the captain and talking about Yeltsin. Once he was out on the street, he felt that his good mood had totally evaporated.

Turning up his collar, he set off towards the subway, thinking about the next day. The grocery order with the two sticks of salami, the phone call to Urengoi, a liter of vodka for the holidays (he should have asked his colleagues where they got the Special, but it was too late now), collect little Anna from the kindergarten, because the wife was going to the gynecologist—the stupid cow, even down there she had something wrong with her—put it all together and he'd have to take a half day off from German Parmenych for taking today off. He was sitting inside the subway car now, opposite a pregnant woman who was staring hard at him from under her head scarf, drilling holes in his bald patch; he just kept on looking at his newspaper until the bastards tapped him on the shoulder, and then he had to get up and give her his seat, but they were already approaching his station. He went over to the doors and looked at his tired, wrinkled face in the glass with the entwined electrical snakes rushing past outside it. Suddenly his face disappeared and its place was taken by a black void with lights in the distance: the tunnel had come to an end and the train had emerged on to the bridge across the frozen river. He could see a sign, "GLORY TO SOVIET MAN," on the roof of a tall building, lit up by crossed beams of blue light.

A minute later the train dived back into the tunnel and the glass was filled with gesticulating alcoholics, a girl with needles who was finishing knitting something blue under the subway map, a schoolboy with a pale face, daydreaming over the photographs in a history textbook, an army colonel in a tall astrakhan hat, invincibly clutching a briefcase with a combination lock, and there on the other side of the glass somebody had traced out the word 'YES' in block capitals.

Then a long and empty street covered in snow appeared in front of him. There was a sharp pain in his leg. He put his hand in his pocket and took out a pin with a big round green head that had gotten in there somehow. He tossed it into a snowdrift and looked upward. In the gap between the houses the sky was very high and clear, and he was surprised to make out the dipper shape of the Great Bear among the fine sprinkling of stars—for some reason he'd been sure it could only be seen in summer.

Tai Shou Chuan USSR

(A Chinese Folk Tale)

A S EVERYONE KNOWS, OUR universe is located in the teapot of a certain Lui Dunbin who sells trinkets at the bazaar in Chanyan. The strange thing is, however, that Chanyan ceased to exist several centuries ago. For many ages already there has been no Lui Dunbin sitting in the bazaar, and long, long ago his teapot was melted down or squashed as flat as a pancake by the weight of the earth above it. In my opinion there is only one rational explanation which may be offered for this strange contradiction in terms—that the universe continues to exist, while its location has already perished: while Lui Dunbin was still dozing at his stall in the bazaar, in his teapot they were already excavating the ruins of ancient Chanyan, the grass was growing thick above his grave and people were launching rockets into space, winning and losing wars, building telescopes and tank factories . . . Stop . . . This is where we shall start. In his childhood, Ch'an the Seventh was called the Little Red Star. Then he grew up and went to work in the commune.

What is the life of a peasant? This is something we all know. Like others, Ch'an lost heart and took to drinking without restraint. He even lost track of time. He got drunk in the morning and hid in the empty rice barn in the yard of his own house, so that the chairman Fu Yuishi, nicknamed "the Bronze Engels" for his great political understanding and physical strength, would not notice him. Ch'an hid because the Bronze Engels often accused drunks of certain incomprehensible offenses—of conformism or degeneracy—and forced them to work without pay. People were afraid to argue with him because he called that a declaration of counterrevolutionary views and sabotage, and counterrevolutionary saboteurs were supposed to be sent to the city.

That morning, as usual, Ch'an and the others were lying around drunk in their barns and the Bronze Engels was riding around the empty streets on a donkey, looking for someone he could send to work. Ch'an was in a really bad way, and he lay with his belly to the ground and his head covered with an empty rice sack. There were several ants crawling across his face, and one even crawled into his ear, but Ch'an was in no state to raise his hand to crush them, his hangover was too bad. Suddenly from far away, from the Party yamen itself, where there was a loudspeaker, he heard the time signal on the radio. Seven times the gong sounded, and then. . . .

Either Ch'an imagined it, or a long black limousine actually did draw up at the barn. It was a mystery how it could ever have gotten in through the gate. Out of it emerged two fat bureaucrats in dark clothing with square ears and little badges in the form of red flags, while a third person with a gold star on his chest and a prawnlike mustache, remained sitting in the depths of the car, fanning himself with a red file for papers. The first two waved their hands and came into the barn. Ch'an threw the sack off his head and stared at his visitors in total incomprehension. One of them came over to Ch'an, kissed him three times on the lips and said:

"We have come to you from the distant land of the USSR. Our Son of Bread has heard much of your great talents and sense of justice and he invites you to visit him."

Ch'an had never even heard of such a country. "Maybe," he thought, "the Bronze Engels has informed against me, and they're taking me in for sabotage? They say they like to play the fool when they do that . . ."

In his fear Ch'an broke into a fierce sweat.

"And who are you?" he asked.

"We are P.A.'s," the strangers replied, then they took Ch'an by his shirt and pants, threw him onto the back seat, and sat on each side of him. Ch'an made as though to leap out again, but he received such a blow to the ribs that he quickly changed his mind and submitted. The driver started the engine, and the car moved off.

It was a strange journey. At first they appeared to be driving along the familiar road, then suddenly they turned off into the forest and seemed to dive down into a pit. The car was jolted hard, and Ch'an squeezed his eyes tight shut. When he opened them again, he saw that they were driving along a broad highway flanked by small houses with aerials on their roofs. There were cows wandering about and tall posters with pictures of the fleshy faces of ancient rulers and inscriptions in an ancient tadpole script. All of this seemed to come together over their heads, and it was as though the road was passing through an immense empty pipe. "It's like inside the barrel of a cannon," Ch'an thought for some reason.

It was amazing. He'd spent all of his life in the village and never even suspected that there were places like this nearby. It was clear now that they weren't going to the city and Ch'an felt calmer. The journey proved to be a long one. After a couple of hours Ch'an began to nod off, and then he fell asleep altogether. He dreamed that the Bronze Engels had lost his Party Card and he, Ch'an, had been appointed chairman of the commune in his place and now he was walking along the deserted dusty street looking for someone he could send to work. As he came up to his own house, he thought:

"Right then, Ch'an the Seventh is probably lying drunk in the barn—I'll just glance inside and see." He seemed to remember that he was the Ch'an the Seventh himself, but he still had this thought. Ch'an was quite amazed at this, even in his dream, but he decided that if he'd been made chairman, he must first have studied the art of Party vigilance, and this was it. He walked up to the barn, opened the door and there, sure enough, he saw himself sleeping in the corner, with a sack over his head. "Just you wait," thought Ch'an, and he picked up the half-empty bottle of beer from the floor and poured the contents straight onto the back of the head under the sack.

Suddenly there was a whirring and screeching and knocking sound above his head and Ch'an waved his arms in the air and woke up. It turned out they'd switched on some gadget on the roof of the car that whirled around and blinked and howled. Now all the cars and people ahead of them began to give way, and the constables with striped batons saluted. Ch'an's two companions flushed in pleasure. Ch'an dozed off again, and when he woke it was already dark, the car was standing on a beautiful square in a strange city and there were crowds of people all around, but a line of constables in black caps prevented them from coming close.

"Perhaps you should go out to the workers?" one of Ch'an's traveling companions said with a smile. Ch'an had noticed that the further they left his village behind them, the more politely the pair of them treated him.

"Where are we?" Ch'an asked.

"This is Pushkin Square in the city of Moscow," one of the P.A.'s answered and pointed to a heavy metal figure that was clearly visible in the beams of the searchlights beside a column of water that glittered as it scattered in drops into the air.

Above the monument and the fountain words of fire blazed across the sky. Ch'an got out of the car. Several searchlights illuminated the crowd, and above their heads he could see immense banners: "GREETINGS TO COMRADE SALAMI FROM THE WORKERS OF MOSCOW!"

Also floating above the heads of the crowd were portraits of himself on long poles. Ch'an suddenly realized that he could read the tadpole script without any difficulty, and he couldn't even understand why it was called tadpole, but before he could come to terms with his surprise a small group of people squeezed through the police cordon and came towards him: there were two women in red sarafans reaching down to the asphalt with semicircles of tin on their heads and two men in military uniform with sawn-off balalaikas. Ch'an realized that these must be the workers. They were carrying something held out in front of them, something small, dark, and round, like the front wheel of a Shanghai tractor. One of the P.A.'s whispered in Ch'an's ear that this was the so-called bread and salt greeting. Following his instructions, Ch'an tossed a piece of the bread into his mouth and kissed one of the girls on her rouged cheek, scraping his forehead on the tin kokoshnik in the process.

Then the police orchestra rumbled into life, playing on strangely shaped *tsins* and *yuahs*, and the crowded square yelled as one: "Hoo-rr-aaah!"

Actually, some of them were shouting that they should beat someone called yids, but Ch'an was not acquainted with the local customs, and so he decided not to ask about that.

"Who is Comrade Salami?" he inquired, when they had left the square behind them.

"You are Comrade Salami now," the P.A. replied.

"Why am I?"

"The Son of Bread has decided," replied the P.A. "The country is short of meat, and our ruler believes that if his deputy has a name like that, the workers will be calmer."

"But what happened to his old deputy?" Ch'an asked.

"The previous deputy," the P.A. replied, "looked like a pig; they often used to show him on the television, and for a while the workers would forget that there wasn't enough meat. But then the Son of Bread learned that his deputy was concealing the fact that his head had been cut off a long time ago, and he was employing the services of a sorcerer.

"But then how could they show him on television if his head had been cut off?" asked Ch'an.

"That was precisely what offended the workers most," the P.A. said, and then fell silent.

Ch'an wanted to ask what happened after that and why the P.A. always called the people workers, but he decided not to, in case he put his foot in it somehow. Soon the car came to a stop at a large brick house.

"This is where you are going to live, Comrade Salami," said one of the P.A.'s.

Ch'an was shown into his apartment, which was decorated in an expensively luxurious style, but which gave him a bad feeling—as if the rooms were spacious and the windows were big and the furniture was beautiful, but somehow it was all unreal; there was something dark and devilish about it, as though you only had to clap your hands hard and it would all disappear. But then the P.A.'s took off their jackets, vodka and meat hors d'oeuvres appeared on the table, and a few minutes later Ch'an could have looked the devil in the eye and spat at him. The P.A.'s rolled up their sleeves, one of them picked up a guitar and began to play, and the other began to sing in a pleasant voice:

We are children of the Cosmos
But first of all
We are your children, Mother Earth!

Ch'an couldn't quite grasp whose children they were, but he was beginning to like them more and more. They juggled and tumbled very skillfully, and when Ch'an clapped and applauded, they recited freedom-loving verse and sang beautiful songs about strong male friendship and the beauty of little girls. And there was a song about something incomprehensible that wrung Ch'an's heart when he listened to it.

When Ch'an woke, it was morning. One of the P.A.'s was shaking him by the shoulder. Ch'an felt ashamed when he saw what condition he had slept in, especially since the P.A.'s were neat and freshly washed.

"The First Deputy has arrived!" one of them said.

Ch'an noticed that his patched blue jacket had disappeared, and in its place on the chair hung a gray jacket with a little red flag on the lapel. He began dressing hurriedly, and had just finished tying the knot in his tie when a smallish man sporting noble gray locks was led into the room.

"Comrade Salami!" he announced, "the foundation of the wheel is the spoke; the foundation of order in the Empire is personnel; the reliability of the wheel depends on the space between the spokes, and personnel decide everything. The Son of Bread knows of you as a noble and enlightened man and he wishes to elevate you to high office."

"How could I dare to dream of such an honor?" responded Ch'an, barely managing to suppress his hiccuping.

The First Deputy invited him to follow. They went downstairs, got into a black car, and set off along the street, which was called Great Armory Street. Then they found themselves in front of a house like the one where Ch'an had spent the night, only several times larger. The house was surrounded by a large park. The First Deputy went ahead along the narrow pathway. Ch'an followed him, listening to the P.A. hurrying along behind playing a small flute in the form of a fountain pen.

The moon was shining. Black swans of amazing beauty were swimming in a pond, and Ch'an was informed that they were all actually enchanted KGB agents. There were paratroopers disguised as marines lurking behind the poplars and willows. There were marines lying in the bushes, disguised as paratroopers. At the entrance to the house several old women sitting on a bench ordered them in men's voices to halt and lie on the ground with their hands on the back of their heads. Only the First Deputy and Ch'an were admitted. They walked for a long time through corridors and up staircases on which happy smartly-dressed children played, and finally they approached a pair of tall inlaid and encrusted doors at which two cosmonauts with flamethrowers stood on guard.

Ch'an was alarmed and crushed by such magnificence. The First Deputy pushed open a ponderous door and said to Ch'an: "After you."

Ch'an heard gentle music and he tiptoed inside, where he found himself in a bright spacious room with windows wide open to the sky. In the very center, seated at a white grand piano, was the Son of Bread, covered in ears of corn and gold stars. He could see right away that this was no ordinary man. He was connected by several pipes to a large metal cabinet beside him which was gurgling quietly. The Son of Bread glanced at the new arrivals, but did not seem to see them; the wind came in at the windows and ruffled his gray hair. In fact he had seen everything, and a minute later he raised his hands from the piano, smiled graciously and spoke:

"In order to strengthen . . ."

He spoke indistinctly and seemed to be short of breath, and Ch'an realized that now he would be an extremely important official. Then came lunch. Ch'an had never eaten anything so delicious. The Son of Bread did not put so much as a single morsel in his own mouth. Instead, the P.A.'s opened a small door in the cabinet, threw in several shovels of caviar and poured in a bottle of wheat wine. Ch'an could never have imagined anything like that happening. After lunch he and the First Deputy thanked the ruler of the USSR and went out.

He was driven home, and in the evening there was a festive concert, at which Ch'an was seated in the very front row. The concert was a magnificent sight—every piece involved an amazing number of players in incredibly close coordination. Ch'an particularly liked the children's patriotic dance "My Heavy Machine Gun" and "The Song of the Triune Goal" as performed by the State Choir, except that during the performance of the song they trained a green floodlight on the soloist and his face became quite corpselike, but then Ch'an did not know all the local customs, so he did not ask his P.A.'s about anything.

In the morning, as he drove around the city, Ch'an saw

crowds of people stretching along the streets. One P.A. explained that all of these people had come to vote for Pyotr Semyonovich Salami, that is, for him, Ch'an. In a fresh newspaper Ch'an saw his own portrait with his biography, which said that he had a third-level education and had previously worked as a diplomat. That was how in year eighteen of government under the motto of "Efficiency and Quality," Ch'an the Seventh became an important official in the USSR.

A new life opened up. Ch'an had nothing at all to do, nobody asked him about anything, and nobody required anything of him. Occasionally he would be summoned to one of Moscow's palaces, where he sat in silence on the presidium as some song or dance was performed. At first he felt extremely embarrassed that so many people were watching him, but then he took a look at how the others behaved, and began acting the same as they did, hiding half of his face behind his hand, and nodding thoughtfully at the most unexpected moments.

He acquired a circle of high-living friends: People's Artists, Academicians, and General Directors skilled in the martial arts. Ch'an himself became a Victor of Socialist Competition and a Hero of Socialist Labor. In the mornings they all got drunk and went to the Bolshoi Theater to indulge in debauchery with the singers. Of course, if someone more important than Ch'an was taking his revels there, they had to turn back, and then they would stagger into some restaurant, and if the simple people or even the bureaucrats saw the sign "Special Party Service" hanging on the door, then they understood that it was Ch'an and his company making merry, and they kept well away. Ch'an also liked making trips to the botanical gardens to admire the flowers. On those occasions, Ch'an's bodyguards would ring the Gardens to make sure the ordinary people didn't get in his way.

The workers respected and feared Ch'an a great deal; they sent him thousands of letters complaining of injustice and asking him to help with all kinds of matters. Ch'an would sometimes pull some letter or other out of the heap at random and then help—this earned him a good reputation with the people.

What Ch'an liked most of all was not the free food and drink, not all his mansions and mistresses, but the local people, the workers. They were hard-working and modest, understanding. For instance, Ch'an could crush as many of them as he liked under the wheels of his immense black limousine, and everyone who happened to be on the streets at the time would turn away, knowing that it was none of their business, and the main thing was that they must not be late for work. They were so very self-less, just like ants. Ch'an even wrote an article for the main news-paper—"With People Like This You Can Do Anything You Want"—and they published it, with just a slight change to the title which became, "With People Like This You Can Achieve Great Things." That was more or less what Ch'an had wanted to say. The Son of Bread was extremely fond of Ch'an. He would often summon him and burble something to him, but Ch'an couldn't understand a single word. In the cabinet something gur-gled and glubbed, and the Son of Bread looked worse with every day that passed. Ch'an felt extremely sorry for him, but there was nothing he could do to help.

One day, as Ch'an was resting on his estate outside Moscow, news arrived of the death of the Son of Bread. Ch'an took fright and thought that now he was bound to be seized and arrested. He wanted to strangle himself on the spot, but his servants per-suaded him to wait for a while, and in fact nothing terrible hap-pened at all. On the contrary, he was appointed to yet another post: now he was in charge of the country's entire fishing indus-try. Several friends of Ch'an's were arrested, and a new leader-ship was established under the motto "Renewal of the Origins." During these days Ch'an's nerves were under such great strain that he totally forgot his own origin, and even began to believe that he really had worked as a diplomat and not spent days and nights at a stretch drinking in a small remote village. During the eighth year of rule under the motto "The Workers' Letters," Ch'an became the ruler of Moscow, and in the third year of rule under the motto "The Radiance of Truth," he married, taking as his wife the beautiful daughter of a fabulously rich academician. She was as elegant as a doll, had read many books, and knew dancing and music. Soon she bore him two sons.

The years passed and ruler followed ruler, but Ch'an only grew stronger and stronger. Gradually a large circle of devoted officials and military officers consolidated itself around him, and they began saying in low voices that it was time for Ch'an to take power into his own hands. Then one morning it happened. Ch'an now discovered the secret of the white grand piano. The Son of Bread's main responsibility was to sit at it and play some simple melody. It was considered that in doing this he set the fundamental harmony which was followed in every other part of the government of the country. Ch'an realized that the difference between rulers lay in which tunes they knew. The only thing he could remember very well was *The Dog's Waltz*, and for most of the time that was what he played. On one occasion he attempted to play the *Moonlight Sonata*, but he made several mistakes, and the following day a rebellion broke out among the tribes of the Far North, and there was an earthquake in the South, in which however, God be praised, nobody was killed. The rebellion caused quite a lot of bother, though: for five days the rebels with their black banners bearing a yellow circle fought with the "Brothers Karamazov" crack paratroop division, until they had all been killed to the last man.

After that Ch'an took no more risks and he played nothing but *The Dog's Waltz*, but he could play it any way at all—with his eyes closed, with his back to the piano, or even lying on it belly-down. In a secret drawer under the grand piano he discovered a collection of melodies composed by the rulers of ancient times, and he often leafed through it in the evenings. He learned, for instance, that on the very day the ruler Khrushchev played *The Flight of the Bumblebee*, an enemy plane was shot down over the country's territory. The notes in many of the melodies had been masked with black paint, and there was no way of telling what the rulers of those years had played. Ch'an had now become the most powerful man in the country. As the motto for his reign he chose the words "The Great Reconciliation." Ch'an's wife built new palaces, his sons grew, the people prospered, but Ch'an himself was often sad. Although there was no pleasure that he did not experience, many cares still gnawed at his heart. He begun turning gray and hearing less and less well in his left ear.

In the evenings Ch'an dressed himself up as an intellectual and wandered about the town, listening to what the people were saying. During his strolls he began to notice that no matter where he wandered, he always came out onto the same streets. They had strange names, such as Little Armory Street or Great Armory Street, they were all downtown, and the most distant street on which Ch'an ever found himself in his wanderings was called Ballbearing Street. Beyond that, they said, there was Machine Gun Street, and even further out, the First and Second Caterpillar Track Passages. But Ch'an had never been there. When he dressed up to go out he either drank in the restaurants around Pushkin Square or dropped in to see his lover on Radio Street and take her to the secret food stores on Corpse Street. (That was its real name, but in order not to frighten the workers, all of the signs there had the "r" missing.) His lover, a young ballerina, was as happy as a little girl when he did this, and Ch'an's heart felt a little lighter, and a minute later they would be back on Great Armory Street.

For some time now the strange narrowness of the world in which he moved had been grating on Ch'an's nerves. Of course there were other streets and even, it seemed, other cities and provinces, but Ch'an, as an old member of the upper ruling echelons, knew perfectly well that they existed for the most part in the empty spaces between the streets onto which he constantly emerged during his walks, simply as a blind. And although Ch'an had ruled the country for eleven years, he was an honest man, and he felt very strange making speeches about meadows and wide open spaces, when he remembered that even most of the streets in Moscow might as well not exist.

One day, however, he gathered the leadership together and said:

"Comrades! We all know that here in Moscow there are only a few real streets, and the rest hardly exist at all. And there's no knowing what lies further out, beyond the ring road. Then why . . . ?"

He had not even finished speaking before everyone there began shouting, leapt to their feet, and immediately voted to remove Ch'an from all of his posts. As soon as they had done that, the new Son of Bread climbed up on the table and shouted:

"Right, gag him and. . ."

"At least let me say good-bye to my wife and children!" Ch'an implored. But no one heard what he said. They bound him hand and foot, gagged him, and threw him into a car. After that things went as usual—they drove him to the Chinese Passage, stopped right there in the middle of the road, opened a manhole in the asphalt, and threw him in headfirst. The back of Ch'an's head struck against something and he lost consciousness.

When he opened his eyes, he saw that he was lying on the floor of his barn. He heard a gong strike twice outside and a woman's voice say:

"Beijing time, nine o'clock."

Ch'an rubbed his forehead, leapt to his feet, and staggered out onto the street, and at this very moment the Bronze Engels rode out from behind the corner. Like a fool, Ch'an panicked and ran, and the Bronze Engels rode after him with a loud clatter of hooves, past the silent houses with the lowered blinds and the locked gates. He overtook Ch'an on the village square, accused him of Ch'ungophobia, and banished him to sort magic mushrooms.

When he came back three years later, the first thing Ch'an did was to take a look around his barn. The wall on one side ran into a fence behind which there was a huge pile of garbage that had been accumulating there for as long as Ch'an could remember. There were large red ants crawling over it. Ch'an took a spade and began digging. He stuck the spade into the heap several times, and eventually it struck iron. It turned out that buried under the garbage was a Japanese tank that had been there since the war. It was standing so that the barn and the fence concealed it from view, and Ch'an could dig it out without worrying about anybody seeing it— especially as everybody was lying around drunk at home.

When Ch'an opened the hatch, his face was struck by a wave of sourness. There was a big anthill inside, and the remains of one of the tank's crew were still in the turret. When he took a closer look, Ch'an began recognizing the shapes of things. Beside the breech of the gun there was a small bronze figure dangling on a green-tarnished chain. Beside it, under the observation slit, there was a puddle where rain water collected. Ch'an recognized Pushkin Square with its monument and fountain; an empty, crumpled American can of Spam was the McDonald's restaurant, and a Coca Cola bottle cap was the same billboard Ch'an had stared at for so long with his fists clenched tight from the window of his limousine. It had all been dumped just recently by American spies on their way through the village.

For some reason the dead driver was not wearing a helmet but a forage cap that had slipped down over his ear—its cockade looked very much like the dome on the World Peace cinema. The remnants of the driver's cheeks bore long sideburns, through which numerous ants were crawling, carrying grubs. When he looked closer, Ch'an could see the two boulevards that came together at Corpse Square. He recognized many streets: Great Armory Street was the front section of armor, and Little Armory Street was the side section. There was a rusting antenna protruding from the tank, and Ch'an realized this was the Ostankino television transmitter. Ostankino itself was the corpse of the gunner and radio operator. The driver had obviously managed to escape.

Ch'an took a long stick and rummaged in the anthill to find the dam, the spot in Moscow where Mantulinskaya Street was located and nobody was ever allowed to enter. He sought out Zhukovka, where the most important dachas were—this was a big burrow, where the fat ants each three *tsuns* long wriggled along. And the ring road was the ring on which the turret turned.

Ch'an thought for a minute and recalled how he had been bound and thrown head first into a sewer shaft, and he felt a mixture of fury and resentment. He made up a solution of chlorine in two buckets and poured it into the hatch. Then he closed the hatch and threw earth and rubbish over the tank the way it had been before. And soon he had forgotten all about the entire story. What is the life of a peasant? This is something that we all know. In order to avoid being accused of bearing arms in support of Japanese militarism, Ch'an never told anyone that he had a Japanese tank beside his house. He told me this story many years later when we met by chance in a train. It seemed to me to have the ring of truth, and I decided to write it down.

May all of this serve as a lesson to those who would aspire to power. If our entire Universe is located in the teapot of Lui Dunbin, then what can be said of the country which Ch'an visited? He spent no more than a moment there, and yet it seemed as though his entire life had passed. He rose all the way from prisoner to ruler, and it turned out that he had merely crawled from one burrow into another. Miracles, no more and no less. How apt are the words spoken by comrade Li Chiao of the Huachous regional committee: "A noble name, wealth, high rank, and power capable of crushing a state are, in the eyes of a wise man, little different from an anthill." In my opinion this is just as true as the fact that in the north China extends to the shore of the Arctic Ocean and in the west to the boundaries of Franco-Britain.

So Lu-Tan.

The Tarzan Swing

I

The wide boulevard and the houses standing along both its sides were like the lower jaw of an old Bolshevik who, late in life, has arrived at democratic views. The oldest houses were from the Stalinist period—they towered up like wisdom teeth coated with the brown tarnish produced by many years of exposure to coarse shag tobacco. For all their monumental quality they seemed dead and brittle, as though the nerves in them had long ago been killed off by arsenic fillings. The sites where the buildings of former years had been destroyed now bore the crudely protruding prostheses of eight-story apartment blocks. In short, it was a gloomy spectacle. The only bright spot against this background of gloom was a business center built by the Turks, its pyramidal form and neon glitter transforming it into the likeness of some immense gold fang covered in drops of fresh blood. Up in the sky the full moon blazed brightly like a dentist's lamp poised on its extending arm to throw all of its light into the patient's mouth.

"Who can you believe, who can you believe?" asked Pyotr Petrovich, turning to his taciturn companion. "Myself, now, I'm a simple man, perhaps even a fool. Credulous and naïve. You know, sometimes I look in the newspaper and I just believe it."

"The newspaper?" his company inquired in a low voice, adjusting the dark hood that covered his head.

"Yes, the newspaper," said Pyotr Petrovich. "Any newspaper, it doesn't matter which. I might be riding in the metro, and somebody's sitting beside me and reading, so I lean over a little bit, peer into it, and already I believe it."

"Believe it?"

"Yes. Whatever it is. Except, perhaps, for God. It's too late for believing in God. If I suddenly start believing now it'll be dishonest somehow. All my life I haven't believed, and then when I get near fifty I suddenly start believing? What have I been living for, then? So instead of that I believe in Herbalife or the separation of powers."

"What for?" asked his companion.

"What a misery!" thought Pyotr Petrovich. "He doesn't talk, he caws. Why am I being so frank and open with him? I don't even really know him." They walked on in silence for a while, one behind the other, stepping lightly and trailing one hand gently against the wall.

"I'll tell you what for," Pyotr Petrovich said at last. "It's like having something to hold onto in the bus. It doesn't matter what it is as long as you don't fall. It's like the poet said: 'to hurtle on into the night and obscurity, gazing with hope out of the black porthole of the window.' There you are, probably looking at me and thinking, so you're a romantic at heart, are you my lad, even if you don't look like one on the outside—Well, you are, aren't you?"

His companion turned round a corner and disappeared from view. Pyotr Petrovich felt he had been interrupted in the middle of an important phrase, and he hurried to catch up. When the hunched black back was in his sights once again, he felt relieved and thought for no particular reason that the sharp-pointed hood made his companion look like a burnt out church.

"What a fine romantic you are, my lad," the back muttered quietly.

"I'm not a romantic," Pyotr Petrovich objected heatedly. "In fact you could call me the exact opposite. An extremely practical man. Nothing but work. Hardly even any time to remember what I'm living for. Certainly not for this work, damn it all—no—not for that, but so that . . ."

"So that?"

"Maybe so that I can go outside in the evening and breathe the air in deep and feel that I'm a part of the universe, a blade of grass in the concrete, you might say—It's a pity I'm not often moved to the core like that nowadays. It's probably because of that up there."

He raised his hand and pointed to the immense moon blazing in the sky, and then realized that his companion was walking in front of him and couldn't possibly see his gesture. But the companion must have had something like an eye in the back of his head, because he mimicked Pyotr Petrovich's gesture almost simultaneously, stretching up his arm in exactly the same way.

"At moments like that I ask myself what I do all the rest of the time in my life," said Pyotr Petrovich. "Why do I so rarely see everything the way I do then? Why do I always make the same choice, to sit in my chamber and stare into its darkest corner?"

The unexpected precision of these final words gave Pyotr Petrovich a certain bitter satisfaction. But then he stumbled, throwing his arms up in the air, and the theme of the conversation went completely out of his head. Keeping his balance with a monkeylike twist of his torso, he clutched at the wall with one hand, while his other hand almost broke the glass in a window close beside him.

On the other side of this window there was a small room illuminated by a red night light. It looked as though it was in a communal apartment—the furniture included a refrigerator, and the bed was half-hidden by a wardrobe, so that nothing could be seen of the sleeper in it except the skinny naked legs. Pyotr Petrovich's gaze fell on the wall above the night light, which was covered by a large number of photographs. There were family snapshots, photographs of children, grownups, old men, old women, dogs; right at the very center of the exhibition was a photograph of the graduating class at some institute, with the faces set in white ovals, making the whole thing look like a carton of eggs cut in half longways. For the single second Pyotr Petrovich was looking into the room, a person turned yellow by the passage of time smiled at him out of each of the ovals. All the photographs looked very old, and they all exuded such a strong odor of vanished life that Pyotr Petrovich suddenly felt nauseous. He quickly turned away and walked on.

"Yes," he said after a few steps, "yes. I know what you're going to say: so better just keep quiet. Exactly. Experience of life. We simply lose the ability to see anything else around us except the dusty photographs of the past suspended in space. We gaze and gaze at them, and then we wonder why the world around us has turned into such a garbage dump. And then, when the moon comes out, you suddenly realize that the world's not to blame at all, it's you that's changed, and you don't even know when or why."

There was silence. Pyotr Petrovich had been very badly affected by what he saw in the room, especially by the yellow-yolk faces. Taking advantage of the fact that it was dark and nobody could see him, he stuck out his tongue and grimaced so that his eyes bulged out, transforming his face into the likeness of an African mask—the physical sensation distracting him for a few brief seconds from his sudden ennui. The desire to talk instantly disappeared—worse than that, even, it was as though their hours-long conversation had been illuminated only by the dull red light of the night light, appearing quite stupid and unnecessary. Pyotr Petrovich glanced at his companion, thinking that he was not in the least bit intelligent and too young.

"I don't even understand what you and I are talking about now," he said in an exaggeratedly polite tone.

His companion said nothing.

"Maybe we should keep quiet for a little while?" Pyotr Petrovich suggested.

"Let's keep quiet," muttered his companion.

II

The farther Pyotr Petrovich and his companion went, the more beautiful and mysterious the world around them became. There really was no need to talk at all. The narrow path beneath their feet gleamed in the moonlight; the wall that kept changing color sometimes marked their right shoulders, sometimes their left, and the windows drifting by were dark, exactly like the ones in the poem that Pyotr Petrovich had quoted. Sometimes they had to walk uphill and sometimes just the opposite, downhill, and sometimes by unspoken agreement they would suddenly stop and stand still for a long time, their gaze fixed on something beautiful. The lights in the distance were particularly beautiful. Several times they stopped to look at them and each time they looked for a long time, ten minutes or even longer. Pyotr Petrovich was thinking something vague, almost inexpressible in words. The lights did not appear to have any particular connection with human beings, they were a part of nature—either a particular stage in the development of rotting tree stumps, or stars that had retired from the sky. In any case, the night was genuinely dark, and the red and yellow spots on the horizon somehow defined the dimensions of the world around them—if not for them there would have been no way of knowing where life was running its course, or whether there was any life at all. Every time he would be roused from his thoughtfulness by his companion's footsteps. When his companion started off again, Pyotr Petrovich woke from his reveries and hurried after him. Soon the photographs from the window they had passed were forgotten completely, his heart felt light and happy once again, and the silence began to bother him. "And another thing," Pyotr Petrovich thought, "I don't even know his name. I ought to ask." He waited for a few seconds and then said very politely:

"Hmm, I've just had a thought. He we are, walking along all this time and talking together, and I don't believe we've even introduced ourselves."

His companion said nothing.

"But then, of course," Pyotr Petrovich said in a conciliatory tone when enough time had passed to make it clear that there would be no answer, "what's in a name, eh? It is but empty sound—After all, if you know someone and they know you, then there's really nothing for you to talk about. You'll just keep on wondering what he's going to think about you, and what he's going to say about you afterward. But when you don't know who you're talking to, you can say anything you like; the brakes are off. How long is it you and I have been talking, two hours now, isn't it? And just look, I'm doing almost all the talking. I'm usually a quiet kind of person, and now it seems like the dam's burst. Perhaps to you I don't seem very intelligent and so on, but I've been listening to myself all this time, especially where the statues were, remember? When I was talking about love—and when I listen to myself I'm amazed. Do I really know and understand as much about life as that?"

Pyotr Petrovich raised his face to the stars and sighed deeply; his face seemed overlaid by a shadow from the invisible wing of some unearthly smile as it flew past. Suddenly he glimpsed an almost imperceptible movement to his left, shuddered and came to a halt.

"Hey," he called to his companion, whispering now, "Stop! Be quiet! You'll scare it off. I think it's a cat—Yes, there it is over there. See it?"

The hood turned to the left, but for all his efforts Pyotr Petrovich failed once again to see the face of his companion, who seemed to be looking in the wrong direction.

"Over there!" Pyotr Petrovich whispered in exasperation. "See, where the bottle is? Half a yard to the left. It's still twitching its tail. On the count of three? You go left, I'll go right. Like the last time."

His companion shrugged indifferently, then nodded reluctantly.

"One, two, three!" counted Pyotr Petrovich, and flung his leg over the low iron barrier gleaming dully in the moonlight. His companion followed him in an instant, and they rushed forward together. God only knows how many times that night Pyotr Petrovich had experienced a sense of happiness. Now it came over him again, and he ran under the night sky, free of all care and torment; all the problems which had made his life unbearable a day or two earlier had suddenly disappeared, and even if he had wanted to he couldn't have recalled a single one of them.

Three shadows rushed across the black surface beneath his feet—one, dense and short, was cast by the moon, and the two others, hazy and asymmetrical, were cast by other sources of light, probably windows. Flanking to the left, Pyotr Petrovich saw his companion flanking to the right, and when the cat was somewhere between them, he turned toward it and accelerated. The figure in the black hood instantly executed a similar maneuver— their movements were so closely synchronized that Pyotr Petrovich felt a pang of vague suspicion, but there was no time for that just now.

The cat was still sitting in the same place, which was strange, because they didn't usually allow anyone to get so close. The last one, for instance, the one they had chased forty minutes ago, just after the statues, hadn't let them come within ten yards. Sensing some kind of trick, Pyotr Petrovich slowed to a walk, and then stopped moving altogether, still several steps away from the cat. His companion repeated all of his movements and halted at exactly the moment he did, about three yards away. What, from a distance, Pyotr Petrovich had taken to be a cat, turned out to be a gray plastic bag with a torn handle that was swaying in the wind—that was what he had thought was a tail.

Pyotr Petrovich's companion stood facing him, but still his

actual face remained invisible—the moon was in Pyotr Petrovich's eyes, and all he could see was the familiar dark pointed silhouette. Pyotr Petrovich leaned over (his companion leaned down
at the same time, and their heads almost bumped) and pulled on a
corner of the bag (his companion pulled on another corner). The
bag swung over and something soft tumbled out of it and
plumped onto the asphalt. It was the half-rotten corpse of a cat.

"Ugh, what rotten garbage," Pyotr Petrovich said, turning
away. "We might have known."

"We might have known," echoed his companion.

"Let's get out of here," said Pyotr Petrovich, and he set off
towards the tin border around the blacktop field.

III

They had been walking in silence for several minutes. The dark
back was swaying in front of Pyotr Petrovich's face once again,
only now he was by no means certain that it really was a back, and
not a chest. To help him gather his thoughts, he half-closed his
eyes and looked down. All he could see was the track of silver beneath his feet. The sight of it calmed him and even hypnotized
him slightly, and gradually his consciousness was flooded with a
not quite sober clarity, and thoughts began rushing through his
mind of their own accord—or rather, it was the same single
thought about time past which constantly plagued him.

"Why does he always repeat my movements?" Pyotr Petrovich wondered. "And everything he says always echoes my last
phrase. He really does act exactly like a reflection. But there are
so many windows around here! Maybe it's just an optical illusion,
and because I'm a little bit agitated, it seems as though there are
two of us? After all, so many of the things that people once used
to believe in can be explained by optical illusions! Almost everything, in fact." This thought unexpectedly cheered Pyotr Petrovich up and lent him confidence. "That's what it is," he thought,

"moonshine, the reflection of one window in another and that provocative scent of flowers—we mustn't forget that it's July now—they could create this effect. And when he speaks, it's simply an echo, a still, quiet echo. Of course, that's it! He always repeats the words that I've just spoken!"

Pyotr Petrovich cast a glance at the back of the figure swaying regularly in front of him. "And what's more," he thought, "I've read in many places that if someone frustrates you or embarrasses you in some way, it's always likely not to be another person at all, but yourself. When you stay still or perform any kind of repetitive, monotonous action without any particular meaning like walking or thinking, then your reflection can always pretend to be an independent being. It can start moving a little bit out of step, and you still won't notice it. It can start doing something you're not doing—provided, of course, that it's not anything substantial. Finally, it can become really rebellious and start believing that it really does exist, and then turn against you. As far as I can recall, there's only one way of checking whether it is a reflection or not—you have to make some sudden and quite unambiguous movement, so that the reflection has to repeat it quite obviously, because it still is a reflection and it has to obey the laws of nature, or at least some of them. That's it then, I have to try to distract him with conversation and then come out with something sudden and unexpected and see what happens. I can speak about anything at all, as long as I don't start thinking about it." He cleared his throat and said:

"It's a good thing that you're so tight-lipped. There's an art in listening. Making the other person reveal themselves and keep on talking. . . . They do say silent types make the very best friends. Do you know what I'm thinking about now?"

Pyotr Petrovich waited a moment for an answer, but none came, so he went on:

"About why I love the summer night so much. Of course, it's dark and quiet. Beautiful. But that's not the main thing. Sometimes it seems to me there is a part of the soul which sleeps all the time and only wakes for a few seconds on summer nights, in order to peep out and remember something as it used to be long ago, in a different place—dark blue skies . . . stars . . . mystery. . . ."

IV

Soon it became noticeably harder to walk. This was because, after turning yet another corner, they found themselves on the dark side, where the moon was hidden behind the roof of the opposite house. Pyotr Petrovich was immediately overwhelmed by weariness and uncertainty. He kept talking, even though pronouncing the words had become a repulsive torment. Something similar seemed to be happening to his companion as well, because he stopped contributing even his brief replies to the conversation— he would just occasionally mutter something incomprehensible. Their steps became shorter and more cautious.

From time to time the companion walking ahead would even stop to spy out the right direction—he always made the decision, and all Pyotr Petrovich had to do was to follow behind. A triangle of dense moonlight appeared on the wall ahead, cast through a gap between the houses opposite. Raising his eyes once again from the path of dulled silver beneath his feet, Pyotr Petrovich saw in the triangle the thick shaft of an electric cable dangling against the wall. His mind instantly formed a plan which seemed to him extremely natural, and even to possess a certain humor.

"Aha," he thought, "that's what I can do. I can grab hold of that thing and push hard off the wall with my feet. If he really is a reflection or a shadow, he'll have to reveal himself. That is, he'll have to do the same, only in the opposite direction. Or even better—that's it!—why didn't I think of it before? I can just clock him; take a really good swing. And if the bastard really is some kind of reflection . . ."

Pyotr Petrovich did not finish verbalizing what would happen then, but it was quite clear that this was a way he could either confirm or dispel the suspicions that were tormenting him. "The main thing is, it must be unexpected," he thought, "I have to take him by surprise!"

"Anyway," he said, smoothly changing the subject of a conversation that was already far behind them, "water skis are all right in their own way, but what's most amazing is that even in the city you can move closer to the world of nature, you just have to distance yourself slightly from the bustle. Of course, we're not likely to be able to manage it—we're too conservative. But I assure you, children do it every day of the week."

Pyotr Petrovich paused to give his companion a chance to say something, but once again he remained silent, and Pyotr Petrovich continued:

"I mean their games. Of course, they are often ugly and cruel; sometimes you can get the impression that they spring out of the filth and poverty children grow up in nowadays. But it seems to me that poverty has nothing to do with it. It's not because they can't afford to buy themselves all those motorcycles or skates. For instance, they're all crazy about that thing they call the Tarzan swing. Have you heard about it?"

"I have heard," mumbled his companion.

"It's a rope they tie to a tree, to a thick branch, the higher the better," Pyotr Petrovich continued, staring at the triangle of moonlight and thinking it would take them less than a minute to reach it now. "Especially if the tree stands on the edge of a steep drop. The main thing is, it has to be steep. By water is even better, then you can dive in. It's named after Tarzan; there was a film called that, where this guy Tarzan spent all of his time swinging on lianas. It's very simple, you take hold of the rope, push off with your feet, and swing out in a long, long curve, and if you like you can let go and go flying head first into the water. To be honest, I've never tried a Tarzan swing like that, but I can easily imagine the moment of that stunning impact with the surface, and then slowly sinking into the rippling silence, into the cool peace—Ah, if only we knew just where those boys fly away to on their lianas."

His companion stepped into the space drenched in moonlight. Pyotr Petrovich stepped over the boundary of the moonlight after him.

"Do you know why I can imagine it?" he continued, obsessively measuring the distance to the cable with his eyes. "It's very simple. I remember how once when I was a child I jumped into a swimming pool from the diving tower. Of course, I hurt my belly on the water, but at that moment I understood something important—so important that when I surfaced I kept repeating to myself: 'Don't forget, don't forget.' But when I got out of the water, the only thing I could remember was those words, 'don't forget.'"

At this moment Pyotr Petrovich drew even with the cable. He stopped and tugged on it to make sure it was firmly attached.

"Even now sometimes," he said, getting ready to jump, his voice calm and sincere, "I'd like to be able to take off somehow. It's stupid, of course, infantile, but I still have the feeling I might manage to understand something or remember something. So here goes, with your permission."

As he said this Pyotr Petrovich took a few quick steps, pushed off hard, and soared up into the warm night air. His flight (if it can be called that) lasted almost no time at all. He swayed out a yard or two from the wall, spun around his own axis as he swung forward, and crashed into the wall just in front of his companion, who jumped back in fright. Pyotr Petrovich lost his balance and had to grab him by the shoulder, which of course made it quite clear that this was certainly no reflection or shadow. It was all very awkward, with lots of puffing and panting. The shock produced a very nervous response from Pyotr Petrovich's companion: he shrugged Pyotr Petrovich's hand off his shoulder, leapt backwards, pulled the hood off his head and shouted furiously:

"Just what do you think you're doing?"

"I'm very sorry," said Pyotr Petrovich, feeling himself turning puce—glad that the night was so dark. "I really didn't mean . . ."

"What did you tell me," his companion interrupted, "that it would be nice and quiet, that you're not violent, you simply had no one to talk to? Wasn't that what you said?"

"Yes," whispered Pyotr Petrovich, lowering his face into his hands, "that's what I said. How could I possibly have forgotten? But I was having such strange thoughts, as though you weren't really you, but just my reflection in the windows or my shadow. Funny, isn't it?"

"I don't think it's funny," said his companion. "Now at least have you remembered who I am?"

"Yes," said Pyotr Petrovich making a strange movement with his head—something between bowing it and pulling it back into his shoulders.

"Thank God for that. So you decided to jump me to check whether I was a reflection, did you? And you babbled on about the Tarzan swing just to distract me?"

"No, of course not!" cried Pyotr Petrovich, removing one hand from the electric cable and pressing it against his chest. "That's to say, at first perhaps I was just trying to distract you, but only at the beginning. But as soon as I started talking, it was about things that have tormented me all my life. The things that I feel in my heart."

"You say some strange things," said his companion. "I'm beginning to fear for your sanity. Just think about it—you walk with me for two hours, you talk with me, and then you start seriously believing that the person with you is your own reflection. Do you think that sort of thing would happen to someone normal?"

Pyotr Petrovich thought about it.

"Nnn-no," he said, "it wouldn't. It does look absolutely crazy from the outside. A talking reflection, walking with his back towards you—the Tarzan swing . . . But you know, from inside me it was all so very logical that if I told you the sequence of my thoughts, you wouldn't be surprised at all."

He looked up. The moon above the opposite roof was hidden behind a long cloud with jagged edges. For some reason this seemed like a bad sign.

"Yes," he began again, "if you analyze the subconscious motivation for my actions, then it looks as though I simply wanted a moment of glory . . ."

"The reflection," his companion interrupted, raising his voice, "that's something I could accept. But what I find really strange is your garbled nonsense about the Tarzan swing. About launching into flight and understanding something or other. Just what is it you want to understand?"

Pyotr Petrovich looked up into the eyes of his companion and immediately shifted his gaze to the other's shaven head.

"How shall I put it?" he said. "I feel uncomfortable speaking in banal clichés. Truth."

"What truth?" asked his companion, pulling his hood back up. "About yourself, about other people, about the world? There are many truths." Pyotr Petrovich thought about that.

"About myself, I suppose," he said. "Or rather, about life. About myself and about life. Of course."

"Want me to tell you about it, then?" his companion asked.

"If you know, yes," Pyotr Petrovich said with sudden hostility.

"Aren't you afraid that this truth will be no more use to you than a dead cat?" his companion asked with equal hostility, nodding back the way they had come. "He's hinting at something," thought Pyotr Petrovich. "Mocking me. Applying psychological pressure. But he's got the wrong man for that. What's up with all this sadism, anyway? All I did was shake him by the shoulder, and I apologized afterwards."

"No," he said, straightening his shoulders and gazing firmly straight into his companion's eyes, "I'm not afraid. Get on with it."

"All right then. Does the word 'lunatic' mean anything to you?"

"Lunatic? What, those people who don't sleep at night and go wandering about on the cornices of buildings? I know about . . . O my God!"

V

More than anything, his sudden enlightenment resembled that plunge into cold water which Pyotr Petrovich had tried to tell his pitiless companion about—and not just because he had only just noticed what a cold night it was. Pyotr Petrovich looked down at his feet and saw that the narrow silvery track that he had been following for so long was actually a narrow tin plated cornice that was deeply bowed under the weight of his body.

Beneath the cornice there was empty space, and beyond the space, about 100 feet below, the lights of the street lamps were duplicated in the puddles, the dark crowns of the trees trembled in the wind above the gray asphalt, and Pyotr Petrovich realized with horror that it was finally and absolutely real, that there was no way of ignoring or avoiding the fact he was standing there barefooted in his underwear at an immense height above the nighttime city, with only some miraculous force preventing him from falling. It was astonishing that he maintained his grip—there was absolutely nothing for his hands to grasp hold of except minute variations in the surface of the concrete wall—and if he leaned out even slightly from its cold, damp surface, then the implacable force of gravity would have pulled him downwards.

Not far away he could see an electric cable, but in order to reach out and grab it, he would have to take several steps along the ledge, and that was quite unthinkable. Squinting downwards he could make out the parking lot far below him, the cigarette-pack-sized cars, and a tiny patch of asphalt that someone might have left open specially for him. The most important evidence that the nightmare he had fallen into was the ultimate truth was the smell of garbage smoldering somewhere close—it was a smell that immediately settled all questions and seemed to carry within itself an entirely adequate proof of the ultimate reality of a world in which such smells are possible. Pyotr Petrovich's soul was swamped by a tidal wave of terror that, for a fraction of a second, washed everything else away. The emptiness at his back was sucking him in and he pressed himself as flat against the wall as an election handbill from some unknown party that has absolutely no chance of victory.

"Well?" asked his companion.

Pyotr Petrovich looked at him—cautiously, so as not to glimpse the abyss under his feet for a second time.

"Stop it," he said, quietly but very insistently, "please stop it! I'll fall."

His companion sniggered.

"How can I stop it? It's happening to you, not to me."

Pyotr Petrovich realized that his companion was right, but a moment later he realized something else, something which instantly filled him with indignation.

"That's just mean and nasty," he shouted, getting really worked up, "you can do that to anyone, tell him he's a lunatic teetering on the edge of a void that he simply doesn't see! Out on the cornice . . . why, just a minute ago, you . . . and now . . ."

"That's true," said his companion with a nod. "You have no idea of just how well you put it."

"Then why are you doing this to me?"

"I can't tell what it is you want. First your head's filled with one thing, then with something else. Just now you were meditating on where you could fly to on a Tarzan swing. It was quite moving, honestly. Then you wanted to hear the truth. And that's still not the final truth, by the way."

"So what do I do now?"

"You? No need for you to do anything," said his companion, and suddenly Pyotr Petrovich noticed that he wasn't really holding onto anything and was even standing at something of an angle. "It will all work out."

"Are you mocking me?" hissed Pyotr Petrovich.

"Not at all."

"You bastard," said Pyotr Petrovich in a weak voice. "Murderer. You've killed me. I'll fall now."

"Now it's begun," said his companion. "Insults, hatred. Next thing I know you'll jump on me again or start spitting, the way some of them do. I'm going." He turned and unhurriedly began to walk away.

"Hey!" yelled Pyotr Petrovich. "Hey! Wait! Please!"

But his companion did not stop—he merely waved a feeble farewell with a pale hand protruding from the sleeve of his cassock or cloak. A few steps more and he turned the corner and disappeared. Pyotr Petrovich closed his eyes again and pressed his damp forehead against the wall.

VI

"Well then," he thought, "that's it. That's the end now. I'm finished. All my life I wondered what it would be like, and this is how it turns out. I'll just sway a little, throw up my arms, and— steady, Pyotr, steady—I wonder if I'll cry out? Pyotr, steady now—don't think about that. Think about anything else, but not about that. Please. The main thing is to keep calm, no matter what. Panic means death. Remember something pleasant. But what is there to remember? What was pleasant about today, for instance? Except perhaps for the conversation by the statues, when I was explaining to that guy with the shaved head about love. Oh God, now I've remembered him again. What an idiot I am. Why couldn't I simply have kept on walking, just looking around and enjoying life. But no, I had to start wondering who he was, whether he was a shadow or a reflection. I got what I deserved. Serves me right for reading all kinds of rubbish. But then who is he, really? Damn it, I'd just remembered. No, I didn't, but he told me himself—Where on earth did he come from?"

Pyotr Petrovich half opened his eyes for a second and saw that the wall beside his face was bright and yellow—the moon had come back out from behind the clouds. Somehow it made him feel a little bit better.

"Right," he thought, "so where did I meet him? Before the statues, that's for sure. When the statues appeared, he was already there. And we chased the first cat before the statues too. That's right, he didn't want to at first, no matter how hard I tried to persuade him. And then I started spouting on and on to him about nature, and about love—I knew I shouldn't be talking to him; that you have to keep these things inside if you don't want to be insulted—How does the Gospel put it—'don't cast your pearls before swine, for they will trample them,' isn't that it? What a life! Even if you really like something, maybe the way the moon lights up statues, you have to keep quiet about it. You have to keep quiet all the time, because if you do open your mouth you'll regret it. It's strange, all right. I understood that a long time ago, but I'm still suffering because of my trusting nature. Just waiting all the time for the insults to start—and this one, what an insulting swine he was—a real swine, swine, swine. He told me everything would be all right. How condescending of him—Damn him anyway, here I am thinking about him for almost an hour, and the moon could go at any moment. He's not worth it."

Pyotr Petrovich turned away from the wall, looked up, and smiled weakly. The moon was shining through a ragged round gap in a cloud, which made it look like its own reflection in a hole in the ice on some nonexistent river. The city below was calm and quiet, and the air was filled with the barely perceptible scent of the blossoms of plants he could put no name to.

In a far-off window Sting began to sing in a piratelike bass—too loud, really, for the nighttime. It was "Moon Over Bourbon Street," a song that Pyotr Petrovich remembered with affection from his younger days. He forgot about everything and began listening, and at one point he even blinked rapidly at the memory of something long forgotten. Gradually his pain and sense of hurt abated. With every second the parting from his chance acquaintance seemed less and less important, until eventually he couldn't even understand why he had been so upset about it only a few minutes ago. When Sting's voice began to fade, Pyotr Petrovich took his hand away from the wall and snapped his fingers in time with the despairing English lyrics, in a gesture of farewell:

And you'll never see my face
Or hear the sound of my feet
While there's a moon over Bourbon Street.

Finally the song ended. Pyotr Petrovich sighed and shook his head in order to gather his thoughts. He turned back, stepped around the corner, and jumped lightly down a couple of yards, where it was easier to walk. The night was still as mysterious and tender, and he didn't feel at all inclined to part with it, but he had a very busy morning tomorrow, and he had to sleep at least a little. He looked around him one last time, then glanced briefly upwards, smiled, and slowly set off along the gleaming strip of silver, kissing the night wind as it touched his lips and thinking that, essentially, he was an entirely happy man.

The Ontology of Childhood

WE'RE USUALLY TOO CAUGHT up in what's happening to us in the present to suddenly shift our perspective and start remembering our childhood. An adult's life is pretty much self-sufficient, and it has none of those empty spaces that can be filled up by experiences with no direct link to things actually going on in the world around us. Only occasionally, very early in the morning, when we wake up and see before us the most ordinary of things—perhaps simply a brick wall—do we remember that things used to be different once, not the same as they are today, even though little has actually changed since that time.

There's that crack between two bricks, and in it you can see that strip of cement that bulges out like a wave. If you don't count those years when, simply for the sake of a change, you lay with your feet pointing in the other direction, or that time so very long ago when your head was still gradually receding from your legs and the view of the wall in the morning changed a little bit every day—if you don't count all of that, then this rigid vertical scroll in the crack between the bricks was always the first greeting of the day from the big wide world in which we live: in the winter, when the wall was saturated with cold and sometimes even covered with an incredibly beautiful silvery coating; and in the summer, when two bricks higher up a triangular spot of sunlight with ragged edges appeared (but only on certain days in June, when the sun moved far enough to the west). Somehow during that long journey from the past into the present, the objects around you have lost something fundamentally important, some absolutely indefinable quality. There's no way to explain it.

Take the way the day used to begin: the grownups went off to work, the door slammed behind them, and the immense space around you and all the different objects in it became yours. All prohibitions ceased to apply, things seemed to relax and stop hiding whatever they had been hiding. Take any kind of object at all, say a bunk, top or bottom; three parallel planks, supported on iron cross braces, three rivets in every brace. If there was even a single grownup around, then for sure the bunk would sort of squeeze itself in, make itself narrow and uncomfortable. But when they went off to work it became wider, or at least it was somehow possible to make yourself comfortable on it. And every one of the planks (they still hadn't started painting them then) was covered with a pattern; you could see the annual rings in the wood that had been sawn through at the most incredible angles. When the grownups were around they disappeared, or else it never entered your head to pay any attention to such things in the heavy atmosphere of conversation about breaks between shifts, work norms, and the nearness of death.

The most remarkable thing, of course, was the sunshine. Not even the blinding spot of light in the sky, but that beam of bright air that started at the window, with the fluffy grains of dust and tiny little coiled-up hairs suspended in it. Their movements were so smooth and rounded (and in childhood you can see the entire swarm from a distance with incredible clarity), that you had the feeling of an entirely separate little world living according to its own laws, a world you either once lived in or can still get into and become one of those weightless points of light.

Then again, that's not really exactly what you feel, but there's no other way of putting it, there's no way of pinning it down exactly.

It's just that you see yourself surrounded by realms of absolute freedom and happiness that are hidden behind masks. The sunlight has an astounding ability to bring out the very best in those few things that it comes into contact with on its way from the upper corner of the first window to the lower corner of the second.

Even the iron plated door communicates something about itself that makes you realize there is no need to be afraid of what might appear from behind it. There's really nothing to be afraid of at all, is what the strips of light on the floor and the walls tell you. There is nothing in the world to fear. At least, not as long as this world carries on talking with you; afterwards, at some undefined moment, it begins talking about you. In your childhood you are usually woken by the abusive morning conversations of the grownups. They always begin the day swearing; their voices drawl thickly and stickily through your continuing dream and you can tell very well from the intonations that neither the ones who are shouting nor the ones who are making excuses are actually experiencing the feelings that their voices are trying to express. It's just that they're barely awake and haven't completely shaken off the grip of what they saw in their dreams, even though they can't remember it anymore. They're trying to convince themselves and everyone else as quickly as possible that the morning, and life in general, and the few minutes they have to collect themselves, are all for real.

And when they manage to do this, they finally slip into gear with each other. The final morning doubts disappear, and they're already trying to find the most comfortable spots in this hell they've just dashed into so impetuously. They shift from insults to jokes. The fact that they all share the same fate becomes unimportant, since there are still the small differences they've learned to see, and it no longer matters that they're all going to die here; what matters is that someone sleeps on the top bunk a long way from the window.

You can understand all of this when you're still little, but there's no way to express it in words; you understand it from the grownups' voices that filter through your early morning drowsiness. It seems amazing and strange, but at that time the entire world is amazing, and everything in it is strange. But afterwards they make you get up with all the others. At first the grownups bend down to you from above, proffering you a face distended into a smile. There's obviously some law in the world which says they have to smile when they turn towards you. The smile is strained, of course, but the most important thing is that you understand they're not supposed to do you any harm. Their faces are terrible—pocked, blotchy, and stubbly—a bit like the moon in the window, the same close details.

Grownups are very easy to understand, but there's almost nothing to be said when they're around. Often they make you feel really rotten by paying such close attention to your life. Not that they seem to be asking for anything—just for a moment they put down the heavy invisible beam that they carry around all their lives in order to bend down and smile at you, then they straighten up and pick it up again to carry it further—but that's only how it looks at first glance. In fact what they want is for you to become just the same as they are. They have to pass on their beam to someone before they die—there must be some reason they've been carrying it, after all.

In the evenings several of them often get together and give someone a beating. The one they beat up usually plays along very subtly with the ones who are beating him, and for that they beat him a little less hard. As a rule they don't let you watch this, but you can always hide behind the bunks and watch everything through the standard one-centimeter gap between the planks. But afterwards—no matter how long it might be after that moment when you hide and watch the entire procedure—afterwards the day will come when you yourself will be squirming there on the floor among the flying feet clad in boots of canvas or felt and trying to play along with the others who are beating you.

When you begin to read, at first it's not the text that guides your thoughts, but your thoughts that direct the text. It always breaks off just at the most interesting point, and when you learn from a scrap of newspaper that the audience applauded such and such comrades' entry, you start thinking such and such must be two really big shots if even their comrades are greeted with applause. Then you close your eyes and start imagining those comrades and that applause, and you have time enough to live through an entire little life that's completely invisible to all the others sitting on the latrines beside you. And all because of a scrap of newspaper no bigger than the side of a packet of tea, with a tread mark from the sole of a canvas boot.

But there's still nothing that can compare with getting your hands on an actual book. It doesn't matter which one, there aren't very many here, only five or six, and you read all of them several times; it doesn't matter because you read each book differently every time. At first what's important about it are the words themselves. Each of them instantly summons up the thing it signifies ("boot," "latrine," "padded jacket") or creates a gaping, meaningless black hole ("ontology," "intellectual"), so you have to go to one of the grownups, which you always try to avoid, so that "ontology" becomes a flashlight and "intellectual" becomes a long wrench with an adjustable head.

The next time, what interests you are entire situations—how someone stumps into a narrow, foul-smelling kitchen, and smashes the waiter Proshka's rotten hypocritical face to a pulp with his strong worker's fists. Every one of the grownups has read this little book, and every time, when they enclose their new victim in the circle of stench breathed from their foul mouths, they each take a little step forward in turn and just for a second they become the young champion of justice, Artyom, investing their blows with all their hatred for the lackey's spirit of the twisted hypocritical waiter as he thrashes about in the center of the circle—probably every beating that ever takes place is a triumph of some imaginary justice. And then, the third time, you find a description of some girl breathing on the top bunks, and that's all you notice. You have to grow up altogether before you realize just how squalid and uninteresting everything that you've read and reread so many times really is.

You're happy in childhood because you think you were when you remember it. Happiness in general is nothing but reminiscence. When you were little they let you go out and wander about all day long, and you could walk along all the corridors, looking into any corner you liked and wandering into places no one else might have visited since the people who built them.

Now this has all become a carefully preserved memory, but then you were just walking along the corridor and feeling fed up because winter was starting again, and it would be dark outside the window almost all the time, and you turn off and wait just in case until two swearing sheepskin-coated guards have gone rumbling past along the adjoining corridor, and then you turn off again through a door that was always closed but today is standing wide open. There's something shining at the end of the corridor. It turns out there are two great thick pipes running along the walls here, all plastered over and even whitewashed. And there at the far end, where the light is and the iron manhole is standing open, you see this huge blue machine trembling ever so slightly and humming, and behind it another two just the same, and there's nobody around—you could easily just go down the ladder and enter that magical space that shudders because of all the power it contains.

You don't, though, because at any moment they could lock the door behind you, and you walk back, dreaming of finding your way back here again some time. Afterwards, when you begin coming here every day, when caring for these metallic tortoises that never sleep becomes the nominal goal of your existence, you're often tempted to recall that first time you saw them, but memories wear out if you use them too often, and so you hold this memory—of happiness—in reserve.

Another memory which you almost never use also has to do with the conquest of space. It was probably earlier: on the side corridors, a winter day (the windows are already blue, twilight is setting in), and the entire immense building is filled with silence; everybody's at work. It seems there really is nobody at all around—you can tell from the way everything looks. Grownups alter the surroundings, but just now the twilit corridor is unusually mysterious, filled with strange shadows, and even a little frightening. They haven't turned the lights on yet, but they should soon, and you can allow yourself a rare pleasure—running.

First you pick up speed moving away from the fire fighting panel along the dark cul-de-sac of the corridor (the panel is very strange: just a board with a glossy painting of an ax, a large hook, and a bucket), then you weave along the corridor for a while, delighting in the freedom and the ease with which you can make the walls lean over, come closer or move away—all with those tiny commands you give your own body. But the most amazing thing, of course, is the turn to the right into the short branch of the corridor that ends in a window covered with wire mesh. Twenty yards before you reach the turn you move in toward the left wall, and then opposite the little plywood door with the inscription PK-15S, you move out and lean over to the right, leaning into a long arc—and then there are just a few seconds, when your right side almost touches the tiles of the floor, that bring you a quite incomparable freedom.

Then you skim easily along the rest of the corridor, insert your fingers into the cells of the wire mesh and look out of the window: it's dark already, a few cold lamps are burning above the wall, and its columns are topped by tall caps of snow. The sounds coming in through the window are quite different in nature from sounds born anywhere in the corridor or beyond the partition. The difference is not so much in the actual quality of the sound—whether it is loud or quiet, shrill or dull—so much as in what gives it its life. Almost all sounds are made by people, but the sounds created inside the building seem like the rumbling of an intestine or the creaking of the joints in some immense organism—they're not interesting because they are so ordinary and easily understood. But what comes flying in at the window is almost the only testimony to the existence of all of the rest of the world, so a sound from out there seems unusually important.

The sound map of the world has also shifted a great deal since your childhood, although its main elements are still the same. There's the usual, legitimate sound—distant heavy blows of iron on iron, at only a half or a third the rate of your pulse. They have an interesting echo, as though the sound is not coming from a single point, but from the entire arc of the horizon.

The first thing that this sound was—back in those days when you could still sleep while everyone had to get up—was a timescale, or some kind of external support structure which lent the grownups' evening arguments and morning beatings the essential qualities of duration and sequence.

Later the measured note was transformed into the beating of the heart of the world, which is what it remained until somebody said it was piles being driven on the construction sites. Other sounds that could be made out included the humming of distant machines, the howling of a shunting engine on the siding, voices and laughter (very often children's laughter), the rumble of airplanes in the sky (there was something prehistoric about that), the noise made by the wind and finally, the barking of dogs. They said there used to be some way of communicating with the person in the next cell (it's hard to believe there could ever have been one to a cell): the person in the first cell began knocking on the wall in a certain way, with his message encoded in the sequence of knocks, and he was answered in the same code from the next cell. It was obviously nothing but a legend—what would have been the point of inventing a special language when you could discuss everything when you met during the general work sessions? But it was the idea that was important, the idea of conveying the essence of meaning through the repetition and combination of the most simple things, such as knocks heard through a wall.

Sometimes you wonder what we would hear if our Creator was to try tapping out a message to us. Probably something like distant blows on piles being driven into the ground—but definitely at regular intervals, Morse code would be quite out of the question. The more grown-up you are, the less complicated this world is, but there are still a lot of things in it you don't understand.

Take, for instance, the two squares of sky on the wall—it's sky if you sit on the lower bunk, but from the upper bunk you can see the tops of fat chimneys in the distance. At night stars appear in them, and in the daytime there are clouds that raise lots of questions. The clouds have been with you ever since your childhood, and so many of them have already been born in the windows that every time you meet with something new you are astonished. For instance, hanging in the right window at the moment is an open pink fan (it will soon be sunset) made up of row upon row of fluffy vapor—as if all the planes in the world had woven it (it's interesting to wonder how people who live out their lives up in the skies see the world), but in the left window there's just a pattern of slanting lines. That puts the infinitely distant point from which the wind blows exactly opposite the right window today. It must mean something, you simply didn't know the code—that's what exchanging taps on the wall with God is like. You can't make any mistakes here. Just as you can't make any mistakes about the meaning of what's happening when a blurred spot, a pale irregular triangle, appears on the blank face of a dark November cloud (you've seen it before on the bricks beside your face on a summer morning), and the sun shines out of its center though the scudding streamers of mist. Or in the summer there's the red hill rising up over the horizon (only from the upper bunk).

There used to be many things and events which were ready to reveal their true nature to your first glance, almost everything around you in fact. When a photograph of the prison taken from the outside (presumably from the watchtower above the bakery zone) was handed round, you couldn't really understand what all the old convicts were so amazed about—was there really nothing more astonishing than that in their lives? There was the piece of miserable cake in the evening, the familiar stench from the latrine and naïve pride in the abilities of human reason. And exchanging messages with God. All you have to do to answer him is to feel and understand it all. That's the way you think in childhood, when the world is still built of simple analogies. Only afterwards do you understand that you can't talk with God because you yourself are his voice, gradually becoming lower and quieter. If you think about it, what's happening to you is the same thing that happens to a shout on its way to you from the yard where they're playing football.

Something was happening to the world where you were growing up—every day it changed slightly, every day your surroundings took on a new shade of meaning. Everything began in the sunniest and happiest place in the world, inhabited by people with a rather funny attachment to canvas boots and black padded jackets—people who were funny, but even more important, who were close to you. It began in the joyful green corridors, in the cheerful glinting of the sunlight on the wire mesh where the paint had peeled away, in the crazed clicking of the swallows who had built a nest under the roof of the metal shop, in the celebratory roaring of the tanks rolling out on to parade—although you couldn't see them beyond the wall, you could tell from the sound when it was a tank going by and when it was a motorized gun; in the friendly chuckling of the grownups in response to some of your questions; in the smile of the guard who came across you in the corridor; in the wagging tail of the huge Alsatian bounding towards you.

Afterwards the colors in the best of all places gradually faded: you started to notice the cracks in the walls, the powerful

stench from the kitchen block, so unpleasant in its very famil-
iarity; you began to realize that beyond the maternal embrace of
the wall with its freshly plastered holes there was a life of some
kind—in other words, every day there were fewer and fewer
questions about your true fate remaining unanswered. And the
less that remained hidden from you, the less the grownups were
inclined to forgive your purity and naiveté.

It turns out that simply to see the world is to be tarnished and become an accomplice to all its vileness, and in the evenings there
are so many things to be afraid of in the dead-ends of the corridors and the dark corners of the cells. And then through the
quivering haze of half-forgotten childhood—like a conjuring
trick—there emerges the realization that you were born and grew
up in a prison, in the filthiest and vilest-smelling corner of the
world. And when you finally understand it, you become subject
to the full force of the laws of your prison.

But what of that? After all, the world wasn't invented by people, and no matter how hard they might try, there's no way they
can make the life of the lowliest convict the least bit different
from the life of the camp quartermaster himself. And what difference does it make what the reason is, if the happiness generated by all souls is identical? There is a set norm of happiness al-
located to a person in this life, and no matter what might happen
to him, this happiness can not be taken away. If you want to talk
about what is good and what is bad, you must at least know who
man was made by and what for.

Objects do not change, but something disappears while you
are growing up. In reality it's you that loses this "something,"
every day you walk on irrevocably past the most important thing
of all, hurrying on downhill, and you can't stop, you can't halt
this slow descent into nowhere; all you can do is select the words
as you describe what is happening to you. The opportunity to
look out of the window is not the most important thing in life,
but still you're upset when they stop letting you out into the

corridor—you're almost grown up and when the holiday comes you'll get canvas boots and a padded jacket as a present.

Of all the multitude of panoramas available for constant use only one is left (the view from both windows is the same from slightly different angles), and you can only admire it by leaning the short bench against the wall and standing on its edge; a yard surrounded by a low concrete wall, two rusty buses—or rather their remains, hollow yellow shells like dead wasps; the long building of the neighboring prison block under its brown semi-circular arched roof; beyond that, prison blocks that are already far away; and the sky, filling the remainder of the rectangular gap.

What you see every day for years and years is transformed into a monument to yourself—as you once used to be—because it bears the imprint of the feelings of a man who has almost disappeared; in you for a few moments, when you see the same thing that he used to see. In reality, "to see" means to superimpose your soul on the standard impression on the retina of the standard human eye. They used to play soccer in this yard, falling and getting up, kicking the ball, and now there's nothing left but rusty buses. In reality, ever since you began joining in the common work sessions you get too tired for anything inside you to come to life and play soccer on your retina. But no matter what national change of underwear may lie ahead, nobody can ever take away from the past what someone has seen (the former you, if that means anything), standing on a swaying bench and looking out of the window: a few people kicking a ball to each other, laughing—their voices and the sound of feet striking leather take a long time to reach you. One of them suddenly makes a break forward—he's wearing a green T-shirt—dribbles the ball toward the goal made of two old floodlights, shoots, scores, and disappears from view—and you hear the players shouting. Remarkable.

A little convict once lived in this cell and saw all this, but he's not here anymore. Obviously escapes are sometimes successful, but where the escapee takes refuge, not even he can say.

Bulldozer Driver's Day

What are they doing here,
These people?
Alarm in their faces,
Pounding with their crowbars,
Pounding and pounding.
          —Isikawa Takuboku

I

Ivan Pomerantsev leaned with his elbows on the cold damp concrete of the windowsill with the three or four zigzag lines running across it (when Valera wanted to frighten his wife, he would bang it with the iron), blew an obese black fly off the windowpane, and looked out into the yard that was bathed in the last rays of the autumn sunshine. It was warm, and from down below there came a faint smell of linseed oil, exuded by the tin roof of a lean-to shed that had been painted several years ago but still stank whenever the sun heated it even slightly. He could smell fuel oil and cabbage soup, too.

In the distance he could hear children shouting and horses neighing, but they didn't seem like natural sounds, more like a tape recording—probably because there didn't seem to be anything alive anywhere nearby, apart from a motionless pigeon on the windowsill several windows further along. The street was somehow lifeless, as though no one had ever lived on it, or even visited it, and the only thing that made sense of its existence was the rank of faded visual propaganda depicting the unified state of the people and the party in the allegorical form of two muscle-bound figures.

The bell in the corridor jangled. Ivan shuddered, put down his crumpled hand-rolled cigarette—it was moist and hard, and looked like a souvenir toy log—and went to open the door. The walk was a long one: Ivan lived in a large communal apartment, converted from a section of a hostel, and between the kitchen and the entrance lay about twenty yards of corridor spread with rubber doormats and crammed with children's sneakers and crude adult footwear. Outside the door he could hear a man's voice rumbling quietly, with periodic interruptions from a woman.

"Who is it?" Ivan asked in an everyday tone. He'd already realized who it was—but you couldn't just open the door right away.

"We're here to see Ivan Ilich!" the man answered.

Ivan opened up. There on the landing stood the so-called "Team of Five" from the Trade Union office, which for their plant consisted of only two people because Osmakov and Altynina, who was wearing a gauzy suit and carrying a package that smelled of herrings which she held well away from her body with both hands, shared all the jobs between them.

"Ivan! My friend!" Osmakov said with a smile as he stepped inside and held out two trembling palms to Ivan. "How are you? Does it hurt? Where does it ache?"

"Nothing hurts," Ivan said, embarrassed. "Let's go through into the room, shall we?"

Altynina's perfume was even stronger than the smell of herrings. As they walked along the corridor, Ivan deliberately dropped back in order not to smell it.

"Well, now, Ivan," Osmakov said in a sad, wise voice as he sat down at the table, "they've worked it all out and it's been accepted that what happened was an accident. The cause, my friend, was a welding defect. On the nose ring. And your name has been entirely cleared." Osmakov suddenly shook his head and looked around as though he was trying to work out where he was—when he managed it he sighed quietly.

"The bomb's body is made of uranium, after all," he continued, "but the ring is steel. You need a special electrode to weld it on. But the lads in shop number two used an ordinary one. Flaming front line May Day heroes! So the ring just broke off, that's all. Can you remember how it all happened?"

Ivan closed his eyes. The memory was somehow dull and merely formal, as though he himself was not remembering, but merely running over the various parts played in a story he'd been told by someone else. He saw himself from the outside, pressing the stiff button that stops the conveyor—the button only took effect after a long delay, and the rough black belt had to be driven backwards. There he was setting the hook of the hoist in the ring of the faulty bomb with the fat chalk tick on its side (the stabilizer was welded on crooked, and the whole thing was somehow twisted) and switching on the hoist. The bomb swayed ponderously as it came away from the conveyor belt and climbed slowly upward; the chain wound onto the drum and the brake went on.

"That's the fourth today," Ivan thought, "if we carry on like this it'll be pissing bonuses come May Day."

He pressed another button, an electric motor came to life, and the hoist began slowly creeping along the I-beam welded across the beams of the ceiling. Suddenly something got stuck and the hoist came to a halt. That happened sometimes—probably a dent in the I-beam. Ivan stepped under the bomb and began to sway it to and fro by the stabilizer—that helped it pick up inertia and force the wheel of the hoist through the dented spot on the rail—when suddenly the bomb seemed to yield strangely under his touch and the next second Ivan realized that his right hand was not just clutching the barbed metal of the stabilizer, but actually holding the bomb above his head. The next picture in his memory was seen through the window of the hospital ward: a pole holding up a washing line and half a tree.

"Vanya," said Osmakov's voice, "what is it?"

"I'm fine." Ivan shook his head. "I'm just remembering."

"Well? Do you remember?"

"Some of it."

"The most important thing, Ivan Ilich" said Altynina, "is that you managed to jump out of the way of the bomb. It fell beside you. But if . . ."

"And you got a belt across the kidneys from the lithium deuteride cylinder," Osmakov interrupted, "the compressed air forced it out when the shell cracked. Good job the cylinder didn't crack open too—it's thirty atmospheres inside there."

Ivan sat without speaking, listening partly to Osmakov and partly to the big black fly beating itself against the windowpane at regular intervals. "Must be the visitors who disturbed it," he thought, "it was sitting there quietly before. What is it they want?"

Soon Osmakov's reflex responses produced the change that always came over him as a result of simply sitting at a table for a certain length of time: the expression of his eyes softened, the tone of his voice became even more emphatically humane, and his words began tumbling over each other—the longer he talked the more noticeable it became.

"Vanya," he said, tracing small circles across the oilcloth with an invisible glass, "you are the genuine article, a hero of truly glorious labor exploits. I wasn't going to tell you this, but I will anyway: the *Uran-Bator Pravda* is going to print an article about you. The correspondent's already been to see us and shown us the draft. It tells the whole story, just like it happened, only they call our plant the Uran-Bator Canning Factory, and instead of a bomb, a hundred liter barrel of tomatoes falls on top of you, but then you manage to crawl over to the conveyor and switch it off.

And you have a different surname, of course. We thought hard about what would sound best—yours is kind of dead, even a bit reactionary-sounding, May only knows. And your first name doesn't have any impact. What we came up with was Konstantin Pobedonostsev. It was Vaska from *Red Half-Life* who suggested it. He's bright all right, no flickering Mayflies on him."

Ivan remembered now—that was the name of the plant's newspaper—he'd seen it a couple of times. It was hard to read, because everything in it had a different name from its real one: the hydrogen bomb assembly line where Ivan worked was re-ferred to as the "medium-soft plush toy shop" or the "electric doll department," but when *Red Half-Life* wrote about the production of a new doll called "Marina" with seven dresses that could be changed and which was intended to decorate the children's corners on excursion steamers, Ivan imagined a black and yellow picture of foreign parts from the cover of *The Jackal* and gloated to himself: "Right now, stuffed your bellies full up in your skyscrapers, have you, you red flag May Day jerk-offs?"

For six months now, though, *Red Half-Life* had been distrib-uted only to people on a special list—as a leading article ex-plained, this was "due to the importance attached to the produc-tion of soft toys"—and so at first Ivan hadn't even realized that they were talking about the plant's in-house newspaper. Osmakov had skipped imperceptibly on to a different topic.

"That woman's a real shim-sham altogether," he said quietly, gazing at something invisible a yard in front of his face. "'Bloody-red labor-mad!' I yelled at her, 'what in fucking May's name do you think you're doing taking that fence down?'"

"Ivan Ilich," interrupted Altynina, "this will be the first time the town newspaper has ever written about our plant. And the television people might come as well. We've already found a place where they can film. And the Sovcom doesn't object."

"How's that?" Ivan was puzzled.

"The Sovcom," Altynina repeated, speaking clearly. "Comrade Parmahamov is busy at the moment—he's handing over a building to the children. But he phoned himself in person."

"What a lot of stupid fuss, Galina Nikolaevna."

"The children have to be educated somehow. Otherwise they're good for nothing but fires and explosions. Yesterday on Sandel Street they blew up another dumpster. They hang around the sandpits."

Osmakov suddenly emitted a gurgling sound and slumped forward so that his head fell onto the table. They began fussing over him—or rather, Ivan ran to the kitchen to get a rag while Altynina fussed over Osmakov, bringing him around and explaining where he was and how he had come to be there. When Ivan arrived with the rag, Osmakov already looked quite sober and he sullenly permitted Altynina to wipe the lapels of his jacket with her handkerchief. The visitors immediately began preparing to leave: they stood up, Altynina picked up the package that smelled of herring from the table (for some reason Ivan had thought it was intended for him) and began repacking it, wrapping it in fresh newspaper because the brown juice had already soaked through the old paper and it was about to tear open. Osmakov stared with feigned interest at the calendar on the wall showing a short naked woman standing beside a snow-covered Zaporozhets car.

At last the herring was packed and the visitors took their leave. Ivan showed them to the door still carrying the rag in his hand, and then carried it back with him to the room, where he threw it on the floor and sat down on the small divan. He attributed the strange feebleness of his condition to the fact that the blow to his kidneys had prevented him from taking a drink for two whole weeks: one week in the hospital and one week at home. But what really bothered him was that he couldn't remember anything about his life before the accident. Although he could more or less recall the facts, the memories were not really alive. For instance, he could remember how he and Valera used to drink Alabashly wine after their shift and Valera would burp out the words "glory to labor" just at the moment when Ivan was setting the bottle to his lips, so that he would laugh and have to spit out an entire mouthful of fortified port onto the tiled floor.

But although Ivan remembered himself laughing, and he remembered the struggle with the muscles of his own larynx for that mouthful of liquid with an aftertaste of Martian oil, and he remembered Valera's laughing face, he simply couldn't recall the sensation of joy or even understand how he could have taken such pleasure in drinking in a storeroom stinking of urine behind the rusty shield of the fifth reactor. It was the same with his own room. Take the calendar with the Zaporozhets, for instance— Ivan was quite unable to imagine the state of mind responsible for the wish to hang that glossy sheet of paper on the wall. But there it was hanging there. He was equally at a loss to explain the large numbers of empty green glass bottles standing on the floor in front of the wardrobe. He knew that he and Valera had drunk them, and thrown a number of empties out the window; what he couldn't understand was why he had drunk all this strong port, and in Valera's company. In short, Ivan could recall all recent events, but he couldn't recall himself as part of them, and instead of the harmonious personality of a Communist or at least a Christian soul seeking redemption, what he discovered within himself was something strange—as though an empty window frame had been slammed shut by the autumn wind.

"Marat," he heard a coaxing woman's voice from behind the wall, "if you pee out the window, they won't take you into the Sandel cubs. You listen to what your ma tells you. . . ."

II

From early in the morning the entire town knew what was on sale in the wine shop. It would have been useless to try to work out how—there were no announcements on the radio or the television—and in some strange fashion it became known, so that even young children pondering their plans for the evening might well think something like: "Aha! Today the wine shop's got port for two ninety. Pa won't be back till after eight. But the vodka's running out. That means, until eleven . . ."

But they never asked themselves how they knew all this, just as they never asked themselves how they knew if it was a sunny day or was pouring rain. The city, of course, had far more than just one or two wine shops, but they all always sold exactly the same thing; even the beer ran out at the same moment in the basement on Spinal Cord Street and the grocery store on Local Ataxia Passage at the other end of Uran-Bator, so that the inhabitants of every region in the city all thought in terms of a single abstract "wine shop."

In the same way, Ivan, figuring out that today the wine shop had cognac at thirteen fifty, while around the back there was dry Bulgarian for a ruble seventy plus fifty on top, decided that Valera, his neighbor and drinking buddy, was bound to buy the dry wine and then hang about the storeroom to chat with the loaders—and as he was walking up to the wine shop, he ran straight into him. Valera wasn't surprised to see Ivan either, as if he had known that he would appear in the triangle of light between the rows of dark-blue crates, against the background of a garland of paper carnations already hanging on the wall.

"Let's go," said Valera. He shifted a clinking bag from one hand to the other, took Ivan by the elbow and led him off down Spinal Cord Street, nodding to his friends and stepping carefully around the stinking pools of vomit.

When they reached their usual spot, a small yard with swings and a sandpit, they sat down—Valera, as always, on a swing, and Ivan on the planking at the edge of the sandpit. Protruding from the sand were several half-buried bottles, a narrow strip of newspaper that fluttered in the wind, and several dry branches. This sandpit was a great favorite among the area's bottle ladies—it yielded magnificent harvests, almost as good as the playhouses on the playground in Mundindel Park, and the old women often fought for control of it, knocking each other down right there on Spinal Cord Street and wheezing asthmatically as they strangled each other with their empty string bags. Out of some strange sense of tact they always fought in silence, and the only audible accompaniment to their battles—which often ended up as mass brawls—was rapid breathing and the occasional jangling of medals.

"Want a drink?" asked Valera, pulling out the plastic stopper with his teeth and spitting it into the dust.

"I can't," answered Ivan. "You know that. My kidneys."

"Mine aren't in any great shape either," said Valera, "but I still drink. You going to act like a jerk for the rest of your life, then?"

"I'll hold out until the holiday," answered Ivan.

"It's sickening just to look at you. As though," Valera grimaced as he searched for the right word, "as though you'd lost your grip on the thread of life."

The dry wine had a bitter smell—Valera threw back his head, tipped up the bottle above his open mouth, and drank down the stream of liquid that swilled from side to side as if from some hydrodynamic effect.

"There now," he said, "and already I can hear the birds. And the wind. Quiet sounds like that."

"You should write poetry," said Ivan.

"Perhaps I do," answered Valera. "How would you know, you flaming red banner?"

"Perhaps you do," Ivan agreed indifferently.

He was rather surprised to notice that the yard in which they were sitting consisted of more than just the sandpit and the swings—it also had a small fenced-off flower bed overgrown with nettles, a long yellow block of apartments, dusty asphalt, and a zigzag concrete wall. Off in the distance where the wall met the building there were children rummaging in a garbage pile, sometimes freezing motionless for long periods and blending with the garbage, which made it impossible to tell exactly how many of them there were. "In town the children are well brought up and there aren't many freaks," thought Ivan as he watched their noisy bustle, "but once you get to the suburbs, they're climbing on the swings, and digging in the sandpits; they might even use a knife. Some of them are so repulsive."

The children seemed to sense the pressure of Ivan's thoughts: one of the little figures that had been entirely invisible stood up on skinny legs, circled for a short while around a dented yellow barrel lying a little to one side of the rest of the rubbish, and then set off uncertainly in the direction of the adults. It proved to be a boy of about ten, wearing shorts and a jacket with a hood.

"Hey, dudes," he said when he was close to them, "got any matches?"

Valera had been busy with his second bottle, which had a stopper that resisted his efforts, and he hadn't noticed the child approaching, but he swung around furiously at the sound of his voice.

"You!" he said. "Didn't they teach you all in school that children have no business by the swings and the sandpits?"

The boy thought about it.

"Yes," he said.

"Then what d'you think you're doing? How'd you like it if the grownups moved in on your dumps?"

"In actual fact," said the boy, "it wouldn't really make any difference."

"How come you're so cocky?" Valera asked with a hostile curiosity. "D'you know, my son's just the same."

Valera was exaggerating slightly—his son, Marat, had three legs and was retarded: the third leg was because of the radiation, but the backwardness was due to his father's drinking. And he was younger, too.

"Haven't you got any matches, then?" asked the boy. "I'm wasting time here talking to you."

"If I had, I wouldn't give them to you," answered Valera.

"Okay, then, successful labor to you," said the boy, and then turned and wandered back towards the dump, where the others were waving to him.

"I'll come after you," yelled Valera, even forgetting his bottle for a second, "and I'll teach you what words you can say and what words you can't. You little bastard, I'll labor your mother!"

"Oh, forget it," said Ivan, "weren't you just the same yourself? Let's you and me have a talk instead. You know, something strange is happening to me. Like I'm going crazy. Seems like I can remember everything about myself—only it doesn't seem to be about me at all, but about someone else—know what I mean?"

"What's so complicated about that?" Valera asked. "How long is it since you had a drink?"

"Two weeks," answered Ivan, "to the day."

"Then what d'you expect? You've got the black shakes coming on."

"No," said Ivan, "that can't be it. The chief quack told me that takes at least six months."

"You know how far you can trust them. Maybe they just figure that in a week's time you'll be celebrating the big May Day upstairs and they're trying to comfort you, so you don't suffer too much."

"Anyway," said Ivan, "that's not the real problem. I can't remember my childhood, all right? That is, I remember things: I can fill in the forms with where I was born, who my parents were, what school I went to, but somehow none of it's real. I can't remember anything for myself, not so that I really feel it. I close my eyes and there's nothing there but blackness, or maybe a yellow pear shape left over from the image of a light bulb. . . ."

The children from the dump ran hurriedly through the yard and out of sight around the corner. The last to leave was the one who had been looking for matches.

"You're really laying it on thick, pal," said Valera, who had taken out the third bottle. "Who remembers their childhood, anyway? I don't remember anything but words either. There's nothing wrong with you. When you start remembering all sorts of images, you'll know you've got the black shakes. Anyway, what do you need to remember your childhood for, for May's sake? What's so good about it? It's exactly . . ."

In the corner of the yard, among the scrap metal, there was a crimson flash and then a deafening bang, as though someone had smacked gigantic palms against both of their ears. Shrapnel whistled through the air above their heads and a piece of yellow aluminum siding lodged itself in the side of the sandpit just a few inches away from Ivan's leg.

"That's childhood for you," said Valera, recovering from the sudden shock. "Let's go. I can't keep on drinking here with this stink they've made."

Ivan stood up and followed Valera. He hadn't managed to express everything he had wanted to say—everything he'd actually spoken out loud had come out confused and stupid, and Valera had been quite right to feel irritated. "I could do with a drink," thought Ivan, scratching the back of his head. Something told him that if he had a drink—not much, just a couple of bottles of dry wine—it would all be over. "But then, what will be over?" thought Ivan—it really wasn't clear just what would be over. What Ivan felt was more like a realization that something was over already, but that he was missing that something. "Okay, so what is it that's missing?"

This was not clear at all, and no matter how hard Ivan tried, the only thing he could tell himself was that he had lost touch with the state in which such questions didn't arise. Worst of all, he couldn't even remember whether before the accident he had possessed any other memory of the past, different from his present one, or whether even then there had been nothing but the colorless formulae of official forms. They came out onto Spinal Cord Street and Valera glanced around at the crimson brick walls and the red cog wheels that had been hung up on the façades in honor of the holiday.

"Well, where to now?" he asked.

Ivan shrugged. It was all the same to him.

"Let's go to the Sovcom," said Valera. "We can drink right there on the square. Maybe some of our buddies will be there.

To reach Sandel Square, where the Sovcom was located, they had to go down Spinal Cord Street. Ivan began thinking and his thoughtfulness led smoothly into a calm state of numbness, so that he found himself on the square before he was aware of it. The gray façade of the Sovcom had already been decorated with the three massive profiles of Sandel, Mundindel, and Babayasin, and opposite them, above the squat building of the Sovcom bath-house, a red cloth banner bearing the words "LONG LIVE THE CAUSE OF MUNDINDEL AND BABAYASIN!" had been unfurled.

"Here, Val," said Ivan, "why's Mundindel got hair here? He was bald. And they've left out Sandel—what's wrong with him all of a sudden? Seems to me they used to write about him too."

"How should I know?" Valera answered. "Might as well ask why grass is green."

Paved with ribbed concrete slabs, the open expanse in front of the Sovcom would have looked more like a military airport than anything else, if not for the huge monument directly opposite the building—a ten-foot-tall mustachioed Babayasin with his legendary saber raised high above his head, between the tiny figures of Sandel and Mundindel which seemed to prop him up from both sides, were almost beautiful in their romantic passion. The sun was shining from the direction of the monument, which in silhouette looked like an immense fork with thick prongs that someone had thrust into the concrete of the square. Several men were sitting in the shade of the monument on white stools brought out of the Sovcom; a newspaper was spread out on the concrete in front of them with gleaming green bottles and red tomatoes.

"Maybe we'll join them, then?" said Valera.

From their suppurating, inflamed eyes it was easy to recognize the men sitting by the monument as workers from the

Loomworker chemical weapons plant on the edge of the city. Two of them nodded to Valera—the entire city knew him as a virtuoso master of obscene language (his nickname was "Valera the dialectician")—and the boys from the "Loomworker" were very proud of their tradition of rhetorical eloquence.

"Who's drinking, boys?" Valera asked.

"Nah," one of the chemical workers answered after a short pause, "we're waiting for the secretary. We've already had a gargle, that'll do for now."

"Ah, well, what kind of May Day is this? I can hardly believe it, they're turning down free drinks now."

Valera sat down on the concrete and leaned back against the low barrier around the monument. The plastic wheel of a bottle stopper skeetered across the surface of the concrete. Ivan sat down beside him, tucking the hem of his padded work jacket under his backside, and screwed up his eyes. He still felt sad and weary at heart for no obvious reason, but at least he was calm, and for a second he even thought he caught a brief glimpse of a memory through some crack—a strange looking red cap and a plastic tabletop.

"Valera!" one of the chemical workers called quietly. "Valera!"

"What?" Valera stopped glugging to ask.

"How's things down at the samovar and matryoshka plant? Will your collective fulfill the plan?"

Ivan started. This was an open challenge and an insult. But then he realized that the chemists were not really looking for an all-out fight, they simply wanted to try their skill against a master of language without having to worry about losing, and he calmed down. Valera had also realized what was going on—he was used to these games.

"We're working our way through it bit by bit," he replied lazily. "And how's the labor discipline around your place? What innovations have you got lined up for the May holidays?"

"We're still thinking about it," answered the chemist. "We'd like to spend a bit of time in your collective and get some advice from top rank workers. The main thing is to keep a peaceful sky over your head—that's right, isn't it?"

"That's right," answered Valera. "Come over and discuss things if you like, but you've plenty of veterans of your own, just look at that honor board of yours—five Stakhanovs up your exchange of experience in a single country."

Someone snorted quietly.

"That's true, we do have our own veterans," the chemist persisted, "but the tradition of competition has put down deeper roots at your place, just look at all those pennants you May Day front liners have collected, shove the weak link up your Rot-Front and a superstructure in behind!"

"Not bad," Ivan observed, "but he's nervous, so he's started off sounding too much like a newspaper. . . ."

"You'd do better to think about material incentives—five symptoms of your mother—than go counting other people's pennants—ten neckties down your open hearth and quantity up your quality," Valera rattled off like a drum beat, "and then you could boast about your counterplan, may each of you receive a plaster Pavlik Morozov from his people's militia according to his labor standards."

Ivan suddenly thought that today's conversation with the boy by the swings must have had an effect on Valera, although he hadn't said anything about it—there was an edge of bitterness in his words. The chemist said nothing for a few seconds while he gathered his thoughts, and then spoke in a reconciliatory tone.

"I wish you'd shut up, Maypole your mother under a wagon shaft in the garden city."

"Then slag off back to May up Ludwig Feuerbach and down Klara Zetkin," Valera answered indifferently.

Ivan could tell that the victory had not brought him any particular satisfaction. This wasn't up to his level.

"Let's have a drink, then," said the embarrassed chemist.

Ivan opened his eyes and saw the chemist accept the bottle

held out by Valera. He turned out to be quite a young guy, but to judge from the color of his face and the purple boils on his neck, he'd already worked with "Bird Cherry" and "Collective-Farm Lily" and maybe even with "Summer Breeze." Nobody spoke. Ivan thought about saying something to warm the atmosphere a little, but he changed his mind and fixed his gaze on the black tip of the shadow from Babayasin's saber as it crept imperceptibly across the concrete.

"You're not bad at scattering the May buds," Valera said after a little while, "but you've got to relax. And not feel any hatred." The boy turned blue in pleasure.

"What are you hanging around here for?" asked one of the chemists. "You waiting for someone?"

"We're just looking for the thread of life," answered Ivan.

"Well, have you found it?" a strong voice boomed behind him. Ivan turned around to see the Secretary of the Sovcom, Parmahamov, who must have crept up on them from the direction of the monument in order to hear the living conversation of the people. Ivan had seen Parmahamov a couple of times at the plant—he was a short, stout man of absolutely undistinguished appearance, who usually wore a cheap blue suit with wide lapels, a yellow shirt, and a purple tie. He used to work in some bank, where he stole a pile of money, for which he was frequently abused in the press.

"I've been listening to you boys," said Parmahamov, rubbing his hands together, "and I was thinking how remarkably talented our people are; the way you, Valery, managed to link dialectics with daily life—we could print that straight off in the newspaper. Next year we'll promote you to the ranks of the people's nightingales. . . . And what was it you boys wanted?"

"We made an appointment," one of the chemists answered.

"Then I'll listen to what you have to say," said Parmahamov. "And don't you go away yet, Ivan, I've got to present you with something. Right then, let's go."

The first thing to strike them inside the Sovcom was the

huge number of children. They were everywhere: crawling up and down the broad marble staircase with its red carpet-runner, hanging on the velvet curtains, clowning about in front of the mirror that covered half the wall, burning something that gave off a stink in the far corner of the hallway, torturing a cat under the stairs—and everywhere screeching intolerably, repulsively. While they were climbing the stairs Ivan twice had to step over bluish, swollen-looking, tightly swaddled infants who moved by wriggling their entire bodies, like worms. Inside the Sovcom there was a smell of urine and boiled buckwheat.

"There, you see," said Parmahamov, turning around, "we've handed it over to the children."

They went up to the fifth floor. Five or six young men were sitting motionless in the deep armchairs at the blind end of the corridor, wearing round flying helmets with condensation misting the transparent visors.

"Who are they?" inquired Valera.

"Those? Young cosmonauts. A subsection of the Palace of Pioneers. Where we are now is the Palace of Pioneers, and downstairs is the nursery and kindergarten."

"But why are they wearing helmets?"

"Stops the acetone evaporating too rapidly. We have to fight for every bottle."

Eventually they reached Parmahamov's office, which proved to be small and sparsely furnished. Almost all of the space was taken up by a long conference table, from beneath which Parmahamov dragged out a dribbling infant by the ear and booted him out into the corridor. Ivan noticed that the curtain at the window was stirring in a suspicious manner—there must be children hiding there too—but he decided not to interfere.

"Sit down," said Parmahamov, pointing to a chair. Ivan and Valera sat down under a portrait of Sandel's mother, who gazed piercingly into the room from beneath a white cotton cap, and the others sat at the table.

"Right, then," said the chemist who had tried to compete

with Valera, "right, we want to go over to balanced bookkeeping. And self-supporting finances. The collective sent us."

"Balanced bookkeeping," said Parmahamov, "is a fine thing. How do you want to do it; which model are you going to choose?"

"May bloody knows," said the chemist after a moment's thought. "You tell us about it. You think we understand it all? If you ask me how much phosgene to add to cyanogen chloride to make Collective-Farm Lily, then I can tell you, but how could I know anything about these models? I've spent my entire life on the shop floor."

"That's right," said Parmahamov. "That's exactly right. And you did the right thing, boys, by coming here. Where else would you go, if not here?"

He got up from the table and began walking to and fro in the narrow space beside it, one hand clutching his belt under his jacket behind his back and the other held in front of him with the thumb extended and palm open, as though in anticipation of some invisible handshake. Ivan recalled a restricted circulation brochure he had once seen, called "Partai-chi," which described an entire complex of movements allowing even an individual of the very sharpest mental acuity to tune his mind for the faultless exposition of the party line. The exercise that Parmahamov was performing was one of them.

"Yes." he said, suddenly coming to a halt.

Ivan looked at him and was amazed at what he saw—Parmahamov's eyes had changed, transforming themselves from cunningly squinting slits into two circles of tin. He was breathing somehow differently now, and his voice was an octave lower.

"What can I say to you," he intoned slowly, and gave a sudden shake of his head as though in bitter comprehension. "I can see it. I can see everything you're thinking after you've read all those newspaper reports! It's true. They lied to us for a long time. But that time is now over. Now we know everything—about how the prowdled sabort sprattled our souperus and the dork lyubyanik condited our rid. Why do we know? Because they told us the truth. Now let me ask you—ought we to think about our children and our grandchildren? You, Valera, our nightingale, you tell me."

"I should think we ought," said Valera. "Of course."

"Right then. Then just work it out: they'll grow up, our children, and by that time there'll be a new truth ready for the telling. Do we want them to be told that new truth, like we're being told now?"

"Of course we do," everyone at the table answered loudly. "Get to the point!"

"The point's very simple. Right now the leadership is watching to see how the people are working. If we're working badly, then what's the point of telling us the truth? And we should work anyway out of simple gratitude, and not go counting other people's caviar and dachas. That's real balanced bookkeeping."

Parmahamov thought about something for a second and his features softened.

"And in general," he said, "to put it in simple human terms, how wonderful it is to be alive!"

He must have pressed a button of some kind—immediately after he finished speaking a crowd of Young Pioneers came tumbling into the room and stood tightly packed around Valera, Ivan, and the chemists. The Pioneers were in smoothly ironed white shirts with ties, they smelled of fruit drops and starch, and in Ivan's smoke-polluted breast a wave of nostalgia rose and fell at the thought of his own childhood—or rather, at the thought of his vanished memories.

"Take them to the Museum of Glory," said Parmahamov.

"Let's go," commanded one of the Pioneers, and in two seconds the flood of red ties had swept Ivan and Valera and the chemists from the floor of Parmahamov's office. Ivan could only vaguely recall what happened next. He retained nothing but scraps of memories from the Museum of Glory—first they were all led up to a small glass display case which housed the first documents of the people's power in Uran-Bator (which had some other name then)—"The Decree on Land," "The Decree on Sky," and the historical "Order No. 1": *From the first day of the month of May of this year entry to the city and exit therefrom are forbidden under pain of capital punishment.* Commissars: Sandel, Mundindel, Babayasin.

For some reason this was followed by the display stand, "The Life of the Peoples of Our Country Before the Revolution," a board covered in canvas to which a horseshoe, a yellow horse's jaw, and a crumpled birch-bark sandal had been attached with wire. Close by, in an illuminated glass box, hung the tiny women's Brownings that had belonged to Sandel and Mundindel, and beneath them Babayasin's notched saber, which turned out not to be so very big after all. Everywhere there were photographs of coarse mustachioed faces, and the voice of the Pioneer acting as guide had continuously explained some incomprehensible difference between them. Then the voice had acquired deep, soft, and velvety tones, and began talking about death and describing its various forms, beginning with drowning. Ivan suddenly understood. . . .

III

"I'll teach you how to talk in front of your mother, you little pup! I'll give you flaming Mayflies!"

That was Valera shouting behind the wall, and he could hear a child crying.

"Marat, love, hold on," said a different female voice. "Hold on love, you know Pa's . . ."

Ivan turned over onto his back and fixed his gaze on the faint gold glimmer of the pretzel-shaped lamp on the ceiling. It was Valera's room, and for some reason he was lying on Valera's bed in his trousers and jacket. But that wasn't what was bothering him, it was the dream he'd just stopped dreaming.

In the dream he'd found himself in a strange place, a gloomy room with lancet windows that had obviously once been a church but was now filled with old battered skis and sodden boots that gave off the smell of a damp prison. Through the narrow slit of a window he could see a patch of gray sky, and occasional gusts of steam. Ivan himself was sitting on a tiny bench and in front of him an old man with a broad beard covering his chest was sleeping on an immense pile of old felt boots—that was how Parmahamov appeared in this dream, where for some reason he was called Ivan Ilich. Ivan tried to get up but realized he couldn't because the legs of his new namesake were lying on his shoulders. Ivan also realized that he was dying, and this had less to do with his bruised kidney than with the legs lying on his shoulders. Death would come when Parmahamov woke up.

Ivan tried cautiously removing Parmahamov's legs from his shoulders and Parmahamov started waking up—he stirred and groaned, even raised one hand a little. Frightened, Ivan stopped moving. The old man began snoring again, but now he was sleeping restlessly, turning his head in his sleep, and it seemed as though he might wake up at any moment. Ivan very much did not want to die—there was something in his life which made it worth bearing the bitter stench of this room, and Parmahamov's legs on his shoulders, and even the terrible thought that there was nothing at all in the world except this room, a thought which seemed to permeate the air along with the smell of soaking leather.

"There must be some way of getting out of this," thought Ivan. "There has to be." And then he noticed that Parmahamov had skis on his feet and their tips reached down to only a little short of the floor. Ivan dragged the bench out from underneath himself and began cautiously stooping down, pressing himself towards the floor. The ends of the skis came to rest on the floor and Ivan sensed that he could creep out from under Parmahamov's legs. No sooner had he crawled out from underneath them and taken two steps to the side, than his bruised kidney stopped hurting. Then Ivan realized that he wasn't Ivan at all—the thought didn't sadden him in the least—and he knew exactly what he had to do. In the wall opposite the lancet window there was a little door. Ivan tiptoed over to it, opened it, squeezed through into a narrow black space, and began feeling his way forward. His hands moved closely over the surface of dusty picture frames, chairs, bicycle handlebars—and then came across a new door ahead of him. Ivan drew breath and pushed against it.

Outside it was a hot sunny day. Ivan was standing in a small yard in which hens and cocks were strutting about. The yard was enclosed by an uneven but sturdy fence, beyond which he could make out rocky orange-colored slopes rising upwards with little blue houses scattered across them. Ivan went over to the fence, grabbed hold of its top and raised his head over it. About three hundred yards away was the sea. And at the edge of the sea a slim white form glinted blindingly in the sunlight . . . Ivan couldn't remember anything after that.

"Pulled out of it?" asked Valera, coming into the room.

"Seems like it," Ivan answered, getting up. "What happened to me?"

"Just pushed yourself a bit too hard around the Maypole. They took us to the museum on the fourth floor, and then Parmahamov came down and started telling us how you'd saved someone from drowning, and he wanted to present you with an illustrated book on behalf of the Sovcom. And then you just keeled over. They brought you here in the Sovcom wagon, like a king. Here's the book."

Valera held out to Ivan a massive tome with a glossy dust jacket, which Ivan could scarcely keep hold of. *My Albania* was written in large letters on the cover.

"What is it?"

"Pictures," answered Valera, "have a look, there's some interesting ones. At first I thought it would be nothing but a load of dusty museum pieces, but then I had a look and it's not bad."

Ivan opened the book and his eye fell on a large, double-page reproduction. It showed a large log with a fat naked man lying on it belly down.

"In search of the internal Pinocchio," Ivan read off the title. "Only it's not clear where he's looking for Pinocchio: in the log or in himself."

"Seems to me," answered Valera, "it's all the same one May or the other."

Ivan turned the page and suddenly almost dropped the book. What he saw—and immediately recognized—was the enclosed yard with the cocks, hens, and the fence and beyond that the little blue houses with the St. Andrew's crosses on their shutters climbing up the orange mountain slopes. In the center of the yard a man was sitting on a cracked bench, wearing a military service jacket with the sleeves rolled up, and playing on a small accordion whose case lay open beside him.

"Waiting for the white submarine," read Ivan, then he snatched up the book and set off back to his own room, without even looking at Valera. He didn't keep the door key under the doormat like everyone else, but in the pocket of a padded jacket hanging on a nail. Ivan realized now why he'd woken up at Valera's place; the people who'd brought him home hadn't been able to open the door.

Everything in the room was just as it had been: the stain from the herrings was there on the tablecloth; the miniature Kremlin made of bottles still stood in front of the wardrobe and, still trying hard to appear nude, the naked woman by the Zaporozhets on the calendar was smiling at the photographer. Ivan collapsed onto the bed and slept.

From the moment his head touched the plastic foam pillow, he began dreaming again. He was standing on a high roof at night and looking down at a city spread out all around him like a jumble of gigantic quartz crystals illuminated from within by thousands of shades of electric light—but he was not in the least afraid that he might fall (in Uran-Bator the tallest building was the five-story Sovcom, but there was no point in even dreaming of getting up there to see the city). Then he was down on the ground, on a broad well-lit street filled with happy, carefree people, and he wasn't immediately aware that it was nighttime and the light was coming from street lamps and shop windows. The next instant he was hurtling along a road supported on slim columns in a quietly growling car with blue, red, and orange numbers and lines flashing on the dashboard in front of him. Then he was at a table in a restaurant, surrounded by several people in familiar military uniform, and on the table, among an incredible display of glasses and bottles, lay several packs of Winston.

"A-a-agh!" Ivan howled as he awoke, "a-a-a-gh!"

The strange dream crumbled and disappeared. When Ivan opened his eyes he was in the familiar room and outside the dark window a guitar was jangling in the usual fashion. His recollection of the shock he had suffered remained unclear; he couldn't remember what was wrong at all. But he was afraid to stay in bed—he got up and began pacing nervously across the painted floorboards. He had to do something to occupy his mind.

"Maybe I should tidy up the room?" he thought. "This is really frightening, I feel like I'm going nuts, I feel totally witless, witless"—he repeated it to himself several times, feeling something inside him rising up in response to the word. The strange sensation gradually passed. He took a look around and decided to start with the bottles. "It was something very odd," he recalled, opening the window and looking out and down into the trash strewn yard, "something about an accordion."

The yard was empty, except for the far end by the swings and the sandpit, where he could make out the lit ends of cigarettes. The children had long ago all gone home, and he could throw his garbage straight out the window, onto the pile, without worrying about hurting anyone. Ivan threw out a few bottles, a few seconds went by, and then he heard an unimaginably piercing feline screech that was immediately answered by jolly catcalls from the direction of the swings and the sandpit.

"Keep up that labor initiative, get that Partcom up your Kollontai!" shouted Valera's drunken voice; some women began giggling. "We're going to give all tomcats a triple Central Committee May Day with bells and whistles!"

"Whistles," repeated Ivan, "witless . . . whistles . . . Winston . . ." He suddenly drew back from the window and clutched his head in his hands—he felt as though he had been struck in the face with a plank.

"My God!" he whispered, then repeated the phrase in English, "My God! How could I have forgotten?"

He dashed over to the wardrobe, pushing aside the remaining bottles which went rolling across the floor, some of them breaking—and flung open its doors. Inside stood a tattered accordion case. Ivan pulled it out, carried it over to the bed, clicked open the locks, opened the lid, and laid his palms on the rough panel of the transmitter. One palm crept to the right, felt its way into another section and found the cold handle of a pistol; the other found a package containing money and maps.

"My God," he whispered again, "I forgot all about it, everything. If that thing hadn't smacked me in the back, I'd be drinking with them now . . . And tomorrow, as well."

He stood up and strode around the room again, running his fingers through his hair. Then he sat back down, pulled the open accordion case toward him and switched on the transmitter. Two eyes, one green and one yellow, seemed to open and gaze out at him.

IV

The next morning Ivan was woken by music. His first sensation on waking was terror at the thought that he had forgotten everything. Leaping to his feet, he was about to dash over to the wardrobe, but he sighed in relief at the certainty that he could remember. The note in pencil on the wallpaper: "FIRST THING IN THE MORNING REMEMBER TO PLAY THE ACCOR-

DION" was superfluous after all. He even found it rather funny and was ashamed of the fear he had felt the previous day. Ivan turned over onto his back, set his hands behind his head, and stared at the ceiling. Through the window he heard another stream of slushy wind instrument music, as if the soloists' thick fatty voices were being stirred into a melody to produce something like a thin soup.

"Why all the music?" wondered Ivan, and then he remembered: today was a holiday, Bulldozer Driver's Day. Demonstrations, cabbage pies, and all the rest of it—perhaps it would be easier to leave the city during the drunken uproar. He could sing a farewell song with everyone else at the Babayasin monument on the way to the station. There was a knock at the door.

"Ivan!" Valera shouted from the corridor, "are you up yet?"

Ivan muttered something loudly, trying not to invest the sounds with any meaning.

"Okay," Valera answered, and trudged off down the corridor in his massive boots.

"He's gone to the demonstration," Ivan realized. He turned to face the wall and became thoughtful as he gazed at the pimply projections on the wallpaper. After a while the happy holiday sounds of building work and subdued banter fell silent in the yard and it became absolutely quiet. Ivan got up, made his bed quickly, and began gathering his things. Putting on his special holiday work jacket with the white nitrolacquer Levi's inscription and the Adidas artificial leather hood, he looked himself over carefully in the mirror. Everything seemed to be fine, but just in case Ivan released a long blond forelock from under his cap, then took an artificial sunflower seed husk out of the accordion case and glued it to his chin.

"That's just perfect," he thought, picked up the case and took a farewell look around his room. Taking his leave was not difficult.

Downstairs by the door Valera was leaning against the wall and smoking. Just like Ivan, he was wearing his special holiday padded jacket, but his was a Wrangler. Ivan hadn't been expecting to meet him here—he was quite startled.

"Right then," said Valera good-naturedly, "slept it off all right?"

"Ughu," answered Ivan. "I thought you were going off with the column?"

"Oh, come on, flaming peaceful May. You yelled through the door for me to wait. Are you completely crocked or what?"

"All right, to May with it," Ivan said vaguely. "Where shall we go then?"

"Where else. To Petya's place. We'll sit for a while with our own buddies."

"That means Maypoling it all the way through town," said Ivan, "past the Sovcom."

"We'll walk it, it won't be the first time."

Ivan trudged off after Valera along the empty and depressing street. Nobody was around, but from somewhere in the distance they could hear the sounds of a wind orchestra, now including the sharp, particularly unpleasant sound of cymbals, which had previously been filtered out by the window. The street merged into another, which in turn merged into a third, and the music grew louder and louder until finally it drowned out the scraping of the two men's boots on the asphalt from Ivan's hearing. Turning one more corner they saw a raised dais upholstered with red cloth, and standing on it a singer with an incredibly ruddy face; he was gesturing to the crowd, moving his arms out from his chest and although his mouth was wide open, in some cunning fashion he managed to smile as if astonished that he was giving away his art to the people so simply. At the same moment he came into view, they heard the words of the song:

My own free land, my beaming nation
Glows bright as nuclear radiation.

At this point their view of the singer was obstructed by another corner, and the music once more became a sticky porridge of wind instruments and baritone. Ahead of them Ivan and Valera caught sight of the tail end of the column making its way to the center of the city, and they quickened their step in order to fall in with the others. He caught a glimpse of Osmakov, looking gloomy with the collar of his raincoat freshly washed, and the smiling Altynina, wearing a ribbon in a bow; they were standing to one side of the stream of people, in a small side street, beside a group of horses harnessed to a huge mobile propaganda display shaped like a bulldozer.

They soon came out into the square in front of the Sovcom. The monument to Sandel, Mundindel, and Babayasin was decorated with paper orchids which were now sodden and heavy with rain. A ballbearing race had been set on the point of the saber raised high above the head of the bronze Babayasin, with hooks set in its outer ring. Festive red ribbons dangled down from the hooks, into the clutching left hands of twenty or so of the city's most active party members. They were all dressed in identical brown waterproof raincoats and caps covered with gleaming raindrops, and they were walking in a circle, around and around the monument, so that if anybody had been watching from above, what they would have seen was something like a reddish-brown toothed cogwheel slowly rotating in the very center of the square. Other living cogwheels, made up of people holding hands, regulated themselves around the movement of the main group. Ivan and Valera shifted from one foot to the other as they waited for their column to form into a long loop in order to file past the central cogwheel. They had to wait for a long time—the leadership had grown very tired since the morning and was now rotating much less rapidly.

"Valera," asked Ivan, "why's it all different this time?"

"Haven't you listened to the radio recently? They've improved the transmission. There's going to be a new model of bulldozer."

Valera apprehensively rubbed a finger over the white letters on his padded jacket to make sure they weren't smudging—it had been known to happen. Finally there were only a few people in front of them and Ivan and Valera joined hands and linked up with their neighbors, slipped between a pair of cops, and were carried towards the center of the square.

The handshake passed off almost without a hitch, apart from the fact that Ivan forgot to shift the accordion case from his right hand to his left, so that he had to linger for a moment in front of the monument. The hand he shook belonged to the editor of *Red Half-Life*, Colonel Kozheurov, but Valera had to be satisfied with the wet artificial limb of the head of the Sovcom's Department of Culture. Valera was upset by this, and when they had left Sandel Square behind them and the people had fallen neatly back into a column, he turned back and waved his fist threateningly at the retreating gray façade with the huge red letters spelling out "PEACE, LABOR, MAY."

Ivan's padded jacket had soaked up a lot of water and grown heavy, but there wasn't much further to go to reach Petya's place. There were fewer and fewer militiamen around and more and more drunks. At last they were surrounded by the tarpaper-roofed greenhouses of Babayasin Prospect, and when Ivan and Valera had drifted with the crowd as far as their destination, they fell out of the column and cut across the line of movement, paying no attention to the whistling and Maying of the parade marshal. They quickly made their way to the familiar entrance and up to the third floor; there was already a smell of hard liquor on the landing by the door of the hostel where Petya lived and Valera, completely forgetting his ominous encounter on the square, livened up and gave Ivan a thump on the shoulder. The hostel was shaking to the sound of music. Petya opened the door and stuck his small head out through the gap—as always, it seemed as though he was standing on a bench behind the door.

"Cheers," he said without any expression.

"That's a tremendous racket," said Valera as he entered the corridor.

"Who is that laboring away?"

"Gentle May," Petya answered, walking off along the corridor.

Pyotr's room differed from Ivan's in the arrangement of the bed and the wardrobe, the number of bottles on the floor and the calendar on the wall—a different naked woman was smiling and holding out a glass of mandarin juice into the room. Ivan thought her green-varnished nails looked like flies that had fallen into the glass and drowned.

Ivan sat on the bed, picked up a magazine from the bedside table, and opened it at random. His eyes met the gaze of of an old musketeer wearing a French beret. Valera and Pyotr had struck up a monosyllabic conversation: Ivan filtered out everything except Valera's occasional colorful *bon mot*.

" 'Communism has a healthy, correct understanding of the life of each individual which is perfectly compatible with Christianity', wrote the musketeer, 'such as serving a transpersonal goal—serving not oneself, but a greater whole.' "

The words somehow filtered very easily into Ivan's mind—so easily, in fact, that their meaning remained entirely unclear. As Ivan began thinking about them, it suddenly grew darker in the room and the conversation at the table stopped dead. Ivan looked up. An immense two-dimensional plywood bulldozer was drifting by outside the window, painted crimson with the cogs of the open motor painstakingly drawn in. It was astonishing, both because it was so big and because it was made out of a single piece of plywood, specially produced for the purpose by the local factory. But there was a strange discrepancy, which Ivan had noticed during the demonstration as he walked past the contraption standing in the side street and glanced at the green magnesium wheels supporting it—it looked like the chassis from a Tu-720 heavy bomber. At the time he hadn't realized what was wrong, but now—probably because he could only see the upper part of the agit-monster through the window—he spotted it: the cabin of the bulldozer was absolutely empty. They hadn't even drawn in the glass. Instead there were just two square holes swan through the wood, showing gray patches of the wet, distended sky.

The bulldozer drifted past and Ivan, nodding his head as thoughts came crowding in, became absorbed in the magazine as he waited for everyone to get so drunk that he'd be able to slip away unseen. The article obviously fascinated him.

"What kind of sickle are you hammering out of that?"

Ivan looked up. Valera and Petya were staring fixedly at him. He suddenly realized that for five minutes the room had been absolutely quiet, and he put the magazine down.

"It's really interesting," he said, moving his hand closer to the pocket with the revolver, just in case, "about the philosopher Berdyaev."

"So what's it say?" Petya asked with a strange smile. "What's he write about?"

"He has one pretty good idea. That the psychological world of the communist is sharply divided into a kingdom of light and a kingdom of darkness—the camps of Ormuzd and Ariman. It's basically a Manichean dualism which exploits the monistic . . ."

Ivan didn't even feel the stool hit his face—he realized he must have caught the blow when he looked up from the floor and saw Petya taking a slow step towards him holding it in his hand. Valera was standing behind Petya trying—just as slowly—to stop him. Fortunately, he managed it. Ivan shook his head and pulled the pistol out of his pocket. The next moment the stool, thrown accurately by Petya, struck him. His pistol flew off into the corner, gave out a quiet plopping sound, and a substantial dent appeared in the ceiling. Plaster scattered down onto the floor.

"Making out like he's a thief, the bloody front line worker," said Petya to the confused and startled Valera, as he bent down for the pistol. "I did a year and a half inside, I know that tune. Now," he turned towards Ivan, "you're in for an epiphenomenon of dehumanization. An accordion across the power tool." He reached out for the case.

V

"It depends on your pay," Ivan said, pressing the crumpled handkerchief to the corner of his mouth, "and what kind of car it is. You're wrong to think you live in the kingdom of darkness and we have the kingdom of light. We have trouble too. All sorts of homeless blacks. They spread AIDS." Ivan couldn't remember anything except a few snatches of the TV program with the gloomy title of "The Camera Looks Out Into the World," but that was enough. Valera and Petya listened with their mouths wide open, and Ivan didn't even want to get up from the table. But it was time to go.

"You tell them over there," Valera said as Ivan was putting on his padded jacket, "that we're not malicious. We want to live with a peaceful sky above our heads too. We want to work in peace and raise children. Okay?"

"Okay," answered Ivan, hiding his pistol in the case with the transmitter and carefully clicking the nickel-plated locks closed. "I'll make sure I tell them."

"And tell them," Petya said as he walked with him along the corridor with the identical rubber mats in front of each door, "that our secret isn't in our bombs and our planes—it's in us, ourselves."

"I'll tell them," promised Ivan, "I've realized that."

"Take the magazine," Petya said in the doorway, "you can read it on the way." Ivan took it. Then he embraced Petya and the subdued Valera in farewell and stepped out onto the staircase without looking back. The door clicked shut behind him. He walked down, stepped onto the dark street and took a deep breath of air that smelled of heavy fuel oil and damp planks. There was a crimson flash in the sky, and Ivan almost made a dash back to the entrance ("Could it possibly be?" was the thought that flashed through his mind), but then he realized it was only a fireworks display.

"Hoorah!" came the ragged cheer from people on the street. "Hoorah!"

"Hoorah!" cheered Ivan.

Another set of rockets exploded in the sky and again everything was lit up—yellow walls, yellow three-story houses, yellow streamers of either smoke or mist across the low shaggy-haired sky. Far, far away in the distance he could hear a sad, drawn-out mechanical howling—as though something huge, rusty, and oily was demanding attention from the people, or perhaps simply wishing them a happy holiday. Then everything turned green. Ivan strode off towards the station.

Prince of
Cosplan

Loading . . .

The little figure runs along the corridor. It is drawn with great affection, perhaps a little too sentimentally. If you press the <Up> key, it jumps, arches its back, and hangs in the air for a second, trying to catch hold of something above its head. If you press <Down> it squats and tries to pick something up from the ground under its feet. If you press <Right> it runs to the right, if you press <Left> it runs to the left. In fact you can use various keys to control it, but these four are the most important.

The space through which the figure runs changes. Most of the time it's no more than a plain stone passageway, but sometimes it turns into an incredibly beautiful gallery with a strip of oriental ornament running along the wall and tall narrow windows. There are torches blazing on the walls and enemies with naked swords standing in the dead ends of side corridors and on the precarious bridges over deep shafts of stone—the little figure can fight with them if you press the <Shift> key. If you press several keys at the same time, the little figure can leap and stretch, hang swaying on the edge of a precipice, and even run and jump over the deep stone shafts with the sharp spikes sticking up down below. The game has a number of levels, and you can pass from lower ones to higher ones, or tumble back down from the higher levels. The corridors change, the traps change, the jars from which the figure drinks to restore its vital energy look different, but still everything remains the same: the figure still runs over the flagstones past the torches, the skulls on the shelves, and the drawings on the walls.

The final purpose is to reach the highest level, where the princess is waiting, but to do that you have to devote a lot of time to the game itself. In fact, to be successful, you have to forget that you're pressing keys and actually become the little figure—only then will it acquire the degree of agility required to fence, jump through the snapping body-scissors in the narrow stone corridors, leap over the stone shafts and run over the collapsing flagstones, each of which can only support the weight of a body for seconds—although the figure has no body, let alone any weight, and neither, if you think about it, do the tumbling slabs of stone, no matter how convincing the sound might be when they fall.

Level 1

The prince was running along the stone ledge: he had to squeeze through under the iron portcullis before it dropped, because beyond it stood a jar with a slim neck, and he had almost no strength left at all. There were already two shafts with spikes behind him, and the leap down onto the floor strewn with stone fragments had cost him a serious effort as well. Sasha pressed <Right> and then immediately <Down>, and by some miracle the prince squeezed under the portcullis, which was already half-lowered. Then the picture on the screen shifted, and in place of the jar there was an obese warrior wearing a turban standing on the bridge and gazing hypnotically at Sasha.

"Lapin!" said a repulsively familiar voice behind his back, and Sasha felt a sudden sinking feeling in his stomach, although there was no real reason for him to feel afraid.

"Yes, Boris Grigorievich?"

"Come into my office."

Boris Grigorievich's office was actually not an office at all, it was simply a section of the room separated off by several bookshelves and cupboards, and when Boris Grigorievich strode around his territory the bald dome of his head could be seen over the top of them, so that Sasha sometimes had the feeling that he was squatting down beside a billiard table and watching the movement of the only remaining ball over the top of the cushion. After lunch Boris Grigorievich usually dropped into one of the pockets, but he spent the golden hours of the morning bouncing around from cushion to cushion, with the part of the cue played by the telephone—every ring it gave made the ivory-colored hemisphere move faster above the paper-cluttered surface of the cupboards.

Sasha hated Boris Grigorievich with the calm, enduring hatred known only to Siamese cats who live with cruel masters, and Soviet engineers who read George Orwell. Sasha had read all of Orwell at college, when it was still forbidden, and every day since then he had found a multitude of reasons to smirk wryly and shake his head. And now, as he approached the passage between two cupboards, he gave a crooked smile at the thought of the conversation ahead. Boris Grigorievich was standing by the window and practicing the "swallow's flight" blow, pausing at length in each of the intermediate positions. He wasn't using a bamboo pole, as he had when he recently began studying Budokan, but a genuine samurai sword. Today he was wearing a "hunting costume" of green satin over a creased kimono of patterned sinobu fabric. When Sasha entered, he lovingly laid the sword on the windowsill, sat down on a straw mat and pointed to another mat beside it. Folding his legs underneath him with a struggle, Sasha sat down and fixed his gaze on the Honda poster showing a motorcyclist in tall leather boots who for more than a year had been riding the wall of death across the cupboard to the right of Boris Grigorievich's straw mat. Boris Grigorievich placed his hand

palm-down on the processor unit of his AT—it was the same as
Sasha's, except that it had an eighty megabyte hard disk—and
closed his eyes, pondering how to begin the conversation.

"Have you read the latest issue of *Arguments and Facts?*" he
asked after a minute or so.

"I don't subscribe."

"You should," said Boris Grigorievich, picking up the folded
sheets of newsprint from where they lay on the floor and shaking
them back and forth, "it's a fine newspaper. What I can't understand at all is just what the communists are hoping for. Killed
fifty million people and still they carry on with their mumbo
jumbo. They can't fool anyone any longer."

"Uh-uh," said Sasha.

"And look at this, about a thousand women in America pregnant by aliens. Plenty of them here too, but the KGB's got them
hidden away somewhere."

"Just what is he after?" Sasha thought wearily.

Boris Grigorievich began thinking and his face darkened.

"You're a strange lad, Sasha," he said at last. "You're always
sullen, never make friends with anyone in the department.
They're people, you know, not just pieces of furniture. Yesterday
you gave Lusya a real fright. She told me today: 'I don't care
what you say, Boris Grigorievich, but I'm scared of being alone in
the elevator with him.'"

"I've never been alone in the elevator with her," said Sasha.

"And that's exactly why she's afraid. Take a ride with her,
grab her by the cunt, have a bit of a laugh. Have you read Dale
Carnegie?"

"What did I do to frighten her?" Sasha asked, trying to recall
who Lusya was.

"Never mind Lusya, that's not the point," said Boris Grigorievich, gesturing impatiently. "You just need to behave like a
normal human being, understand? All right, we'll continue this
conversation some other time, right now I've got an important
question for you. How well do you know *Abrams?*"

"Fairly well."

"How do you turn the turret in it?"

"First you press <C> and then use the cursor keys. The vertical ones raise the barrel."

"You sure? Let's take a look."

Sasha went over to the computer. Boris Grigorievich whispered something to himself as his fingers stumbled uncertainly over the keyboard while he loaded the game.

"That turns it right, and that turns it left," said Sasha.

"So it does. I'd never have guessed in a hundred years."

Boris Grigorievich picked up his phone and began dialing a number.

"Boris Emelianovich," he purred, "we've worked it out. Press <C> and then use the arrow keys . . . Yes, yes . . . You reverse it using <C> too . . . Oh no, not at all, ha ha ha . . ."

Boris Grigorievich turned to Sasha, curved his lips into an imploring smile and without giving the slightest hint of offense, twirled his fingers in the direction of the exit. Sasha stood up and went out.

"Ha ha ha . . . On paper? *Populos?* I've never even heard of it. We'll do it. We'll do it. We'll do it. Take care now."

Level 2

Sasha always went out onto the dark staircase to smoke, to a window from which he could see a tall building and some ramshackle but beautiful earth terraces below it. When he had lit his cigarette, he usually stared for a long time at the skyscraper—his view of the star perched on its pinnacle was slightly from one side and the wreaths framing it made it look like a double headed eagle. As he looked at it, Sasha often imagined a different version of Russian history—or rather a different trajectory, leading to precisely the same point—with the construction of exactly the same tall building, but with a different symbol on its summit. But right now the sky looked particularly repulsive, and seemed even grayer than the building.

On the landing one floor below, two men dressed in identical overalls of fine English wool were smoking: each of them had a gold wrench sticking out of his breast pocket. Listening to their conversation, Sasha realized that they were from the game *Pipes*. Sasha had seen the game, he'd even gone to install it on some deputy minister's hard disk, but he didn't like its total lack of romanticism, its superficiality of feeling, and especially the fact that up in the top left corner it had an image of a loathsome-looking plumber who began laughing every time one of the pipes burst. These two, however, seemed to be seriously involved.

"They won't deliver under the old contracts," complained the first set of overalls, "they want hard currency."

"Try going back to the beginning of the stage," answered the other set, "or simply reload."

"I've tried that. Yegor even took a trip to the plant, three times he tried to get to see the director before he went down."

"If he goes down, you have to press <Control-Break> or <Reset>. You know what Yevgraf Emelianovich says, 'Fix your woes with <Reset>.'"

The two sets of overalls looked up simultaneously at Sasha, glanced at each other, tossed their cigarette butts into the bucket, and disappeared off down the corridor.

"I wonder," thought Sasha, "whether they're just pretending to each other or they really find it interesting playing with those pipes?" He set off down the staircase. "My God, just what is it I'm hoping for?" he thought. "What will I be doing here a year from now? They may be very stupid, but they see everything— and they understand everything. And they never forgive anything. What a chameleon you have to be to work here."

Suddenly the staircase under his feet shuddered, a heavy concrete block with four steps on it fell away from under his feet, and a second later smashed into the flight of steps a floor below, without causing the slightest harm to the two girls from the administration office who were standing at the precise point of its impact. The girls raised their pretty birdlike heads and looked at Sasha, who had just managed to save himself by grabbing the edge of the step that was still in place.

"Your shoes need cleaning," said the younger one, moving away to avoid Sasha's swaying legs, and the girls giggled. Sasha squinted down at them and saw they were standing on the lower edge of a pyramid of small multicolored cubes. That must be *Crazy Bird*, a pleasant enough game with amusing music, but with an unexpectedly stupid and cruel ending. He could hang there like this for as long as he wanted, there was even something pleasant about the monotonous swaying to and fro, but Sasha thought it must look stupid. He pulled up his legs and clambered onto an unfamiliar stone landing that broke off abruptly above an abyss, while its opposite edge was concealed behind the left edge of the screen—he could just make out a buzzing sound from that direction. The other edge of the landing was flanked by a high wall built of coarse blocks of stone. Sasha sat down on the cold, rough surface of the floor, leaned back against the wall, and closed his eyes. Somewhere in the distance he could hear a flute playing quietly. Sasha didn't know who was playing it, or where they were, but he heard that music almost every day. At the beginning, when he was still finding his bearings on the first level, he had been irritated by the monotony of the distant quavering sound, its seeming pointlessness, but in time he had gotten used to it and even began to discover a certain beauty in it—it was as though the single long, drawn out note contained an entire complex melody, and he could listen to the melody for hours at a time. Just recently he had even begun stopping in order to listen to the flute and would go on standing motionless for some time—just as he was now—after its sound had faded away.

He looked around. There was only one way out—a leap into the unknown beyond the left edge of the screen. He could take a run and jump, or just push off as hard as possible from the edge of the platform with both legs. All of the abysses in the labyrinth were the right width for either a running jump or a standing jump, and naturally the first seemed the most reliable, but for some reason intuition prompted him to try the second. Sasha walked over to the abyss and stood on its very edge, then launched himself as hard as he could into buzzing obscurity. After landing on his haunches he straightened up, and beads of cold sweat sprang out on his forehead at the thought that he had almost taken a running jump. Right there in front of him a dead body hung, twisted in torment on a sharp steel spike. It was already crimson and swollen, covered with hordes of fat, slow moving flies. When some of them flew up into the air to take a break they made the buzzing sound that was audible in the picture to the right. In life the corpse had been a middle-aged man; he was wearing a respectable suit and still clutching a briefcase in his hand. He must have been a novice in this game who decided it would be safer to take a running jump. But then, Sasha could easily have ended up on the bottom of a deep stone shaft, while the man in the suit might have continued on his journey toward the princess. There was no way of guessing for sure—at least Sasha didn't know of any.

Carefully stepping around the corpse, he ran on along the corridor. At one point he reached up, clambered onto a platform supported by two coarse pillars and ran on along another corridor—at three points of which he had to leap across deep stone shafts. What he found surprising was that all of this was happening on the second level, which he thought he knew like the back of his own hand, and it was only when a control slab clicked under his feet and he heard the clanking of a portcullis rising in the corner that he realized what had happened.

Not far from the exit to the third level there was a portcullis which he had never found out how to open, and once he had managed to get onto the next level, he had decided it must be purely decorative. Now it turned out there was an entire section of the labyrinth behind it, only it was a dead end. Sasha ran under the raised portcullis and dashed on—he was in familiar

territory now and the surroundings didn't threaten any more surprises. He stepped on one more control slab, then jumped over
another—otherwise the portcullis ahead, which had begun to
rise, would drop back down—and then set off along the corridor
as fast as he could. He had to hurry because once it was fully
raised, the portcullis immediately began to descend. He just
managed to squeeze through under the spikes when they were
less than a yard from the ground and found himself beside the
staircase on the third floor, very close to the spot where only a few
minutes before a section of the stairs had collapsed underneath
him. The door to the next level was close now. "Damn," thought
Sasha, shaking himself and finally realizing just how fast his heart
was beating, "the staircase here never used to collapse before! It
collapsed on the fourth floor, but not here. It must do that every
now and then."

"Sasha!"

He turned around. Emma Nikolaievna was peeping out of
the door of the second section of the timber department. Her
face was thickly coated with powder, reminding Sasha of a large
pink patch of ringworm sprinkled with streptocide.

"Sasha, give me a light, will you?"

"What's the matter, can't you manage it yourself?" Sasha
asked rather coldly.

"I'm not in *The Prince*, am I?" answered Emma Nikolaievna.
"I haven't got any flaming torches on the walls."

"What, did you play it before then?" Sasha asked a little
more kindly.

"There was a time, but those guardians, you know. They
could do anything they liked with me. Anyway, I never got further than the second stage."

"You have to use the <Shift> key for that," said Sasha, taking the cigarette from her and striding toward the flickering
image of a torch blazing on the wall. "And the cursor keys."

"It's too late for me now," sighed Emma Nikolaievna, taking
the lighted cigarette and gazing at Sasha with moist eyes. He was

on the point of opening his mouth to express polite protest when he spotted a seminaked monster, complete with a chest covered in red hair and a thoughtful expression on its large snout of a face, peeping out from behind her shoulder—monsters like that are only encountered in small foreign trade organizations or on the bottom of the well of death in the game *Targkhan*. He blenched, nodded awkwardly, and went back to his own section.

"The dame's done for," he thought, "she'll end up in DOS soon. Or maybe she'll pull through somehow, who can tell?"

In his section the phone was ringing loudly and Sasha jumped impatiently onto the slab that opened the entrance, in order to make the door to the next level rise as quickly as possible.

Level 3

"Lapin! You're wanted on the phone!"

Sasha hopped across to the desk and picked up the receiver.

"Sasha? Hi!"

It was Petya Itakin from Gosplan.

"Are you coming over today?"

"I wasn't really planning to."

"The boss said that someone from state supplies was coming by with some new programs, so I just thought it must be you."

"I don't know," said Sasha, "nobody's said anything to me about it yet."

"But you're the one who's got the three extra files for *Abrams*, aren't you?"

"Yes."

"That means they're bound to send you. Be sure to wait for me if I'm out, okay?"

"Okay."

Sasha hung up and went to his desk. Beside him at the reserve computer a temporary consultant from Penza was absorbed in firing his laser gun at an Ergon rocket ship that had almost turned into position to fire back; on every side the joyless sands of *Starglider* extended as far as the eye could see.

"How're you getting on there?" Sasha inquired politely.

"Not good," answered the visitor, frowning as he hammered at the keyboard. "Not good at all. If that thing just . . ."

Suddenly a blinding whirlwind of fire hid everything from sight. Sasha pulled back and covered his face with his hands, quite instinctively; when he realized that nothing could happen to him and opened his eyes, the visitor was no longer there beside him—nothing was left but the flaps of his jacket, which were smoldering on the floor.

Boris Grigorievich bounded out from behind the cupboard and flung his sword on the floor, then held up the sides of the long padded cloak he had draped over his body armor before combat and began stamping on the lump of cloth that was giving off vile-smelling smoke. His horned helmet represented a sullen Japanese deity and in combination with the fussy, rather woman-ish movements of his large, flabby body, the scowl stamped into the metal was actually rather frightening. When he had liqui-dated the remains of the fire, Boris Grigorievich removed his helmet, wiped his wet bald patch and glanced inquiringly at Sasha.

"Done for," said Sasha, and he nodded at the DOS prompt blinking in isolation on the screen.

"I can see that. Just load him up again, we've got a document here that still needs to be signed."

Boris Grigorievich's telephone began ringing, and he dashed back behind the cupboard without finishing what he was saying. Sasha moved over to the next computer, went into drive A, where the visitor's rotten Bulgarian diskette was sitting, and called up the game. The disk drive buzzed quietly and a few seconds later the man from Penza reappeared in his chair.

"When you're targeted by rocket fire, you should gain as much height as you can," said Sasha. "You can't get more than one of them with the laser, and that thing fires in salvoes."

"Don't try to teach me," growled his neighbor, attacking the keyboard. "It's not my first year out in deep space."

"Then at least you should set up auto-exec for yourself," said Sasha, "nobody's got the time to keep on reloading you."

The visitor didn't answer—he was under attack simultaneously from two walking tanks, and had no time for idle chatter. Suddenly there was a loud rumble followed by shouting in the boss' office.

"Lapin!" Boris Grigorievich roared from his cupboard. "Come here immediately!"

When Sasha came running in Boris Grigorievich was standing on the desk and using his sword to keep at bay a tiny Chinaman with a childish face who kept thrusting a pike at him with the speed of a sewing machine. Realizing at once what had happened, Sasha dashed over to the keyboard and jabbed his finger at the <Escape> key. The Chinaman froze in his stride.

"Phew!" said Boris Grigorievich, "that was a close one. Loaded the fifth dan by mistake—just pressed the key without thinking about it, thought it was asking me for the type of monitor. Never mind, we can sort him out now. But then, we'd better deal with him later. You've got a job to do. Go save that extension to *Abrams* onto a diskette and get over to Gosplan. You know Boris Emelianovich?"

"I installed *Abrams* for him," Sasha answered, "deputy manager on the sixth floor."

"Good. You can get a contract signed at the same time—take it over with the file. And he'll give you a diskette . . ."

From the other side of the cupboards there came a blinding flash of flame, a series of bumps and a sudden smell of scorched flesh.

"What's that?"

"The guy from Penza again. Looks like he hit a pyramid mine."

"Okay, we'll reload him tomorrow morning. We've suffered his noise and stench for more than an hour already. On your way.

He'll give you a diskette with *Arkanoid.* Take a look around to see what they have that's new, okay?"

Sasha was about to turn toward the door, but Boris Grigorievich pulled him back by the sleeve.

"Wait," he said, putting on his helmet. "I need you for a moment. When I shout 'kiyai,' press a key."

"Which one?"

"It doesn't matter."

He went around behind the Chinaman, who was still frozen in his furious attack, assumed a low stance and measured his sword against the Chinaman's neck.

"Ready?"

"Ready," said Sasha, turning away.

"Kiyai!"

Sasha poked at the keyboard; there was a sharp whistle and a crunching sound and something struck the floor.

"Now you can go," said Boris Grigorievich in a hoarse voice. "And be quick about it, there's a lot of work to do."

"I wanted to go to the cafeteria," said Sasha, trying to look away.

"Better get across to Gosplan right away. You can get lunch there."

Sasha emerged from behind the cupboards, went over to his seat, shoved the visitor's fused spectacle frames under the radiator with his foot, then sat at his computer and dumped everything he needed onto a diskette. He put the diskette in his bag, stood up, and slowly made his way across the debris-scattered stone slabs of the corridor, jumping in his usual fashion over the trap, swung on his hands, jumped down to the lower stage, raised a slim, decorated jar from the floor and pressed it to his lips, thinking that he still didn't know who set out these jars in the quiet corners of the underground terrain—or where each jar disappeared to after he had drunk its contents. Sasha knew every detail of the path to the fourth level and he walked, leapt, clambered, and stretched quite mechanically, thinking about all kinds of nonsense.

First he recalled Kudasov, deputy manager of the second section, who had reached the eighth level in the game *Throatcutter* ages ago, but still hadn't managed to jump over some kind of green locker—he always said that was why he was the permanent deputy manager for several high-flying bosses who shot past him to promotion like rockets, all of them managing the locker, if not immediately, then at least without any great struggle.

Then Sasha began thinking about the strange things Itakin had said one evening recently—that some young guys had cracked his game a long time ago; it wasn't quite clear just what Itakin had been thinking of, since the game had already been cracked when Sasha installed it on his hard drive. Then the door to the fourth level slowly rose and Sasha stepped into the subway car that happened to be behind it.

Level 4

"Just where is it I'm trying to get to?" he thought, staring into the black mirror of the subway door and adjusting the turban on his head. "I've already reached the seventh level—well, maybe not quite reached it, but I've seen what's in there. It's all the same stuff, only the guards are fatter. So I'll reach the eighth level— but it's going to take so long—and what comes after that? Of course, there's the princess . . ." Sasha had last seen the princess two days before, somewhere between the third and fourth levels. The corridor on the screen had disappeared and been replaced by a room with a high vaulted ceiling, its floor spread with carpets. Immediately the music started playing, plaintive and wailing, but only at the beginning, and then only so that one note at the very end would sound particularly beautiful.

On the carpet stood an immense hourglass. From the stone floor a spoiled palace cat gazed at Sasha as though through the lens of a monocle, and on the scattered cushions in the very center of the carpet sat the princess. From that distance he could not make out her face—she seemed to have long hair, unless it was a dark scarf falling across her shoulders. She could hardly be aware that he was watching her, or even that Sasha existed as such, but he knew that if he could just reach that room, the princess would run to throw her arms around his neck. The princess stood up, crossed her arms on her chest, took a few steps across the carpet, and went back to sit down on the scattered cushions. Instantly it all disappeared, a heavy door clanged shut behind him and Sasha found himself beside the tall rocky projection with which the fourth level began.

"I wonder what she's thinking about now? Maybe she's thinking about the one who's making his way to her through the labyrinth? That is, about me—without even knowing that she's thinking about me?"

The columns of a station flickered past beyond the glass of the door. The train stopped. Sasha allowed himself to be caught up in the crowd and drifted slowly toward the escalators. Two of them were working. Sasha branched into the section of the crowd that was making for the one on the left. His head gradually filled with the slow, gloomy thoughts about life that usually came in the afternoon. "It's strange," he thought, "how I've changed over the last three levels. It used to seem as though I just had to leap over the next gap and that was all. My God, how little I needed in order to be happy! And now I do it every morning almost without looking, so what? What have I got to hope for now? That at the next level everything will change and I'll start wanting something the way I knew how to want before? Well, just suppose I do get there. I almost know how to do it already: after the fifth portcullis I have to jump—there must be a way through in the ceiling, the stone slabs there are odd. But when I do get through, where shall I find the me who wanted to get through?"

Hearing a familiar clanking sound, Sasha suddenly turned cold. He looked up and saw that a body-scissors had been switched on ahead of him on the escalator—two sheets of steel with sharp-toothed edges that clashed together every few seconds with such force that the sound was like a blow on a small church bell. The other passengers passed straight through it quite calmly—it existed only for Sasha, but for him it was absolutely real: he had a long ugly scar running the full length of his back, and on that occasion the body-scissors had barely touched him, ripping a patch of cloth out of his expensive denim jacket. It wasn't very difficult to get through a body-scissors—you just had to stand close and then step through the moment it opened. But this time Sasha was riding on an escalator and there was no way he could guess at just which moment he would reach the scissors.

Without pausing to think, he turned and dashed back downward. It was hard to run—the escalator was packed with drunkards who only let Sasha past with great reluctance. A woman in a red shawl clutching two big bundles in her arms held Sasha up for so long that he found himself closer to the scissors than when he started, but eventually he managed to get through the crowd. Then a portcullis dropped down in front of him and Sasha realized that he was lost. He turned limp and screwed up his face, but instead of seeing his entire life flash before his eyes in a single second, for some reason he recalled in great detail a singing lesson in the fourth grade when he had pushed the young music master so far that he had stopped playing Kabalevsky on the piano, got up, walked over to Sasha, and smacked him on the face. The clanking of the body-scissors was very close now, and Sasha instinctively stepped backwards, thinking that perhaps he might just. . . .

Autoexec.bat—level 4

"Just where is it that I'm going?" Sasha thought, staring into the black mirror of the carriage door and adjusting the turban on his head. "I've already reached the seventh level—well, maybe not quite reached it, but I've seen what's there. It's the same old stuff, only the guards are fatter. So I'll reach the eighth level—but it's going to take so long. And what comes after that? Of course, there's the princess."

Sasha had last seen the princess two days before, between the third and fourth levels. The corridor on the screen had disappeared and been replaced by a room with a high vaulted ceiling, its floor spread with carpets. Immediately the music started playing, plaintive and wailing, but only at the beginning, and then only so that one note at the very end would sound particularly beautiful. He stopped thinking about the princess and began looking around at the people. Most of them were the filthy types that usually hung around railway stations. There were lots of drunks and identical-looking women carrying big bags. There was one Sasha particularly didn't like the look of—wearing a red shawl and clutching two big bundles. "I've seen her before somewhere, for sure," thought Sasha. He'd often had that feeling recently, the feeling that he'd already seen what was happening, only just where and in what circumstances he couldn't recall. But he'd read in some journal that the feeling was called déjà vu, from which he had drawn the conclusion that the same thing happened to people in France. The columns of a station flickered past beyond the glass of the door. The train stopped. Sasha allowed himself to be caught up in the crowd and drifted slowly toward the escalators. Two of them were working. Sasha branched into the section of the crowd that was making for the one on the right. His head gradually filled with the slow, gloomy thoughts about life that usually came in the afternoon.

"It seems to me now," he thought, "that nothing could be worse than what's happening to me. But after another couple of levels I'll start feeling nostalgic even about today. And it will seem to me that I had something in my grasp, without even knowing what it was, but I had it in my grasp and I threw it away. My God, how awful things must become afterwards, to make you start regretting what's happening now. And the strangest thing of all is that life keeps on getting worse, more and more meaningless—but on the other hand, absolutely nothing in life changes. What have I got to hope for? And why do I get up every morning and go somewhere? I'm a bad engineer, a very bad one. I'm simply not interested in any of that. And I'm a poor chameleon as well, soon they'll take me and throw me out, and they'll be quite right too . . ."

A familiar clanking sound made Sasha turn cold. Looking up he saw that a body-scissors had been switched on on the next escalator. For the first moment the sense of fright was so strong that Sasha didn't grasp that it was no threat to him. When he realized the situation he sighed so loudly that the woman with the bundles, the one who had attracted his attention in the train, looked over at him from the next escalator. She passed through the scissors without any idea of what would have happened if he had been in her place. Sasha found her gaze unpleasant and he turned away.

The next body-scissors stood at the exit from the subway and Sasha got through it without the slightest difficulty, but he didn't drink from the small jar standing beyond it—it looked suspicious somehow, decorated with a strange triangle design. He had drunk from a jar like that once and then had had to take two weeks off work to get over it. Intuition told him that somewhere in the vicinity there must be another jar, and Sasha decided to look for it. His attention was caught by a hairdresser's on the other side of the street: the first two letters in the shop sign were not lit and Sasha felt sure that must mean something.

Inside was a small room where clients waited their turn. It was quite empty now, which was the second strange thing. Sasha walked around the room, moved the armchairs about—late last year he had sat on a chair in the corridor at the army office, which he'd tumbled into from the third level, when suddenly a rope ladder had fallen down from above him and he'd made good his escape to a two month business trip. Then he jumped up and down a bit on the coffee table with the magazines (they sometimes controlled sections of the walls that swung open) and even tugged on the coat hooks. But it was all in vain. Then he decided to try the ceiling, climbed back up onto the coffee table and leapt upward, raising his hands above his head.

The ceiling proved to be solid and the table somewhat less so: two of its legs gave way at the same time and Sasha's outstretched hands were thrust against a color photo of a smiling half-wit with red hair hanging on the wall. Suddenly a trap door creaked open in the floor, revealing the brass neck of a jar standing on the stone surface about two yards below.

Sasha leapt down onto the stone platform and the trap door slammed shut over his head. Looking around he saw at the other side of the corridor a pale warrior with a mustache wearing a plumed red turban. The warrior cast two diverging trembling shadows, because behind his back two smoky torches framed a tall carved door complete with a black sign which read "USSR GOSPLAN."

"Well, well," thought Sasha, snatching out his sword and dashing forward to meet the warrior, who had drawn a crooked yataghan, "and like a fool I always took the trolley."

Level 5

"Itakin?" a female voice asked on the telephone. "He's at lunch. But you can come up and wait. Is it you who was supposed to bring the new programs from State Supply?"

"Yes," replied Sasha, "but I want to go to the cafeteria as well."

"Do you remember the way up? Room 622, turn left along the corridor from the elevator."

"I'll find it," said Sasha.

The cafeteria was noisy and crowded. Sasha walked between the tables, looking for his friend, but he couldn't see him. Then he joined the line. In front of him there were two Darth Vaders from the first section: they breathed with a noisy whistling sound as they discussed some magazine article in their mechanical voices. It was very hard to understand anything at all from their unnatural speech. The first Darth Vader put two plates of sauerkraut on his tray, and the second took borscht and tea. Of course, the food in Gosplan wasn't what it had been before the troubles began: all that remained of its former magnificence were the lovely five-pointed stars of carrot—cut with a special Japanese apparatus—which occasionally found their way into the cabbage.

Sasha was very curious about how the first Darth Vader would manage to eat his cabbage—he would definitely have to remove his hermetic black helmet for that. But the black-clad pair sat at a small table over in the corner and closed themselves off with a black curtain bearing the image of a sword and shield: all that could be seen beneath it were their gleaming calfskin boots, the pair on the left thrust motionless and firm against the floor, while the pair on the right were constantly swirling about, one boot rubbing against the other and wrapping its sock around the other's calf. Sasha thought that if he happened to be playing *Spy* he would have recruited the Darth Vader on the right.

He looked around and carried his tray over to the farthest corner, where a dozen or so elderly men in flying uniforms were sitting at a table by the window. He sat politely at the edge of the group. They glanced at him, but didn't say anything. One of the pilots, a stocky white-haired man with two unfamiliar medals on his light-blue flying suit, was standing holding a glass in his hand. He had just begun pronouncing a toast.

"Friends! We have the pleasure of marking a double celebration today. Today Kuzma Ulyanovich Staropopikov marks twenty years of service in Gosplan. And this very morning over Libya Kuzma Ulyanovich shot down his one-thousandth Mig."

The pilots applauded and turned toward the hero of the hour, who was sitting at the center of the table. He was short, stout and bald, wearing thick glasses with frames held together with black tape. There was absolutely nothing distinctive about him—quite the contrary, he was the least remarkable of all the people gathered around the table, and Sasha had to look closely before he saw the rows of medals and ribbons—equally unfamiliar—on his chest.

"I make so bold as to assert that Kuzma Ulyanovich is the finest pilot in Gosplan! And the 'Purple Heart' which he was recently awarded by Congress will be the fifth that he bears on his chest."

People began applauding again, and Kuzma Ulyanovich was slapped on the shoulder several times. He turned a deep shade of red, waved his hand in the air, removed his glasses, and wiped them thoroughly with his handkerchief.

"And that's not all," continued the white haired man, "in addition to the F-15 and F-16, Kuzma Ulyanovich recently mastered a new fighter plane, the B-2 'Stealth' fighter. His record also contains numerous technical improvements—after pondering the lessons of the conflict in Vietnam, he asked his mechanic to create two files in Assembler so that the cannon and the machine gun could be operated by a single key, and now we all use this method. . . ."

"That's enough now, surely," the hero of the hour mumbled shyly.

Another pilot got to his feet—he also had a lot of medals on his chest, but not as many as Kuzma Ulyanovich. "Our Party organizer has just informed us that today Kuzma Ulyanovich shot down his thousandth Mig. In addition to that he has, for instance, destroyed the radar installation outside Tripoli 4,500 times and if we were to add in all the rocket ships and airports, his hit total would be quite staggering. But a man can't be measured by numbers alone. I know Kuzma Ulyanovich well, perhaps better than the others here—I've been his flying partner for six months now—and I want to tell you about one of our raids. It was my first time on an F-15, and as you all know, it's not an easy machine to handle: you only have to hurry a little bit too much, try turning just a little bit too fast, and it goes down. Before takeoff

Kuzma Ulyanovich said to me: 'Vasya, remember, don't get nervous, fly behind and below and I'll cover you.' Well, I was inexperienced then, and full of pride—why should he be covering me, I thought, when I've been all around the Persian Gulf on an F-16? Yes, indeed. . . . Well, we got into our cockpits, and we were given the command to take off. We were flying from the aircraft carrier *America* and our mission was first to sink some ship in the port at Beirut, and then wipe out a terrorist camp near Al-Benghazi. So we took off, and we're flying low, on autopilot. Down there near Beirut there are maybe eight radar units—well, you know, you've all been there . . ."

"Eleven," said someone at the table, "and there are always Mig-25s on patrol."

"Right. Anyway, we got there flying low with our sighting devices switched off, and then with about ten miles left we went into manual, climbed a thousand feet and switched on the radar. They spotted us right away, naturally, but we'd already locked on, let go one Amraam each, taken evasive action against rockets, and set off westwards, losing altitude. The ship had been blasted to smithereens, they told us over the radio. So there we are again flying low and blind, and we seem to have made it without any problems, but then I spotted a Mig-23 and like an idiot I went after it—let me just stick a Sidewinder up his nozzle, I thought. Kuzma Ulyanovich could see on the radar that I'd moved to the right and he yelled at me over the radio: 'Vasya, get back in line, fuck you!' But I'd already switched on my sights, locked onto the bastard, and fired my rocket. What I should have done then was to fly back down toward the ground, but no way—I started watching the Mig falling. Then I looked at the radar and I saw an SA-2 coming straight for me, I'd no idea who launched it."

"That's the radar site near Al-Baidoi. When you're flying west from Beirut you should never move to the right," said the Party organizer.

"Sure, but I didn't know that then. Kuzma Ulyanovich yelled over the radio: 'Cut in the baffle!' But instead of the thermal baffle—you have to press <F> to do that—I go and press <C>. So I caught it right under the tail. I pressed <F7> and ejected. As I'm falling I look down and see a desert and a highway, and some kind of vehicles on the highway, and I'm being carried toward them. Then before I'd even landed, what do I see, damn it, but Kuzma Petrovich coming in for a landing on the highway? So I'm wondering who's going to get there first . . ."

Sasha drank his last mouthful of tea, got up, and went to the door. The flagstone just outside the door of the cafeteria looked a little strange—it was a different color and jutted up about half an inch above the others. Sasha stopped one step short of it, stuck his head out into the corridor and looked upwards. He was right: a yard above his head hung the gleaming steel spikes of a portcullis.

"Oh, no," Sasha muttered.

He took a careful look around the cafeteria. At first glance the other exit was nowhere to be seen, but Sasha knew that it was never obvious. The way might lie, for instance, behind the huge picture on the wall, but he would have to swing from the chandelier in order to be able to jump into it, and that would require piling several tables on top of each other. There were also several projections on the wall which he might use to climb upwards, and Sasha had already made up his mind to try that when a woman in a white overall coat called out to him.

"You're supposed to take your tray over to the washer, young man," she said, "that's no way to behave." Sasha went back for his tray.

". . . The entire section started searching for mistakes," Kuzma Ulyanovich's junior flying partner was saying. "Remember that? Then the late Eshagubin comes over and asks a question: 'How,' he says, 'can an F-15 fly on a single motor?' And you know what Kuzma Ulyanovich answered him?"

"That's enough, now, really," said Kuzma Ulyanovich, embarrassed.

"No, no, let me tell them . . ."

Sasha didn't hear any more. His attention switched entirel
to the moving conveyor belt that was carrying the plates and tray
to the washer. It ended at a small opening, which he could easil
climb through, and he decided to try it. Putting his tray on th
conveyor, he looked around and then quickly clambered up him
self. Two tank crew members standing by the belt glanced at hir
in amazement, but before they could say anything Sasha ha
squeezed through the opening, leapt over a gap in the floor, an
set off as fast as his legs would carry him toward a slowly risin
section of the wall with a large plaster shell covered in peelin
paint. Beyond it, by the light of blazing torches, he could see
narrow staircase leading upward.

Level 6

Itakin's boss, Boris Emelianovich, turned out to be one of th
tank crew who had stared at Sasha with such astonishment in th
cafeteria. Sasha ran into him right in the doorway of room 622
and since Sasha had just clambered up maybe a dozen cornice
that you had to climb by jumping and then pulling yourself up
he was tired and panting, while Boris Emelianovich had come u
in the elevator, so he was fresh and smelled of eau de cologne.

"Are you from Boris Grigorievich?" Boris Emelianovicl
asked, not showing the slightest sign that he recognized Sasha a
the young hooligan from the cafeteria. "Let's move, I have t
leave in five minutes."

Boris Emelianovich's office was part of an immense hall sec-
tioned off with cupboards like Boris Grigorievich's office, but inside, occupying almost all of the space, stood a huge tank, an
Abrams M-1, gleaming with lubricant. By the wall stood two bar-
rels of fuel with a telephone and a four-megabyte Super AT with
a VGA color monitor that made Sasha's mouth water when he
looked at it.

"A 386 processor?" he asked respectfully. "And that must be a 1.2 megabyte hard drive?"

"I don't know all that," Boris Emelianovich replied dryly, "ask Itakin, he's my mechanic. What do you need me to sign?" Sasha stuck his hand into his bag and pulled out the papers, which had gotten slightly crumpled on the journey. Boris Emelianovich signed the first two right there on the armor plating with a flourish of his gleaming Mont Blanc pen shaped like a machine gun shell with a golden bullet tip, but he paused at the third and started to think.

"I can't do this one," he said at last, "I have to call the directorate. I shouldn't sign this, Pavel Semyonovich Prokurin should."

He glanced at his watch and dialed a number.

"Get me Pavel Semyonovich. When will he be there? No, I'll call back." He turned to Sasha and looked at him significantly.

"You've come at rather a bad time," he said. "We're advancing in five minutes. And if you want your paper signed, you'll have to go to the directorate. Hang on though. It might be quicker. You can ride a bit of the way with me." Boris Emelianovich leaned over the computer.

"Damn," he said, "where's Itakin gone? I can't start the engine."

"Try changing directory," said Sasha, "you're in the root directory. Or go into *Norton* first."

"You try it," answered Boris Emelianovich, moving aside.

Sasha jabbed at the keys in his accustomed manner: the hard drive whirred into action and almost immediately the tank's electric transmission began humming powerfully and the air was filled with the bitter fumes of diesel exhaust. Boris Emelianovich leapt up agilely onto the armor plating; Sasha preferred to drag a chair up to the tank and step from that onto its slightly raised nose.

It was roomy and very comfortable in the turret. Sasha looked into the sight, but it wasn't working yet; then he looked around. Inside, the turret looked liked the cabin of a bus which had been lovingly decorated by the driver—on both sides of the cannon's breech hung key rings, pennants, and little monkeys, and the armor plating had been adorned with several girls in bathing suits cut out of a magazine. Boris Emelianovich threw Sasha a microphone helmet and disappeared into the driver's compartment. The engine roared and the tank rolled out onto an immense plain, complete with a mountain that looked like a volcano far ahead in the distance, its summit cut off by the edge of the screen. Sasha rose waist-high out of the turret and looked around. He could see twenty or so similar tanks, two or three of which had appeared while he had been watching.

"What's that formation called?" he asked into the microphone.

"What formation?" Boris Emelianovich's voice asked, distorted by the earphones.

"When the tanks are all in a single line. If it was soldiers it would just be called a line, but what's it called for tanks?"

"I don't know," said Boris Emelianovich. "It's always like that after lunch—we just all come out together. You'd do better to count how many tanks there are."

"Twenty-six," Sasha counted.

"Fair enough. Babarakin's out sick, Skovorodich is in Austria, and the rest are all here. It's going to be hot today."

"Twenty-one, twenty-one, who's that you're talking to?" said a voice in the helmet phones.

"Twenty-one here, twenty-one calling seventeen, come in."

"Seventeen here."

"Seventeen, I've got a young guy from State Supplies here, he needs to get a piece of paper signed. This way he doesn't have to go all the way across town."

"Understood, twenty-one," replied the voice. "At the farm in ten minutes."

Boris Emelianovich's tank turned sharply to the right and Sasha was jolted in the turret. Taking several ruts at full speed, Boris Emelianovich moved out onto the highway, turned and set off at about eighty miles an hour toward a distant grove of trees where the road forked at some kind of sign hanging on a post.

"Climb up the turret," ordered Boris Emelianovich "and close the door. There's a grenade launcher sitting up on that hill over there."

Sasha followed orders—and just in time: there was a blow against the tank's armor plating and a loud, sharp, whining sound.

"There he is, the bastard," Boris Emelianovich's voice whispered in the earphones, and the turret began slowly turning to the right. On the sighting screen Sasha saw a small square positioned on the top of the hill and the words "gun locked." But Boris Emelianovich was in no hurry to fire.

"Go on!" Sasha said under his breath.

"Wait," whispered Boris Emelianovich, "let me get a shrapnel shell loaded . . . We'll need the armor-piercing shells later."

Once again there was a whining sound and something hit the armor plating. Then the next moment the Abrams cannon barked and a huge black and red tree sprang up on the top of the hill. Soon a farm surrounded by a low fence appeared to the left of the highway and began rushing rapidly toward them—it looked like an abandoned government dacha. Boris Emelianovich braked three hundred yards short, and so sharply that Sasha, who was gazing into the sights, would probably have gotten a black eye if not for the soft rubber surrounding the eyepieces.

"I don't like the look of that window," said Boris Emelianovich, "now just let me . . ."

The turret turned to the left and once again the cannon barked. The farm was shrouded in smoke and flame, and when the air cleared all that was left of the comfortable two-story house was a smoke-blackened foundation and a small piece of wall, in which an open door led into mysterious space. For good measure Boris Emelianovich gave a long burst on the machine gun, shooting through several boards in the fence, and then drove slowly up to the farm.

"You can get out and stretch your legs for a while," he said to Sasha, when the tank stopped at the burnt-out ruin. "It all seems quiet enough."

Sasha climbed out of the turret, jumped down to the ground, and turned his head to and fro. There was a buzzing in his ears, his knees were trembling, and he felt he wanted to grab hold of a handrail like the ones inside the turret.

"Feeling a bit strange?" Boris Emelianovich asked in a friendly voice. "You should try it five days a week, eight hours a day, or all on your own with three T-70s at a time moving against you. That'll make your knees shake. This is a quiet spot, paradise."

It really was a beautiful spot—tall trees stood here and there in the even field, and Sasha could hear the birds chattering in the green grove beyond the highway. The sun came out from behind a cloud and everything assumed the gentle hues that are only to be seen on a well-tuned VGA monitor assembled in Europe or America—but never on a Korean model, let alone a monitor from Singapore. There was a roaring sound from the direction of the highway.

"Pavel Semyonovich is on his way. Get your document ready."

The black dot on the highway was approaching rapidly and soon it had turned into a tank exactly like Boris Emelianovich's, except for the howitzer sticking up above its turret. The tank drove up and stopped, and out of the turret jumped a thin, gloomy-looking soldier wearing gold-framed spectacles and a black pilot's jacket.

"Let's see what you've got there," he said to Sasha. Then he squatted on one knee beside a sheet of roofing metal torn away by the shell blast, placed Sasha's piece of paper on the flat section, and wrote on the top of it "No objection."

"And as for you, Boris," he said to Boris Emelianovich, "no

more of this. You're always got some kind of fucking nonsense to be dealt with just before battle."

"Never mind," said Boris Emelianovich, "we'll catch up. This young guy's as good a mechanic as Itakin, he got my engine going in a second."

The gloomy soldier glanced at Sasha under his eyebrows, but he said nothing. They heard a roaring sound approaching rapidly from the direction of the distant blue hills on the horizon. Sasha looked up and saw a squadron of F-15s hedge-hopping toward them. They flew just above the tanks, and the lead pilot, who had a red eagle's head drawn on his wing, performed a roll only fifty feet above the ground, then shot up almost vertically in a steep climb; the others divided into two groups and, gaining height, set off toward the distant mountain with the truncated summit. For the second time that day Sasha had the feeling that something had happened to him before—perhaps a bit differently, but it had happened, he was sure of it.

"Not a single Mig will stick its nose out today," said Boris Emelianovich. "Kuzma Ulianovich is in the air. That's his plane with the eagle. You can leave your howitzer here."

"I'll hang onto it for while," answered his morose companion. Somewhere in the distance by the mountain there was a flash and they heard a rumble.

"It's begun," said the gloomy soldier. "Time to be going."

"I brought you a howitzer just like that," said Sasha, remembering the diskette he had in his pocket and taking it out.

But Boris Emelianovich was already lowering himself into the tank.

"No time now. Give it to Itakin."

One turret door clanged shut, then the other, and the tanks sprang into motion, throwing up clods of earth with their caterpillar tracks. Sasha watched them move away until they were just two dots and then walked toward the farm, where the two transparent torches he had noticed some time ago were blazing by the door in the only wall which was still standing.

Level 7

When the door closed behind him, Sasha realized that at last he had got out of the underground labyrinth and was now somewhere in the interior palace chambers. The walls around him no longer consisted of crudely hewn stone blocks, but of fine openwork arches, supported on light carved columns. The ceilings receded upward into twilight, the bright southern stars twinkled in the black velvet sky outside the windows, and even the torches on the walls burned in a different way—without any crackling or sooty smoke. There were two identical lowered portcullises, one on each side of Sasha. Patterned Persian carpets were hanging on the wall above his head—yet another thing he had never seen on the lower levels. He moved toward the portcullis on the left, in front of which the slab controlling the lifting mechanism protruded slightly above the floor; but when he stood on it, it was the portcullis behind his back that began to rise.

Sasha spun around and ran back that way. Beyond the portcullis the path divided. He could jump, draw himself up, and run on—there were several body-scissors clanking away and that meant there was a jar hidden somewhere close by, maybe even two—that had happened once on the third level. On the other hand, he could go down the steps, and after hesitating for a second, that was what he decided to do.

At the bottom of the steps was the beginning of a long gallery with a mural running in a narrow strip along the wall. Torches were smoking in the bronze rings screwed into the wall and up ahead, guarding the entrance to a staircase, stood a guard in a scarlet caftan, with a curling mustache, holding a long sword. Down in the bottom right corner of the screen Sasha noticed the six triangles that indicated the life force of his opponent, and he turned cold at the sight; he'd never encountered anything like that before. The most he'd seen so far was four triangles. Sasha took out the sword he had found once beside a heap of human bones, and assumed the position. The warrior began to approach, gazing straight into his eyes, and stamping his green Morocco-leather boot on the stone slabs. Suddenly he lunged with incredible speed and Sasha barely managed to deflect his sword using the <PgUp> key, before immediately pressing <Shift>, but that surefire move didn't work either—the warrior managed to leap back before advancing again.

"Hi there, Sasha!" said a voice behind his back.

Sasha felt a sharp surge of hatred for the unknown idiot who had decided to distract him with conversation at such a moment, feigned a lunge, then aimed his sword directly at his enemy's throat and sprang forward. Once again the warrior in the scarlet caftan had time to leap back.

"Sasha!"

Sasha felt someone's hands turning him around bodily on his revolving chair, and he almost stuck his sword into the person who appeared in front of him. It was Petya Itakin. He was wearing a green sweater and old jeans, which surprised Sasha greatly, given what he knew of the etiquette at Gosplan.

"Let's talk," said Itakin.

Sasha glanced at the little figure frozen motionless on the screen.

"I've been waiting for you for an hour," he said. "I started up your boss' *Abrams* for him."

"I've seen it already," said Itakin. "Five minutes ago a T-70 got him right on the turret. He's come in for repairs."

Sasha stood up and followed his friend out into the corridor. Every now and then Petya jumped over something, and at one point he dropped to the floor and froze. Sasha noticed a huge blue eye that drifted over their heads and guessed it must be the third or fourth stage in the game *Tower*. He'd once gotten halfway up the first tower, but when he heard that after you climbed the first tower you had to start on the second and nobody had any idea what came after that, he gave up and became the Prince instead. Petya had been climbing his tower for well over a year at this stage. They went out onto the staircase, where Petya deftly dodged something like a flying boomerang, and then onto the long, empty balcony, with its heaps of sun-bleached stands bearing colored photographs of pale and flabby faces. Sasha tested the floor with his feet—there didn't seem to be any suspicious slabs. Petya leaned his elbows on the rail of the balcony and gazed at the lights of the city below.

"What is it?" asked Sasha.

"Okay," said Petya, "I'm leaving Gosplan soon."

"Where are you going?"

Petya nodded vaguely to his right. Sasha looked in that direction and saw thousands of glowing points, all different colors, burning all the way off to the horizon. Itakin could also have meant that he was planning to jump from the balcony.

"Like the stars in *The Prince*," Sasha said unexpectedly, gazing at the lights, "only they're all upside down. Or downside up."

"Maybe it's in your *Prince* that they're all upside down," said Petya. "Haven't you ever wondered why the picture there sometimes reverses?"

Sasha shook his head. As always, the view of the city in the evening induced a feeling of sadness in him. Long-forgotten memories would surface before being immediately forgotten again—most of all it seemed like an oath he had sworn to himself a thousand times and already broken 999 times.

"What's the damn point of living anyway?" he asked.

"Well, now," said Petya, "I haven't done any drinking today, but anyway, why don't you ask the guard? He'll explain all about life to you."

Sasha fixed his gaze on the lights again.

"You've been running through that labyrinth for more than a year now," said Petya, "but have you ever wondered whether it's really there or not?"

"What?"

"The labyrinth."

"You mean, whether it really exists or not?"

"Yes."

Sasha thought about it.

"I think it does. Or rather, it would be correct to say that it exists to the same extent that the Prince does. Because the labyrinth only exists for him."

"To put it absolutely correctly," said Petya, "both the labyrinth and the figure only exist for the person watching the screen."

"Well, yes. . . . I mean, why?"

"Because both the labyrinth and the figure can only appear in him. And the screen as well, come to that."

"Well," said Sasha, "we did that in second year."

"But there's one more detail," Petya continued, paying no attention to Sasha's words, "one very important detail. The dopes we did the course with forgot to mention it."

"What detail?"

"You see," said Petya, "if the figure has been working in State Supply for a long time, then for some reason it starts thinking that it is looking at the screen, although it is only running across it. And anyway, if a cartoon character could look at something, the first thing he would notice would be whoever was looking at him."

"And who is looking at him?"

Petya thought for a moment.

"There is only one . . ."

The next instant something struck him hard in the back and he tumbled over the rail and hurtled down toward the ground. Sasha saw the thing like a boomerang that he had seen before on the stairs. It was spinning as it swung away in the direction of the chimneys on the horizon with their crown of motionless smoke. Sasha hadn't even enough time to feel scared, it had all happened so quickly. Leaning over the edge of the balcony he saw Petya clinging tightly to the railings of the balcony one floor below.

"It's all right," shouted Petya, "the spinners never drop you more than one story. I'll just . . ."

At this point Sasha spotted a huge eye like a round aquarium, overflowing with blue liquid, slowly creeping toward Petya along the wall.

"Petya! On your left!" he shouted.

Petya freed one hand and threw two small red spheres the size of a ball of wool at the blue eye—the first made the eye shudder to a halt, and when the second hit it, the eye dissolved into the air with a popping sound.

"Go back to room 620," shouted Petya, clambering over the railings. "I'll be there in a minute, and we'll polish off your game."

Sasha turned toward the balcony's exit and suddenly a steel portcullis came rattling down right in front of him, its sharp spikes splitting several of the tiles on the floor. He stepped back, and a second portcullis clanged down onto the railing of the balcony. Looking up, Sasha saw a small square manhole in the low cement ceiling. He jumped in his accustomed fashion, pulled himself up and climbed into a narrow stone corridor.

Ahead of him a square patch of reddish light fell on the floor. Sasha walked up to it and looked cautiously upwards. There was a narrow four-sided shaft, and high above him he could see a burning torch and a section of smoke-blackened ceiling. It was obviously an ordinary corridor trap, but this time Sasha was at the bottom. There could be guards up above, so he stood on tiptoe, and stepping carefully over the dust that had accumulated over the centuries, he walked on.

Some way ahead he came to a turn and a few yards further on, a dead end. He was about to go back, but he heard a portcullis clank down at the far end of the corridor and he stopped. He'd fallen into a trap. There was only one thing left for him to do—carefully test all the slabs in the floor and the ceiling: any of them might control portcullises or sliding sections of the wall. Holding his hands above his head, he jumped. Then again. And again. The third slab gave slightly. After that it was simple: he jumped again, pushed against the slab with his hands and immediately sprang back. There was a rumbling sound and he squinted in the usual fashion to prevent the dust stirred up from the floor obstructing his vision.

After a little while he stepped forward. There was now a gaping rectangular hole in the ceiling, through which he could climb, and towering up above him was a wall with wooden cornices every two and a half yards—the distance was the same on all of the levels. Standing on one of those cornices he could jump up and catch hold of the next one, stand on it, and repeat the process, and so on all the way to the top. This wall had six cornices, so the entire process took a little over a minute, and he wasn't even slightly tired. Now he was standing in a corridor between walls of crudely dressed stone blocks. Ahead of him there was a well shaft, with the bitter smell of torch smoke rising out of it.

Sasha looked down—about five yards below he could see a brightly lit floor. He sighed, lowered one leg over the edge of the hole, hung there on his hands, and then with a certain effort forced himself to open his fingers. The height was not very great, but the slab he landed on fell away under his feet and went tumbling downward. He didn't have time to grab the edge of the hole and after an agonizingly long fall he crashed into the floor on top of the broken pieces of the shattered slab. He didn't break anything, but he was stunned at the shock of the blow. For several seconds he squatted there on his haunches, remembering how long ago, one terrible dark winter in his childhood, he had bruised his coccyx badly jumping down from the dormer window of a gas substation onto a frozen mattress.

When he shook his head and opened his eyes, Sasha found himself in the same gallery with the strip of decoration on the walls that Itakin had dragged him out of, and standing there staring at him with his arms crossed on his chest was the same guard in the red caftan—Sasha made sure it was him by glancing at the lower corner of the screen, where he spotted the six triangles indicating the warrior's vital energy.

Sasha leapt to his feet, assumed combat position, and pulled out his sword. The warrior pulled out his own and came toward him; his gaze was so menacing that Itakin's advice to have a talk about the meaning of life seemed like a malicious joke. Sasha swung the end of his blade through the air, preparing to strike, but the warrior suddenly struck the sword from Sasha's hand with a swift, unexpected blow, and hit Sasha across the head with the flat of his heavy blade.

Level 8

Lying on the floor, Sasha opened his eyes and gazed uncomprehendingly around the twilit room. He could feel a soft carpet underneath him. An oil lamp was burning on the wall, and beneath it was an incredibly beautiful chest bound with repoussé sheets of copper. Clouds of smoke hung under the ceiling and Sasha was aware of a strange smell, like scorched feathers or burnt rubber, but rather pleasant all the same. Sasha tried to sit up, but realized that he couldn't move—he was stitched up to the neck in a sack made of something like mattress ticking, and bound with thick rope.

"Are you awake now, shuravi?"

Looping himself up like a worm, Sasha turned over onto his other side. He saw the warrior in the red caftan sitting on a pile of cushions. Beside him smoke was rising from a large hookah, whose long pipe and copper mouthpiece were lying on the carpet. On the other side of the warrior lay Sasha's bag. The warrior drew a crooked knife out of the folds of his caftan and held it up, laughing, for Sasha to inspect.

"Don't be afraid, shuravi," he said, bending over Sasha. "If I didn't kill you right away, I won't touch you now." The loops of rope around the sack relaxed. The warrior sat back down on his cushions and puffed thoughtfully on the hookah as he watched Sasha disentangle himself from the sack. When he had finally freed himself from it and was sitting on the carpet rubbing his swollen legs, the warrior held out the smoking hose of the hookah toward him. Sasha took it meekly and inhaled deeply. The room instantly narrowed and twisted out of shape, and suddenly he could hear the crackling of the oil in the lamp—an encyclopedic collection of different sounds.

"I am called Zainaddin Abu Bakr Abbas al Huvafi," said the warrior, pulling Sasha's open bag toward himself and thrusting his hand into it. "You may call me by any of these names."

"My name is Alexei," Sasha lied, without knowing why. Of all of those incomprehensible words the only one he had been able to make out was "Abbas."

"Are you a spiritual man, then?"

"Me?" said Sasha, following the room's transformations with fascination. "Yes, I suppose I am spiritual."

For some reason he felt quite safe.

"I was looking here at the books you read."

Abbas held up John Spencer Trimmingham's *Sufic Orders in Islam,* which Sasha had bought recently at the Academy book shop and had already read more than halfway through. The cover of the book bore a mystic symbol: a green tree made of interwoven Arabic letters.

"I wanted very much to kill you," Abbas confessed, weighing the book in his hand and gazing tenderly at the cover, "but I cannot kill a spiritual man."

"But why would you want to kill me?"

"Why did you kill Maruf today?"

"Who is Maruf?"

"So you have forgotten already?"

"Ah, you mean the one with the yataghan, and that feather in his turban?"

"That one."

"I didn't want to kill him," Sasha answered. "He came straight at me, or did he? Anyway, he was already standing there at the door with his yataghan. It just all happened automatically."

Abbas shook his head in disbelief.

"What do you take me for, some kind of monster?" Sasha asked, feeling quite disconcerted by this time.

"And why not? In our villages, shuravi, they frighten the children with your name. And this very Maruf, whose throat you cut, came to me this morning and said: 'Farewell, Zainaddin Abu Bakr. I feel in my heart that today the shuravi will come. . . .' I thought he had taken too much hashish, but this afternoon they brought him to the guardroom with his throat cut."

"Honestly, I didn't really want to . . ."

"Perhaps you wanted and perhaps you didn't want. Every man has his fate, and Allah holds all the threads in his hand. Is this not so?"

"Indeed it is," said Sasha, "precisely so."

"I once spent five days here drinking with a Sufi from Khorasan," said Abbas, "and he told me a little story—I don't remember now exactly how it all happened, but someone had his throat cut by mistake, and afterwards it turned out he was a murderer and a thief, and at that very moment he was preparing to commit the most horrible atrocities. I enjoy drinking with spiritual men; and so I remembered this story and thought perhaps you might know some stories as well."

Abbas went over to the trunk and took out a bottle of White Horse whisky, two plastic cups, and a handful of crumpled cigarettes.

"Where did you get those from?" Sasha asked in amazement.

"The Americans," Abbas replied. "Humanitarian aid. When they started putting computers into your ministries, they started helping us as well. And they also trade for hashish."

"And you mean to say the Americans aren't monsters too?"

"They are all different," Abbas replied, filling the two plastic cups. "But at least it is possible to come to an understanding with them."

"Come to an understanding? How?"

"It is very simple. Whenever you see one of the guards, you

just press the <K> key, then he'll pretend to be dead and you can carry on your way."

"I didn't know that," said Sasha, taking a plastic cup.

"How should you know," asked Abbas, raising his own cup in salute to Sasha, "when all of your games have been broken open and you have no instructions? But you could have asked, couldn't you? I even came to believe the shuravi didn't know how to talk."

Abbas drank and sighed loudly, then suddenly began to speak in quite a different tone of voice.

"You know, you have something called the Moscow Housing Construction Office," he said, "and in that place there is a certain Semyon Prokofievich Chukanov—a short, fat little swine, a nasty piece of work. He comes into the first level, but he's too afraid to go any further because of the traps. He just stops and waits for our men. You know how things are on our side—no matter what you might think about it, it's your duty and you just go in and do it—and what experience have the boys got down there, they're still nothing but kids? So he kills five men a day. He has his norm—he goes in, kills a few, and then withdraws. Then he does the same thing all over again. But you know, if he should ever get to the seventh level!"

Abbas set his hand on the handle of his sword.

"Do the Americans supply you with weapons?" Sasha asked in order to change the subject.

"They do."

"Can I have a look?"

Abbas went over to his chest, took out a small scroll of parchment, and tossed it over to Sasha. When Sasha unrolled it he saw a short column of microassembler commands written in an ornate, curly hand in black ink.

"What's this?" he asked.

"A virus," answered Abbas, pouring them another drink.

"Well, well . . . and I was wondering what it was that keeps wiping out our system. What file is it sitting in?"

"All right, now," said Abbas, "enough of this nonsense. It's time to tell your story."

"What story?"

"One with a moral. You're a spiritual man, aren't you? So you must know one."

"But what about?" Sasha asked, squinting at the long sword lying on the carpet close beside Abbas.

"Whatever you wish. The important thing is, it must have wisdom."

In order to gain time to think, Sasha picked up the hookah from the carpet and inhaled deeply several times in rapid succession, trying to recall what he had read in Trimmingham's book about Sufi stories. Then he closed his eyes for a minute.

"Do you know the story of the Maghrib prayer carpet," he asked Abbas, who had prepared himself to listen.

"No."

"Then listen. A certain vizier had a small son by the name of Yusuf. One day he left his father's estates and went off walking until he came to a deserted road where he loved to walk alone, and set off along it, gazing around him on all sides. Suddenly he saw an old man dressed in the robes of a sheik, wearing a black hat on his head. The boy greeted the old man politely and the old man stopped and gave him a sweet sugar cockerel. When Yusuf had eaten it, the old man asked: 'Boy, do you like stories?' Yusuf liked stories very much indeed, and he said so. 'I know a certain story,' said the old man, 'it's the story of a Maghrib prayer carpet. I would tell you it, but it's much too terrible.'

"But the boy Yusuf, of course, said that he was not afraid of anything, and he made himself ready to listen. Then suddenly there was a sound of bells ringing loudly and shouting from the direction of his father's estate—that always happened when anybody arrived. The boy immediately forgot all about the old man in the black hat and dashed away to see who had arrived.

"It turned out to be only one of his father's junior subordinates, and the boy ran back as fast as he could, but the old man was no longer there on the road. Yusuf was very upset and went back to the estate. Choosing his moment carefully, he went up to his father and asked: 'Father! Do you know anything about a Maghrib prayer carpet?' His father suddenly turned pale, began shaking all over, fell down on the floor and died. At this the boy was frightened and he ran to his mother. 'Mother!' he shouted. 'A terrible thing!' She came up to him, smiled, put her hand on his head and asked: 'What is it, my son?' 'Mother,' cried the boy, 'I went to father and asked him about something, and he suddenly fell down dead!' 'What did you ask?' she said with a frown. 'About a Maghrib prayer carpet!' he answered, and suddenly she also turned deadly pale, shook all over, and fell down dead.

"The boy was left all alone, and soon his father's powerful enemies had seized the estate and driven him out into the wide world. For a long time he wandered the length and breadth of Persia until finally he found himself in the khankah of a renowned Sufi and became his pupil. Several years went by, and Yusuf approached this Sufi when he was alone, bowed and said: 'Teacher, I have studied with you now for several years. May I ask you one question?' 'Ask it, my son,' said the Sufi with a smile. 'Teacher, do you know anything about a Maghrib prayer carpet?' The Sufi turned pale, clutched at his heart, and fell down dead.

"Then Yusuf fled as fast as his legs would carry him and became a wandering dervish who walked through Persia in search of renowned teachers. But all those he asked about the Maghrib carpet fell down on the ground and died. Gradually Yusuf grew old and feeble. He began to be tormented by the thought that soon he would die, and leave no trace behind him on the earth.

"One day, when he was sitting in a tea house and thinking of all of this, he suddenly saw the same old man in the black hat. The old man was exactly the same as before; the years had done nothing at all to age him. Yusuf ran up to him, sank to his knees, and implored him: 'Most venerable sheik! I have sought you all of my life! Tell me about the Maghrib prayer carpet!' The old man in the black hat said: 'Very well. Have it your own way.' Yusuf prepared himself to listen. The old man sat opposite him, sighed deeply, and died. For a whole day and night Yusuf sat in silence facing his corpse. Then he got up, took the black hat from the old man's head, and placed it on his own. He had a few small coins left, and before leaving he used them to buy a sugar cockerel from the owner of the tea house."

Abbas said nothing for a long time, then he asked:

"Tell me the truth, are you a hidden sheik?"

Sasha didn't answer.

"I understand," said Abbas. "I understand everything. Tell me, are you certain the old man's hat was black?"

"Yes."

"Maybe it was green? I think it might have been the Green Khidr."

"And what do they know here about the Green Khidr?" Sasha asked. He hadn't read about this person in Trimmingham's book yet, and he was curious.

"Everybody says different things. For instance, the dervish from Khurasan that I drank with. He said that the Green Khidr rarely appears in his own form, he assumes the appearance of others. Or he puts his words into the mouths of different people—and anybody who wishes to may hear him speaking all the time, even when they are talking with idiots, because some of their words are spoken for them by the Green Khidr."

"That is true," said Sasha. "Tell me, Abbas, who is it that plays the flute here?"

"Nobody knows. Time and again we have combed the labyrinth from end to end, but all in vain."

Abbas yawned. "It's time I was at my post," he said. "I have to set out the jars. The Americans will be here soon. I don't know how to thank you . . . except . . . perhaps you would like to have a look at the princess?"

"I would," answered Sasha, draining what was left in his cup at a single gulp.

Abbas stood up, took a bunch of big, rusty keys from a nail

on the wall, and went out into the dimly lit corridor. Sasha followed him. The door of the room where they had been sitting was painted to match the wall, and as Abbas closed it, Sasha realized that he would never have suspected that this dead end—he had been in hundreds of dead ends just like it—was actually a disguised door. They walked in silence as far as the exit to the following level, which proved to be very close.

"Just be quiet," said Abbas, handing Sasha the keys, "or else you'll frighten our men."

"Shall I give you the keys back afterwards?"

"Keep them. Or throw them away."

"But won't you need them?"

"If I need them," said Abbas, "I'll take them off the nail. This is your game. I have my own. If you want anything, just drop in."

He held out a piece of paper with something written on it.

"It is written here which way to go," he said.

Level 12

The climb to the upper level took no more than ten minutes, and if Sasha had managed to get the key into the keyhole immediately, it would have taken even less. A narrow servants' staircase set into the thickness of the stone walls led from one level to another. It was very difficult to tell what kind of stone it was—it was very crudely defined, and it didn't exist for very long—but when the final door closed behind Sasha, reality once again acquired precise outlines and clear colors. In front of him Sasha saw a wall towering up in the distance, with the same kind of cornices he had recently scrambled up toward his encounter with Abbas. He automatically stepped forward, jumped, and reached up.

Suddenly remembering that he was carrying the keys, he screamed in exasperation, came back down, and then for no reason at all jumped straight at the blank wall. Colliding with the stone surface, he collapsed, jumped again, and fell again. He tried to stand up normally, but instead he jumped, and hung, shuddering, in the air for a second with his hands extended above his head. Only then did he come to his senses and think shamefacedly to himself: "This time I really overdid it!" This was the final level, and the servants' staircase ended here. Sasha ran down the long gallery with torches and bronze rings—it seemed to him as though someone had stuck them where there ought to be flags—and after a while he ran into a carpet hanging on the wall.

Turning around, he ran in the opposite direction, winding his way through corridors and galleries until he came up against a heavy metal door like the ones that led from one level to another. He bent down toward it, holding the keys at the ready, but the door had no lock. The princess should have been behind this very door, but in order to open it he would have had to wander for ages through the vast warren of the twelfth level, with the risk of breaking his neck at every step. He found the other entrance ten minutes later when he glanced behind the carpet hanging in the dead end of the corridor: the black staring pupil of a keyhole was visible in one of the slabs. Sasha pushed the smallest key from the bundle into it and a tiny iron door opened, no larger than a manhole. Sasha squeezed through with some difficulty.

He was facing a hall with a tall vaulted ceiling; on the walls there were lighted torches and carpets, and at the far end he could see a raised portcullis, beyond which began a dimly lit corridor. In another wall there was a heavy metal door—the one which had no keyhole—through which Sasha would have entered if he had reached this level on his own. He recognized this place—this was where he had seen the princess when she occasionally appeared on the screen. But she wasn't here now, and neither were the carpets with the pillows, or the potbellied sand clock or the palace cat. There was nothing but the bare floor. The raised portcullis in the wall was something Sasha had not seen before—that part of the hall never appeared on the screen when the princess was shown. He set off toward it. The corridor behind the portcullis unexpectedly ended in an ordinary wooden door like those that lead into the bathroom or toilet in a communal apartment, and Sasha felt his heart fill with unpleasant foreboding. He pulled the door toward himself.

The room which confronted him resembled a large empty shed. There was a smell of something sour and musty, and the floor was littered with trash: empty medicine bottles, an old boot, a broken guitar without any strings, and scraps of paper. In several places the wallpaper had peeled away from the wall and was hanging down in strips, and the window looked straight out onto a brick wall, no more than a yard away.

Standing in the middle of the room was the princess. Sasha looked at her for a long time, walked around her several times, and then suddenly lashed out at her with his foot. All the junk she was made of tumbled onto the floor and fell apart—the head, made from a dry pumpkin with the eyes and mouth glued on, fell over by the radiator, the cardboard arms crumpled in the sleeves of the long cotton caftan, her right leg fell off while the left slumped to the floor still attached to the waist-length tailor's dummy and its iron shaft. Sasha left the room and set off back along the corridor, but the portcullis which separated the corridor from the vaulted hall was now lowered. He remembered he had heard it fall a moment after he had kicked at the dummy, but at the time he had paid no attention.

He went back and looked again at the floor and the walls, and spotted the outline of a door that had been papered over. Going over, he pressed against it with his shoulder. The door gave a little, but it didn't open, though it was obviously very thin. Then Sasha drew back, clenched his fists, took a run and shoulder-charged the door so hard that it burst open. He tore through the wallpaper and hurtled on through the air for a yard or two before he stumbled over something and crashed to the floor, catching a fleeting glimpse as he fell of a pair of shoulders and a head above the back of a chair.

"Careful," said Itakin, turning away from a flickering screen which showed a high vaulted hall with a princess in the center lying on a carpet and stroking a cat, "you'll disturb Boris Emelianovich. He's about to go into battle again. They suffered heavy losses today."

Sasha raised himself up on his arms and looked around— behind him the door of a cupboard set in the wall stood open and various papers were still slithering out of it onto the floor.

"Well I don't know, Petya," he said as he rose to his feet. "What was all that about?"

"You mean the princess?" asked Itakin.

Sasha nodded.

"She was the goal you were striving for all that time," said Itakin. "I told you, your game's been cracked."

"But hasn't anyone else ever reached her?"

"Of course, lots of people have."

"Then why didn't they say anything? So that the others would . . . To conceal their own disappointment?"

"I don't think that's the reason why. It's just that when a man spends so much time and effort on a journey and finally gets to its end, he no longer sees everything the way it really is. . . . Although that's not exactly it either. There is no such thing as the way everything 'really is.' Let's just say he can't allow himself to see."

"Then why could I see?"

"Well, you went in by the back staircase."

"But how is it possible to see something else? And then, I've seen her so many times myself—when you move from one level to another she sometimes appears on the screen, but that's not what she looks like at all!"

"Perhaps I didn't express myself very well," said Itakin. "This game is arranged so that only a cartoon prince can reach the princess."

"Why?"

"Because the princess herself is a cartoon too. And you can draw absolutely anything you like in a cartoon."

"What happens to the people who are playing? Where does the person controlling the prince go?"

"Do you remember how you got to the twelfth level?" Itakin asked, with a nod at the screen.

"Yes."

"Can you tell who it was beating his head against the wall and jumping up and down? You or the prince?"

"The prince, of course," said Sasha. "I can't jump like that."

"And where were you all that time?"

Sasha was about to open his mouth and answer, but he stopped short.

"That's where they go as well," said Itakin. Sasha sat down on a chair by the wall and thought for a long time.

"Listen," he said at last, "who is it that plays the flute in there?"

"Nobody's discovered that yet."

Sasha glanced at the clock and suddenly hiccuped.

"The shop down at the corner is still open," he said. "I'll just get a bottle. Will you wait? Just a glass each, eh?"

"I'm in no hurry," said Itakin. "You're the one they won't let back in."

"I'll be quick," said Sasha, pressing <Escape>. "I'll be back in fifteen minutes." The picture on the screen froze, showing a view through a Moorish arch of an immense oriental palace made up of ranks of towers and turrets reaching up toward huge stars gleaming in the summer sky.

Game paused

The line in the shop was so long that Sasha realized it would be very difficult, if not impossible, for him to buy a bottle. If he'd been sober, it would definitely have been impossible, but it turned out that he had drunk enough for several minutes of Brownian motion across the crowded shop floor to bring him within a reasonable distance of the cash desk. People leaned on him and swore at him from all sides, but soon Sasha realized that the apparent chaos was actually four lines scraping against each other because they were moving at different speeds. The line for cheap wine was on the left, while the line he had found his way into was for sardines in tomato sauce—the kind that gaze up at you with a dozen beady little eyes as soon as you open the can. Sasha's line was moving faster than the line for wine, and he decided to move a yard or two forward in his present company and then jump across to the next one. The maneuver was successful, and Sasha found himself sandwiched between a building laborer's jacket bearing the mysterious inscription "KATEK" on its back, and a brown sports jacket which its wearer, a man of about fifty, was wearing directly over his naked torso.

"Ech-ech-ech . . ." said the man in the brown sports jacket when Sasha looked at him. A quite unbelievable stench issued from his mouth and Sasha hastily turned away and began staring at the wall, where a triangular pennant of red cloth hung beside a head of Lenin constructed out of painted plywood.

"My God," he thought. "I actually do live here in this . . . in this . . . I'm standing here drunk in a line for cheap fortified wine amongst all these filthy pigs—and I think that I'm a prince!"

"Out of sardines!" shouted frightened voices in the neighboring line.

"No sardines!"

Sasha felt someone behind him tugging at his shoulder.

"What I think," the man in the sports jacket said, "is that we should withdraw to our ancient territory in Vladimir and Yaroslavl and . . . and then give the people arms and conquer the whole of Russia all over again."

"And then?"

"And then we march against the Khan Kuchum," said the man, waving his fist in Sasha's face.

"The wine's running out," the people began whispering in alarm.

Sasha squeezed himself out of the line and began pushing his way toward the door. He no longer had even the slightest desire to drink. Two women were standing by the door in white coats and caps, glancing at the clock, and discussing something with quiet passion. Suddenly somewhere behind him, up beneath some invisible ceiling which was about three times the height of the shop, he heard a strange sound that instantly began to swell, like dozens of aviation engines all working together. After a few seconds it had become so loud that the people who only a few moments before were peacefully swearing at each other began, first, to stare upwards in astonishment, and then to squat down on their haunches or simply collapse to the floor, blocking their ears with their hands. The sound reached a peak, then just as suddenly began to fade, finally disappearing completely, before being replaced by the rumbling of tank motors from some other mysterious source, which in turn disappeared just as mysteriously a few seconds later.

"Same thing every evening," said one of the women in the white coats, "right at a quarter to six. We've tried ringing everyone you could think of. Zoya from the Novoarbatsky Supermarket told me it's the same there too."

People were picking themselves up from the floor, glowering at each other suspiciously as they tried to remember who had been where in what line. But that didn't matter now anyway, because the sardines and the wine had both run out. Sasha went out into the street and wandered slowly toward the cheerful electric lights in the windows of the Gosplan building. Ahead of him a body-scissors clicked into action, but from the painful, squeaking way it worked and the large gaps between its bent saw teeth Sasha guessed that it wasn't from his game—it was just an ordinary Soviet body-scissors, old and inefficient, that someone had either dumped in the street or which was still standing in its appointed place.

He was about to walk past, but following the habit he had acquired in his game, he turned back and looked to see whether there was a jar full of revitalizing liquid just beyond it, as there usually was in the labyrinth. There was no jar, but there were three bottles of fortified wine No. 72 standing there. Sasha walked on, listening to the knocking and squeaking behind his back and picking out in it a few notes, repeated over and over again, from "Midnight in Moscow"—as though a record had gotten stuck on a gramophone and a rusty, hopeless voice kept repeating some eternal question addressed to the dull Moscow sky.

Sasha reached Gosplan and realized that he was too late. The working day was coming to an end and the tall, Assyrian door was disgorging wave upon wave of people into the street. He made an effort to go in anyway, managed a few yards of progress against the current, and was just about to grab hold of the cold railing of the turnstile when he was swept away and carried back out into the street by a group of cheerful women. Kuzma Ulyanovich Staropopikov went slouching by holding his briefcase and Sasha automatically set off after him. Staropopikov turned off into a maze of dark side streets—he obviously lived somewhere close by. Sasha didn't know why he was following Staropopikov—he just needed something to do, something to hang onto for a while so that he could think in peace.

Ten minutes later—or perhaps it was more, he seemed to have lost all track of time—Staropopikov reached a large deserted yard and headed for the entrance in the corner. Sasha decided that following him any further would be even stupider than following him this far and he was just on the point of turning back when Staropopikov was suddenly confronted by two lanky youths in fashionable NATO jackets. Sasha would have bet any of his extremities that a moment ago they had not been in the yard. Sensing something was wrong, he ducked swiftly behind the fire escape, which was masked with planks right down to the ground—nobody could see him there, even though he was right beside the entrance.

"Are you Kuzma Ulyanovich Staropopikov?" one of the youths asked in a loud voice—he spoke Russian with a strong accent and, like his companion, he had dark curly hair, swarthy skin, and unshaven cheeks.

"Yes," Staropopikov answered in surprise.

"Did you bomb the camp outside Al-Djegazi?"

Staropopikov shuddered and removed his spectacles.

"And who might you . . ." he began, but his interlocutor cut him short.

"The Palestine Liberation Organization has condemned you to death," he said, drawing a long-barreled pistol from his pocket. His companion did the same. Staropopikov jerked back and dropped his briefcase, and an instant later there was a deafening roar of shots followed by the sound of spent shells clattering against the asphalt. The first bullet threw Staropopikov back against the door, but before he fell the Palestinians had emptied the magazines of both their pistols into him, turned on their heels, and hurried away. Sasha was astonished to notice that he could see the trees and benches through them—by the time they reached the corner, they were almost completely invisible and didn't even seem to make any pretense of turning around it.

An eerie silence fell. Sasha came out from behind the fire escape, looked at Staropopikov, who was quietly rolling to and fro on the pavement, and then glanced around in confusion. A man wearing a tracksuit came out of the next doorway and Sasha dashed toward him as fast as he could run. The man stopped in astonishment and Sasha suddenly felt stupid.

"Didn't you hear anything just now?" he asked.

"Not a thing. What should I have heard?"

"Nothing—There's someone in a bad way over there."

The man finally caught sight of Staropopikov.

"Drunk, probably," he said, going over and taking a closer look. "But then maybe not. Hey, what's wrong with you?"

"My heart," said Staropoikov in a weak voice, pausing between words. "Call an ambulance, I mustn't move. Or get my wife. Second floor, apartment forty-two."

"Maybe we should carry you in?"

"No," said Staropopikov. "I've already had two heart attacks. I know what to do."

The man in the tracksuit dashed up the stairs and Sasha turned and walked quickly away. He wasn't aware of how he reached the subway and then rode back to the State Supply Building. When he found himself in front of the familiar, friendly five-story building with the columns on its façade, he was already completely sober. Two windows on the third floor were still lit and he decided to go up.

The third floor was empty and dark, and it seemed as though everyone had left already, but there was still someone working in the first timber section. Sasha stepped up to the half-open door and glanced inside through the gap. Boris Grigorievich was standing in the center of the office, dressed in a worn, light-blue kimono and green khakama, with the cap of a fifth-rank official on his head and a fan in his hand. He couldn't see Sasha out in the dark corridor, but just at the moment when Sasha glanced in, Boris Grigorievich raised his fan above his head, folded and unfolded it, pressed it against his chest, and thrust it out toward Sasha. Then slowly, pulling up one half-bent leg to the other at each small step, he glided toward the door, holding up the open fan with its red silk face turned toward him. It seemed to Sasha that his boss was crying—or howling quietly—but a moment later he made out the poem that he was reciting:

Like to a drop of dew
That gleams a second's space
Upon the stalk
And flies in vapor
Up to the clouds—
So do not we

Wander all eternity
In darkness?
Oh, hopelessness!

Boris Grigorievich spun around on the spot and froze, with the fan raised high in the air. He stood like that for several minutes and then, as though regaining consciousness, he straightened his jacket, smoothed down his hair, and disappeared into the narrow passageway between the cupboards. Soon Sasha heard a sword whistling through the air and he realized that his boss had begun his usual evening Budokan practice in the second hall to the left after the gates. Then he went in, cleared his throat and called out:

"Boris Grigorievich!"

The whistling of the sword fell silent.

"Lapin?"

"I got everything signed, Boris Grigorievich!"

"Aha. Put it all on the cupboard, I'm busy just now."

"D'you mind if I do a bit of work, Boris Grigorievich?"

"Go ahead, go ahead. I'll be here till late today."

Sasha put the papers on the cupboard, sat at his own desk, and was about to set his finger to the switch that turned on his computer. Then he grinned, took down the telephone book from the shelf above the desk, and leafed through it before pulling the telephone toward him.

"Hello," he said, "is that the Moscow Housing Construction Office? Is Semyon Prokofievich Chukanov still there? What's his number?" He wrote down the new number and dialed it immediately.

"Semyon Prokofievich? I'm calling from Gosplan, on the instructions of Comrade Staropopikov. . . . What's more important is that he remembers you. . . . As you wish. It's up to . . . No, about *The Prince*. He asked me to let you know how to get directly to the seventh level . . . I don't know, perhaps at some meeting in the ministry. I'm sure you'll be able to remember who

saw whom and where, but in the meantime can you write this
down . . . All right, first . . ."

Sasha unfolded the piece of paper Abbas had given him.

"Enter the words 'prince megahit seven'. In Latin letters. A
Russian 'N'—no, the number. Not at all, not at all. All the best.
now."

He got up and went out into the corridor for a smoke. When
he returned a few minutes later, he dialed the same number again.

"Semyon Prokofievich, please . . . What—But I was just
talking with him. How awful. I'm so sorry."

Sasha put down the receiver and switched on his monitor.

Level 1

Jumping down from the stone cornice, he set off along the corridor toward the dead end where he had taken all the things he had
found. It was a long time now since he had come in here, but
everything was just the same—the couch made of broken fragments of stone slabs, covered with old, rotten rags for softness,
someone's shin bone, which he had begun to shape into a cigarette holder and then abandoned, a pair of slim copper jugs, one
of which still held some of its contents, and lying on the floor, a
State Supply Office form with a plan of the first level, now covered with a thick layer of dust. Sasha lay down on the couch and
closed his eyes and almost immediately, from somewhere far, far
above him, beyond innumerable ceilings of stone, there came the
faint sound of a flute being played. He began remembering the
day's events, but he was too sleepy, and pulling some of the old
rags over himself, he found a niche where he was not in a draft
and fell asleep.

At first he dreamed of Petya Itakin, sitting on the top of a
tower and playing on a long reed flute, and then he dreamed of
Abbas, wearing a shimmering green caftan, who explained to
Sasha at length that if he pressed the <Shift>, <Control>, and

<Return> keys simultaneously, and then reached for the key with the arrow pointing upwards and pressed that as well, then wherever the little figure might be, and no matter how many enemies it was facing, it would do something very unusual—it would jump, stretch up, and a second later dissolve in the sky.

Have a nice DOS!